D1111584

OTHER TITLES IN THE SMART NOVELS SERIES:

Bus

ted

BY EMMA HARRISON

smart novels
SAT VOCABULARY

SPARKNOTES is a registered trademark of SparkNotes LLC.

Spark Publishing
A Division of Barnes & Noble
120 Fifth Avenue
New York, NY 10011
www.sparknotes.com

ISBN-13: 978-1-4114-0081-8
ISBN-10: 1-4114-0081-X

Library of Congress Cataloging-in-Publication Data

Harrison, Emma.
  Busted / by Emma Harrison.
    p. cm.—(SAT vocabulary novels)
  Summary: A Stanford University freshman finds her first winter break at home in Connecticut to be a difficult adjustment.
  ISBN-13: 978-1-4114-0081-8
  ISBN-10: 1-4114-0081-X
  [1. Vacations—Fiction. 2. College students—Fiction.] I. Title. II. Series.
PZ7.H2485Bu 2004   2004000028

Please submit changes or report errors to www.sparknotes.com/errors.

Printed and bound in the United States

10

SAT is a registered trademark of the College Entrance Examination Board, which was not involved in the production of, and does not endorse, this book.

ACT is a registered trademark of ACT, Inc., which was not involved in the production of, and does not endorse, this book.

Ask anyone—well, anyone who *knows* me—and they will tell you that I have this **uncanny** ability for finding the fun. It doesn't matter how **sedate** the situation, how **staid** the participants, I, Kim Stratford, will inspire laughter where there is only misery. I can bring **effervescence** to places where boredom seems to **permeate** the very walls. I am the **indomitable** mistress of mayhem.

Examples? You ask for examples? No problem. I have a **plethora** of good stories.

How about last year when we were all forced to sit through career planning with Mr. Winters, the guidance counselor of doom, and I reduced the entire classroom to hysterics by repeatedly insisting I wanted to pursue a career in high-end porn? (I know. It was **ingenious**.) Or when my mother and I went to Aunt Renee's for Thanksgiving, and I refused to give up until I persuaded even my **execrable** Uncle Morgan to play charades. (He did a killer *Jaws*, by the way.) Last summer, I even got the crowd giggling at the funeral of my best friend, Corinne, when I brought up her macaroni-and-cheese obsession during my **eulogy**. Okay, so maybe I didn't find the fun for myself that day—it was next to impossible—but I did find it for other people.

So why, I ask you, *why* was I sitting there for the fifth afternoon in a row, watching yet another **appalling**, mind-numbingly stupid soap opera? Had I really sunk so very low?

It was my first ever winter break from college. One month back at my house in Connecticut, where there was virtually nothing to do, I was facing four whole weeks **sequestered** from all the new friends I'd made at Stanford University in the first few months of

---

uncanny: unnatural or extraordinary
sedate: dull
staid: serious or dull
effervescence: sparkle
permeate: penetrate

indomitable: unconquerable
plethora: excess or large number
ingenious: clever or inspired
execrable: terrible or disgusting

eulogy: speech given at a funeral
appalling: awful or dreadful
sequestered: isolated or apart

my freshman year, and I was **wallowing**. I'm not proud to admit it, but I was. It was about twenty degrees outside and I **abhor** the cold, unless, of course, I'm on the slopes with my snowboard, sporting some sleek, sexy and **impervious** boarding gear. I had already read every last book I would be required to read in next semester's American Writers course—ten heavy and mostly **tedious tomes** that were a serious pain to lug across the country—including the **unabridged** version of *Moby-Dick*, which, let me tell you, will make you want to scratch your brain out through your ear canal, it's so **oblique**.

My high school friends had been **expunged** from my life over the past semester, for which I take the **brunt** of the responsibility. I hadn't been very **fastidious** about returning phone calls and emails, preferring not to be reminded of senior year and of Corinne. I was ready to move on. And when I first stepped off the five-hour flight to California I was overjoyed by my **fortuitous** choice of schools. Stanford was so far away from the Ivies on the East Coast where most of my friends were going that I'd never be expected to see them. It was a new life for me. A new start.

Now, of course, I was paying for it. They all had given up on me, for good reason, and there was no one I could call, no one to distract me from the talk shows and the **turgid** dramas of these horrid over-actors. My life had become so **insipid** I could hardly even stand to be around myself.

I glanced around the impeccably kept living room—my mother is a neat freak while I tend toward the messy—looking for something to inspire me. Mom's many awards of service, **extolling** her virtues as a policewoman, lined the walls. My karate and track trophies were displayed with pride along the mantle. The **eclectic** collection of books and videos we had amassed since I was a kid—everything from *Free to Be You and Me* to *Charlie's Angels 1* and *2*—packed the shelves **adjacent** to the fireplace, but none of them was interesting

wallowing: remaining helpless or self-pitying	**unabridged:** full-length	**fortuitous:** lucky
abhor: hate	**oblique:** indirect or meandering	**turgid:** stiff or stilted
impervious: solid or watertight	**expunged:** wiped out	**insipid:** dull
tedious: boring or tiresome	**brunt:** weight or burden	**extolling:** praising
tomes: books	**fastidious:** careful or attentive	**eclectic:** varied or quirky
		adjacent: next to

enough to stir me from the comfort of the couch. The **effulgent** sun glinted off the snow-covered lawn outside, blinding me whenever I made the mistake of looking toward the window. I squinted and covered my eyes. This was sad. I was becoming allergic to sunlight.

Okay, Kimbo, time to get off your ass, I told myself. **Mustering** all my energy, I pushed myself from the comfy faux-suede cushions and padded over to the mirror to check my reflection. It was beyond **mortifying**. My skin was so pasty you'd think I was a **nocturnal** being. Très vampiric. My short brown hair was mussed into spikes on one side. I even had the pattern of the plaid throw pillow imprinted on my cheek. It was time, as they say, to get a life.

At that moment one of those **ebullient** commercials came on the TV, touting the energizing effects of some nutritional supplement for the elderly. I saw the reflection of the screen in the mirror and caught a glimpse of an ancient couple riding their bikes along a path, smiling all the way. Suddenly I had an **epiphany**. I could do that. I had a bike . . . somewhere. So what if it was sub-zero temperatures out there? I had to do *something*.

I changed into a pair of warm leggings, my favorite Stanford sweatshirt, and my windbreaker, then got my hair under control with a ski hat and headed out to the garage. It took a few minutes to **excavate** my dirt bike from the back of the room, which served as a storage place for all **discarded** furniture, appliances, and sundry items that my mother couldn't seem to part with but refused to keep in her **meticulously** clean house. By the time I'd filled the tires with air and checked the brakes, I was raring to go.

As soon as I was out on the road I felt a million times better. The cold air in my lungs and the pumping of my muscles brought on a light-headed kind of **euphoria**. How had I forgotten how much better exercise always made me feel? I definitely needed to get out more. I rode to the end of my block, slowing down as I passed the houses of my former friends—homes where I'd attended dozens of

---

effulgent: bright or beaming
mustering: gathering
mortifying: shameful
nocturnal: active at night

ebullient: bright and cheerful
epiphany: sudden realization or awakening
excavate: dig out

discarded: thrown away
meticulously: carefully or thoroughly
euphoria: exhilaration or joy

slumber parties, obsessive *Buffy* viewings, and countless junk food fests. When I came to Corinne's house I pedaled a little bit faster. There were certain things I just couldn't **ruminate** on.

I turned down Morrison Street, the main avenue of Morrison, Connecticut, my **quaint** hometown, which was lined with mom-and-pop businesses, the town library, and the **obligatory** Gap. The wind was biting against my face, but I couldn't help smiling. I felt like I was riding down memory lane as I zoomed by Häagen-Dazs and the Morrison Diner, the only two hangouts for kids in this town. I rode through Veterans' Park and passed the bench where Chad Martin had given me my first ever kiss—and the last kiss for a long time. (It was so *sloppy*! Who wanted to do *that* again? Little did I know that Chad was just a smooching **novice** like me. Over the last couple of years I've definitely improved, though I don't know if Chad can say the same.)

Finally I came to Morrison High School where class was in session. The American flag on the front lawn whipped around in the wind, and as I looked up at it, I couldn't help recalling when it had flown at half-mast last year for a month after the senior prom.

If it hadn't been for me, it never would have been lowered, a little voice in my head taunted me. I pulled my cap down to cover my ears and raced away, pushing the thoughts from my mind. (I'm an expert at issue-avoidance.) As I hit the corner the bell **pealed** behind me, signaling the end of classes. I pedaled even harder. The last thing I wanted was a reunion with some of this year's seniors. I took the Donnybrook hill at a rate that would have made Lance Armstrong proud.

On the other side of the hill, I normally would have just coasted, but I felt the need to escape—to put as much distance as possible between myself and the school—so I pedaled just as hard as I had on the way up. My insane **momentum** toward the bottom of the hill sent my heart into my throat, and I slammed on the brakes, stopping

---

ruminate: think over
quaint: old-fashioned or charming
obligatory: unavoidable or necessary
novice: beginner
pealed: rang
momentum: force of motion

just seconds before hurtling into traffic at a four-way intersection. I placed my feet on the ground and caught my breath. Wanting to escape was one thing. **Endangering** my own life was another.

Get a grip, I told myself. If I couldn't be out on the streets of Morrison without having a nervous breakdown, then I was in for one tough winter break.

Across the street was the Morrison Police Station, my mother's home away from home. I saw her Taurus parked in the spot marked "Reserved for the Chief of Police" and smiled, my heart swelling with pride. My mother had worked so **diligently** to become the first female chief in the county. I bet she grinned to herself every morning when she pulled into that space.

When the light turned green I pushed my bike through the intersection, deciding to surprise my mother with a visit. She had gone in early that morning and would be off in about an hour. I thought maybe I could hang out for a while, and then we could go chow down on a pizza together. The only thing better than the **bliss** of a good ride was the reward of a steaming pepperoni pizza afterward.

I locked my bike up outside and barreled through the front door of the station and into the **rustic** front office. Chief Knox, the man who had **abdicated** the position of police chief to my mother, had been an avid hunter and fisherman. He'd had the station outfitted like a log cabin with wood-paneled walls, benches made of cut logs, and paintings of various fish **indigenous** to the lakes and streams of Connecticut. My mother had taken the helm only last year, and redecorating hadn't been her top priority, so the **vestiges** of Chief Knox remained.

"Hey, Selma," I said to the **diminutive** female officer who always worked the desk.

She was the only other woman on the squad and couldn't have been more different from my mom. Short, skinny, and sweet, Selma had managed to **infuse** her immediate area with some feminine

---

endangering: putting in danger
diligently: thoroughly or industriously

bliss: pleasure or enjoyment
rustic: old-fashioned or rural
abdicated: abandoned
indigenous: native

vestiges: traces or remnants
diminutive: tiny
infuse: fill or introduce

touches, placing framed pictures of her kids and her cats on the front desk and always making sure there was a candy jar full of M&Ms for the taking. She even changed them with the seasons, making sure to buy the orange and black ones in October, the pastel ones around Easter, and the red and green ones at Christmastime. You had to love that kind of attention to detail—or be slightly afraid of it.

It was January now, so the M&Ms were back to being multi-colored. She'd probably tossed any **superfluous** red and green candies first thing in the morning on December 26. But even for all her quirks, I liked Selma. She always had a smile for everyone.

"Kim! It's so good to see you!" she **trilled**, grinning up at me. "How's school?"

"Fantastic, thanks," I replied honestly, wishing I was back in my dorm right about then. The emotional bike ride had taken a lot out of me.

"Here to see your mom?" Selma asked.

"Yep," I replied, pulling off my knit hat. Selma's eyes traveled up to my hair, which I was sure was sticking out in a million directions due to static. "Is she busy?"

"She's in with Tad and Quincy," Selma said. "So probably not," she added with a little wink.

Tad and Quincy were the two detectives on the Morrison squad, and there was no love lost between them and Selma. The two men were always **derisive** of Selma's positive outlook, mocking her love of animals and her tendency to believe everyone was innocent. Selma thought they were **sophomoric** and annoying, and she never missed an opportunity to point out that they had yet to solve a case together.

I wasn't fond of Tad myself. I could tell he was jealous of my mother's **ascent** to power, and their relationship was **acrimonious**. Quincy, however, was harmless. He respected my mom and was

---

superfluous: extra or unnecessary
trilled: spoke musically or warbled

derisive: scornful or mocking
sophomoric: immature

ascent: rise
acrimonious: unfriendly or bitter

always nice to me. He just wasn't very self-assured and was therefore **malleable**. He thought Tad's **ribald** sense of humor was hysterical and went along with whatever he did, just like those sorry kids at school who followed the "cool" kids around like they were the end-all be-all.

I grabbed a few M&Ms, thanked Selma, and wound my way through the desks to get to my mom's office at the back of the station. When I was a few feet away, I heard raised voices on the other side of the shuttered glass walls that surrounded her office. I paused, **flabbergasted**. It was completely **bizarre** to hear yelling in the normally **serene** office. (Not much happens in a sleepy town like Morrison.) **Intrigued**, I paused outside the window-walls to listen.

"The headmaster says the problem has just been **exacerbated** since Christmas break," I heard Quincy say in his high-pitched voice. He sounded **tremulous**, like whatever he was talking about was a serious and somewhat scary issue. "They just had to expel five kids, and they've officially requested our help."

"Well, I still say the best way to flush out a drug problem in a teen population is to send someone in undercover," my mother replied firmly. "Kids talk to kids."

I felt my heart skip a few nasty beats. A drug problem? And if they were talking about a headmaster, they had to be discussing Hereford Academy, the upscale private school at the edge of town. The place was populated by overprivileged snobs and brainiacs— the kind of people who probably did drugs just to get Mummy and Daddy's attention. Why was I not surprised they had a drug issue that had grown into a **predicament** worthy of police involvement?

"Yeah, Jenna, that's the problem," Tad said.

"I'd prefer it if you'd address me as Chief Stratford," my mother snapped. "Or just plain 'Chief' would be fine."

I grinned. Go, Mom.

---

malleable: flexible or manipulable
ribald: vulgar or bawdy
flabbergasted: stunned
bizarre: strange

serene: peaceful or calm
intrigued: interested or absorbed
exacerbated: intensified or made worse

tremulous: unsteady or trembling
predicament: problem or dilemma

"Sorry, *Chief*," Tad **amended acerbically**. My mother wisely chose to ignore his tone. The last thing she needed right then was a pointless **altercation**. "But we've been over this already. None of us is going to pass as a high school kid. We don't have anyone in the precinct under thirty."

"If you're about to suggest yet again that we call in the State Police, save your breath," my mother said.

"I'm sorry to say it, Chief, but it looks like we're gonna have to," Quincy replied, sounding like he didn't want to **contravene** but felt it was his only option. "There's no other way."

"There has to be," my mother insisted.

I knew my mother was being **obstinate** because of her out-of-control pride. When she'd been promoted to chief, a lot of people had predicted she would fail—that she didn't have enough experience to take over. The last thing she wanted to do was call for help and prove all those **incendiaries** right—prove that a woman couldn't hack it as chief of police.

"We're just going to have to find someone who can pass as a teenager and deputize them," my mother said.

Suddenly I felt a rush of excitement crash over me. *Someone who could pass as a teenager . . .* Hell. I *was* a teenager. Maybe *I* could do it. I wouldn't mind spending a few days at Hereford finding out what it was really like. My friends and I had always speculated about what the classes were like, how the place was run, whether they had a Miss Minchin–type headmistress policing the halls. I would *kill* to get inside Hereford. Not to mention how cool it would be to collar one of those trust-fund babies for dealing.

But was I up to the job?

You so know you can do this, I told myself, my palms beginning to sweat and causing the M&M dye to smear all over my skin. Last summer I'd participated in the county's Law Enforcement Intern program and had been their number-one recruit. I'd learned all

---

amended: revised or corrected
acerbically: bitterly or sarcastically
altercation: argument

contravene: disobey
obstinate: stubborn

incendiaries: people who stir up trouble

about the various enforceable laws, how to question a witness, when to call for backup—all kinds of things. And then I'd aced the written Police Academy exam. Everyone said I could've joined the force last August if I'd wanted to. Even Tad had been impressed with my performance.

This was **serendipity**! I *could* do this. I *had* to. It was exactly what I needed. An answer to my **ennui**. No more **sedentary** afternoons in front of the TV for me. I was about to become Deputy Stratford.

I popped the last few M&Ms into my mouth and thrust open the door to my mom's office. Tad, tall and **sinuous**, was hovering over my mom's desk. Mom and the **rotund** Quincy both stood the moment I walked in. My mom's face was lined with surprise and confusion over the clear sense of purpose on my face.

"I'll do it," I announced, bubbling over. "Deputize me, Mom. I'm going in."

---

serendipity: luck   **sedentary:** inactive   **rotund:** fat or round
ennui: boredom   **sinuous:** graceful

It took my mother a few seconds to recover from her shock, but when she did, she was **adamant**.

"Uh-uh. No way, no how," she said. Quincy and Tad stepped out of her way as she rounded the desk. My mother is an **imperious** woman, to say the least. Tall and strong, she has a square jaw that's even more pronounced when she's at work because she always has her red hair pulled back in a bun. I'd obviously taken after my father more. **Heredity** could be weird that way. I hadn't laid eyes on my dad in eleven years, but I saw him every time I looked in the mirror. Besides, I kept a photo album **replete** with family photos under my bed, so I knew he was short, dark, and pudgy like me.

Well, I'm not usually pudgy, but that "freshman fifteen" thing is no myth, let me tell you.

"Come on, Mom," I said, crossing my arms over my chest and looking up at her, trying to **convey resolution** with my eyes. "I'm all over this. You know me. I'll be walking out the front gates of that dump with your suspect in hand in less than a week."

Audacious, I know, but I had to be. She was looking at me all **dubious** like I was some kind of **feeble** little girly-girl. So not the case. I don't even own one article of pink clothing, let alone a bottle of nail polish. And even if I did decide to go out tomorrow and wipe out the Betsey Johnson section at Lord & Taylor, I could take care of myself, lace skirts and all.

"Kim, I don't know what you overheard, but I'm not sending you in on this case and that's final," my mother said, her jaw clenching. "You're not even on the force."

"But you said yourself you could deputize somebody," I said,

---

adamant: stubborn
imperious: bossy or commanding
heredity: inherited traits

replete: filled or full
convey: express or get across
resolution: determination or firmness

audacious: bold or daring
dubious: doubtful
feeble: weak

throwing out a hand as she turned her back on me and went behind her desk again. I could feel the adrenaline mounting in my veins, and I refused to be **deterred**. "I'm eighteen. I'm totally deputizable."

Okay. Sometimes I make up words.

My mother sighed as if she was suddenly **encumbered** by the weight of the world. She did that around me a lot. Sometimes I think she would have rather had a more **acquiescent** daughter, but I knew she loved me. Deep down she **appreciated** my **fervent** spirit. I could tell by the way she looked at me whenever I kicked ass in a karate match or came home with another detention for talking back to my misogynistic high school history teacher, Mr. Conroy. She was proud of me. I just wore her out sometimes.

"Kim, this is not even an issue," my mother told me, looking me in the eye. "I'm not sending my only daughter into a potentially dangerous situation."

I **scoffed**. "How dangerous could it be? It's Hereford. What are you afraid they're going to do to me—make me wear Burberry?"

Tad laughed, and my mother shot him a **reproving** look that could have melted steel. Quincy, meanwhile, cleared his throat and started to grow flushed and patchy around his cheeks and neck. I could tell there was something he wanted to say, and from the almost **penitent** way he was looking at my mother, I had a feeling he was going to agree with me.

Nice!

"What is it, Quincy?" my mother demanded.

"Well, Chief," he said, shifting from one foot to the other. "I think Kim would be perfect for the job."

"Oh, you do, do you?" my mother asked, lacing her fingers together. Her face went flat, and Quincy's only reddened further.

"I'm with Quincy on this," Tad put in. "Kim was a stellar recruit in last year's summer program. She can handle those tarts over at Hereford."

---

deterred: discouraged
encumbered: burdened
acquiescent: passive or unresisting

appreciated: valued
fervent: hot-blooded
scoffed: jeered or laughed at

reproving: disapproving
penitent: apologetic

I smirked at his use of the word "tarts." Tad was nothing if not politically incorrect and, well, **crude**. But everyone in Morrison had the same opinion of the kids who attended Hereford. It was a well-off town, but compared to the students at the private school, we were practically **indigent**. It wasn't just about the money either. These kids were *total* snobs. All they ever did was come into town in their brand-spankin' new BMWs and toss out insults to all of us "townies," as they so originally called us. Either that or race their rides out on Route 23 and put each other in the hospital. They were nothing but a bunch of jerks.

"Come on, Chief," Quincy said. "Give Kim a chance."

I had to **preen** slightly. It was kind of cool how both Quincy and Tad had such confidence in me. If only my mother could jump on the bandwagon.

I grinned at my mother and received a blank stare in return. Apparently Tad and Quincy's arguments hadn't exactly been **efficacious**. Not that I was surprised. My mother's hide was as hard as rock.

"Would you two gentlemen excuse us, please?" my mother asked, keeping her eyes on me.

"Sure, Chief," Quincy said quickly, exhibiting a clear **propensity** for escape. He smiled at me as he walked by, and Tad gave me an encouraging wink. I steeled myself as the door closed behind me. My heart was still fluttering with excitement, and I wasn't about to give up this fight.

I wanted to take part in this case. I felt like I was meant to take part in this case.

"Kim, I don't think you understand the seriousness of the situation," my mother began. "I know you're a very self-sufficient person, and I know you did well in the course last summer, but that does not mean you are prepared to take on a case like this on your own."

---

crude: vulgar or offensive
indigent: poor or needy

preen: swell with pride
efficacious: effective or successful

propensity: tendency

"I won't be on my own," I told her. "You guys will help me, right? It's not like you're going to drop me off in the **hallowed** halls of Hereford and just leave me to my own devices."

"Of course not. If I were to send you in, we would be in constant contact," my mother replied. "But Kim, going undercover is a very delicate skill. It takes **finesse** . . . it takes **cunning** . . . it takes imagination—"

"Like I don't **exemplify** all those things," I said, rolling my eyes.

"Kim—"

"Mom, listen," I said, **curtailing** whatever she had planned for her next **harangue**. I walked over and leaned my hands on her desk so I could look down on her. It wasn't often I got to take the **domineering stance** with my mother. I knew I was being **pertinacious**, but I had to do what I had to do.

"If there's a drug problem at Hereford, I want to help." She blinked, and I could tell she was starting to understand exactly why I was so **resolute** about this. "I *have* to help," I added, just to drive the point home.

"Kim . . . ," my mother said in a tone that told me she was breaking.

"Please, Mom," I said. "Just give me a chance. I swear I won't let you down."

My mother took a deep breath and let it out very slowly. "Fine," she said finally. "But one thing goes wrong up there on that campus, and you are outta there. No questions asked."

"Yes!" I said, jumping up. A pack of butterflies went wild in my stomach. "Yes! Thank you, thank you, thank you!"

I ran around the desk and gave her a big hug, and my mother squeezed me back a bit **reluctantly**. I knew she was doing this against her will, but I'd show her. I was going to bring home the bad guys and clean up that school.

Whoa. Did I just say that?

---

hallowed: sacred or respected
finesse: grace or flair
cunning: slyness or sneakiness

exemplify: serve as an example of
curtailing: holding back
harangue: lecture or criticism
domineering: dominant

stance: position or viewpoint
pertinacious: constant
resolute: firm or steadfast
reluctantly: unwillingly

*   *   *   *   *

"Okay, these are your suspects," Tad told me, laying three photographs on the table in front of me. It was the following morning, and I was sitting in the conference room at the police station, my back **rigid**. I had worn my most boring brown sweater and my cleanest jeans to **engender** an air of responsibility, but Tad's business-like demeanor only served to make me feel like the **inept** rookie I was.

I'd woken up with slightly less confidence than I'd exhibited the day before. Maybe that rush of **aplomb** I'd had was just an **extension** of the roller-coaster emotions I'd been experiencing, but by the light of a new day the truth was clear.

I mean, yeah, I was a good actress. (Witness the lightheartedness at the funeral and the total dupe I'd pulled on my guidance counselor. The man is a **dunce**, but still.) So maybe I could make the population of Hereford believe I was just another rich student, but who knew if I was a good detective? What if I went in there and tanked? What if I let my mother down and embarrassed her? This was so important to her. What was the headmaster of Hereford going to think if the **emissary** from the local police department couldn't even navigate the school or keep the suspects straight? (I don't have the greatest attention span.)

I couldn't do this. Who was I kidding?

I sipped my Dunkin' Donuts coffee and glanced at the closed door as Tad momentarily turned his back on me. What were the chances I could **abscond** with a jelly donut and make a clean getaway?

"Kim, have you even looked at the photos?" Tad demanded.

I glanced up at him with **trepidation**. For all the **acclaim** he'd heaped upon me the day before, he was back to being **abrasive** today. Talk about **fickle**. But if Tad was having his doubts, maybe

rigid: firm or stiff	**extension:** product or outgrowth	**trepidation:** fear or nervousness
engender: produce		
inept: clumsy or unskilled	**dunce:** fool or idiot	**acclaim:** praise
aplomb: self-confidence or ease	**emissary:** representative or agent	**abrasive:** grouchy or irritating
	abscond: run away	**fickle:** unpredictable or unreliable

my doubts were well founded. Still, somehow I didn't want to let him see me sweat.

"Sorry," I told him, setting the coffee aside. I used my finger-tips to slide the three photographs toward me. The first **depicted** a handsome guy with curly brown hair, broad shoulders, and an open, **genial** smile. It was clearly his class picture, because he was posed in an uncomfortable position in front of a featureless background. The piece of tape slapped on the bottom of the picture read "David Rand."

"David has a record," Tad began, sitting down across from me. "He's from Brooklyn, and he's got two arrests under his belt. One for breaking and entering, although no charges were brought. The other for possession of marijuana."

Possession of marijuana. Like that was such a shocker in this day and age. Not that I would ever say that to Tad, who would definitely go on a **tirade enumerating** the evils of drug use. I didn't need to hear it because I was right there with him. My generation may have been all about the easy high, but I had never touched the stuff, nor anything harder. I kind of wished no one around me had.

I looked at David's sweet face again. He hardly seemed like a hardened criminal.

"Why were no charges brought on the first arrest?" I asked.

"Good question. See? Now you're with me," Tad said, check-ing a file. "It says here that it was the house of a family friend." He scanned the page. "Oh, here it is—a quote from the lady of the house. 'We know Davey didn't mean any harm. This is just the kind of thing he does.'"

"Huh?" I said, my question mirroring Tad's **dumbfounded** expression.

He flipped a page and read on. "This is from his statement. 'They just got the new Protector 2000 alarm system, and I wanted to see if I could get past it. I wasn't going to take anything.'"

---

depicted: showed
genial: friendly

tirade: outburst
enumerating: listing or naming

dumbfounded: astonished or speechless

I let out a guffaw. "Interesting guy."

"No doubt," Tad said. "And it gets even more interesting. Hereford just got a new firewall installed on their computer system, and while the tech guy was in there setting it up, he found out somebody's been hacking all the school's secure files for months. Guess who?"

"David Rand," I said under my breath.

"Got it in one," Tad replied with a wink. I shuddered. Someday I was really going to have to tell him how inappropriate that was.

We moved on to the next picture.

"That would be Marshall Cone," Tad said with a **sardonic** smile. "Big Man On Campus."

"In what way?" I asked.

"That kid is an all-star football, basketball, and baseball player," Tad **clarified**. "*And* get this—he runs an intramural karate league."

"Cool," I said, looking down at the photo. Somehow, even though he was a fellow **devotee** of the martial arts, I took an instant dislike to Marshall. He had one of those **haughty** expressions I expected from kids at Hereford. His chin was slightly raised, and his smile was almost a smirk. He was handsome, no doubt. Broad and athletic with dark skin and dark eyes, but I could practically hear him in my head going on and on about how great he was.

I'm so hot . . . I'm so cool . . . I'm so rich I could buy you and *your family . . .*

"Now, Marshall's a suspect because he's at Hereford on full scholarship," Tad said.

My line of thought was **disrupted**, and I flushed with embarrassment. Okay, so he wasn't rich. So much for jumping to conclusions.

"Why does that make him a suspect?" I asked.

"It's not that. It's the fact that even though he's dirt-poor and on scholarship, he's always walking around with all the same toys the other Hereford kids have," Tad explained, leaning both elbows

sardonic: mocking or scornful	**devotee:** fan or enthusiast	**disrupted:** interrupted or disturbed
clarified: explained or made clear	**haughty:** proud or conceited	

on the table. "PalmPilot . . . iPod . . . laptop computer and on and on."

"So where's he getting the money?" I said, my brain starting to come to life. I felt like I was beginning to **hone** my investigative skills right here. My level of confidence mounted, and I shifted forward in my seat.

"Exactly," Tad said with a satisfied smile. "Could be drug money."

I laid Marshall's picture on top of David's and grabbed the next one. This kid had juvenile delinquent written all over him. **Pallid** skin, a **furtive** expression. You could practically feel the tension in the picture, like as soon as it had been snapped he'd bolted for the nearest door. He had dark, shaggy hair and a bit of stubble around his chin. He sported a leather jacket over the **requisite** shirt and tie.

Even though he was rough around the edges, I thought he was totally hot. His green eyes were intense, and I've always liked the bad-boy type. Or, more accurately, the guys who *looked* like bad boys but underneath were simply misunderstood, tortured-artist types just waiting for someone who really *gets* them. You know, like James Dean or Pacey Witter or Angel.

Of course, he may not have *been* a bad boy. I'd made assumptions on the last picture that had proved to be **fallacious**. I didn't want to make the same mistake twice.

"Who's this guy?" I asked.

"Jonathan Wisnewski," Tad replied with a sneer. "In my opinion, he's your number one. He hangs out with the only rough crowd at Hereford, and he's always looking over his shoulder. He just has that quality, you know?"

"Wait, so no arrests, no suspicious behavior?" I asked.

"Nah. The administrators just think he's hiding something," Tad replied.

---

hone: sharpen   **furtive:** sly or sneaky   **fallacious:** incorrect
pallid: pale   **requisite:** required or necessary

Great. It looked like I wasn't the only one judging books by their covers around here. Still, *I* couldn't help it. I was just a **peer** of these kids, and we always jump to conclusions about each other. But Tad was an adult and a police officer. His behavior seemed a bit **precipitate**, to say the least.

"Can a person really be a suspect based on their appearance?" I asked.

He opened a folder and read from it. "Student exhibits **persistent** exhaustion, paranoia, and **shiftlessness**. His eyes are often glassy and rimmed with red. He is **sullen**, withdrawn, and lashes out when **provoked**."

I blinked. "You just described half my graduating class," I told him.

"Well, we decided he's a suspect, so he's a suspect," Tad shot back, **eschewing** the issue.

"All right, all right," I said, not wanting to get into a big blowout. "So it's just those three? No other possibilities?"

"These are the three suspects we've weeded out after a careful review," Tad said. "It's one of these guys. Don't waste your time elsewhere."

"Gotcha," I said.

At that moment Quincy walked in and handed me a brown folder with an ID clipped to the top. I smiled when I saw that it was a Hereford Academy ID, complete with my senior-year photo and a whole new **alias**—Kim Sharpe.

"Cool," I said, yanking the ID free. With it came a freshly laminated Connecticut driver's license and an ATM card, both with Kim Sharpe's name on them. "Wow, you guys are good," I said, impressed.

"Thanks for the **compliment**," Quincy said, blushing. "Now, in that file is your new history. You've gotta learn that backward and forward."

---

peer: colleague or equal
precipitate: reckless or hasty
persistent: constant
shiftlessness: laziness

sullen: gloomy or morose
provoked: irritated or aggravated
eschewing: avoiding

alias: false name
compliment: praise or flattery

"No problem," I said, opening the file and flipping through the pages.

"He's not kidding, Kim. Backward and forward," my mother said, appearing in the doorway. "Sideways wouldn't be a bad idea either."

I took a deep breath and placed the folder down in front of me. "I got it, Ma," I said. I didn't want her to treat me like I was just her kid around the office. It **undermined** my credibility—if I had any.

"This isn't a joke, Kim," my mother told me, walking into the room. "There's someone at that school dealing a whole hell of a lot of Ecstasy, and they're going to be on the lookout for anyone out of the ordinary."

I straightened up at my mother's tone and pulled the file toward me again. "Okay," I told her. Then, noticing her scolding expression, I added, "I'll study it tonight. I'm going to be a **paradigm** of an undercover officer. I swear."

"All right, then, good," my mother said. She pulled a folded sheet of paper from her back pocket and opened it before laying it in front of me. Quincy smiled and placed a fatherly hand on my shoulder. My heart started to pound **frenetically** as I looked down at the certificate.

This certifies that Kimberly Ann Stratford is hereby instated as a Deputy Officer of the Law in the town of Morrison, County of Morris, State of Connecticut.

It was really happening. I was about to become an Officer of the Law. Kickass!

"You'll have to sign this before we can **dispatch** you on any assignment," Quincy said, clearing his throat in an official way as he handed me a pen.

I grinned at all of them, feeling like some kind of **maverick** young lawmaker—the type of woman they made bad Lifetime movies about. Any doubts I had about my abilities were **allayed** as I saw

---

undermined: damaged
paradigm: example or model

frenetically: wildly or frantically
dispatch: send out

maverick: rebel
allayed: put to rest

the confidence in their eyes. There was no way I could walk away from this now. I signed the certificate with a **flourish**.

David, Marshall, and Jonathan had better watch their backs, I thought. Deputy Kim Stratford was on their tails, and they were never going to see me coming.

*   *   *   *   *

As I followed Ms. Bean—yes, Ms. *Bean*—through the halls of Hereford, I felt like I had been almost **prescient**. The school was everything I had predicted it would be and more. The walls were fashioned out of dark, gleaming wood, just as I'd imagined. The floors were glossed to such a high shine I could almost see my reflection in them. Everywhere I looked there was another painting or photograph of an **aloof** headmaster or a **decorously** dressed faculty member. Every now and then I'd hear a **medley** of voices or a peal of laughter, but the volume was **muted** by the thickness of the walls.

"You will be sharing your room with Danielle Fisher, one of our finest pupils," Ms. Bean told me, her heels clip-clopping as she took a set of stairs to the second floor. The woman had a pointed chin and glasses with tiny round frames, and she wore a black turtleneck. We'd been right about the Miss Minchin idea—she looked just like the headmistress in *Sara Crewe or What Happened at Miss Minchin's* by Frances Hodgson Burnett.

"She has had her room to herself since the **commencement** of the school year, but I'm sure she'll be **amenable** to this new arrangement."

Yeah, right, I thought. I knew *I* would be psyched if I had my own room and some new chick came swooping in and took over. This Danielle girl was about to **forsake** her swingin' single-room lifestyle thanks to me. I could just imagine how a spoiled, stuck-up Hereford

---

flourish: showy gesture
prescient: prophetic
aloof: distant or cold

decorously: properly or decently
medley: jumble or mix
muted: muffled or quieted

commencement: start or beginning
amenable: agreeable
forsake: abandon

girl would feel about *that*. She'd probably be on the phone to Daddy in two-point-five seconds. Just what I needed—instant **enmity**.

Ms. Bean rapped on a door marked "217" and smiled a tight smile in my direction.

"Come in," a quiet voice called out.

"Danielle, I'd like you to meet your new roommate," Ms. Bean said crisply as she opened the door.

Danielle stood up from her computer, turning her back to it as if to hide the screen from us. (Probably carrying on a **passionate** email affair with her ski instructor in Switzerland.) She swung her long blond hair behind her back, and to my surprise, she smiled. Her expression was welcoming, even happily surprised. She was wearing a black V-neck sweater and hip-slung jeans and looked like she would fit right in with me and my friends. I was surprised by the **affinity** I felt for her. After all, she was a Hereford girl. I was supposed to feel nothing but disgust.

"Hi," she said, lifting her hand in an almost-wave.

"Hi. I'm Kim Sharpe," I said, proud of myself for getting even that little bit right. I **bustled** into the room and placed my bags on the empty bed that was shoved against the far wall along with an empty desk and a dresser.

"Oh, we can rearrange the furniture. It's just like that because I've been alone," Danielle said.

"Thanks," I replied.

I noticed that Danielle's room, while not a total disaster, was far from **antiseptic** like my mother's house. Her open closet was jampacked, and there were some sweaters bunched up on the floor on top of her shoes. The garbage was in desperate need of an emptying, and her bed looked slightly mussed, as if she'd recently been napping or reading over there. I had a feeling we were going to get along just fine.

---

enmity: hostility or ill will

passionate: hot-blooded or fervent

affinity: liking

bustled: hurried

antiseptic: sterile or bland

"Well, I'll leave you girls to get acquainted," Ms. Bean said. "Good evening."

Danielle laughed the instant the door was closed and sat down on her bed, facing me.

"She's a **convivial** person, isn't she?" I said lightly.

"*Convivial*," Danielle repeated, sounding impressed.

I flushed. "Yeah, back home they call me the walking dictionary," I told her with an apologetic shrug. "Hope you don't mind, cuz I can't control it."

"Are you kidding? It's fine!" Danielle told me. "I'm always slipping and using big words myself. The kids here think I'm showing off, but I'm not. It's just the way I talk."

"Me too!" I said, grinning. See? I knew I liked this girl.

"So! Tell me all about yourself!" Danielle prompted, leaning back against the wall.

"All about myself?" I repeated uncertainly. She had to be the inquisitive type, didn't she? I could probably **regurgitate** everything I knew about Kim Sharpe in the space of ten minutes, but then what were we going to talk about?

"Oh, sorry. I don't mean to be **presumptuous**," she said, flushing so fast I thought her skin was about to burn off. "I guess I'm just excited to have a roommate. There's kind of a **dearth** of people to talk to around here. At least for me."

"Really?" I asked.

Leading questions, I remembered Quincy telling me. *Always be interested in others, but don't give up too much about yourself.*

"What do you mean?" I **pressed**.

"Well, let's just say I'm not Miss Popularity at Hereford Academy," Danielle replied, getting up and crossing to her dresser. She toyed with the scalloped edge of a frame that was propped up there. The picture appeared to be of her and a guy, but it was hard to tell from that distance.

---

convivial: warm or friendly
regurgitate: repeat

presumptuous: conceited or presuming
dearth: shortage or lack

pressed: questioned persistently

My heart instantly went out to her. She seemed so **forlorn**.

"It's really just me and David," Danielle added, regaining some of her spark.

"David? Is that your boyfriend?"

Danielle laughed. "Uh . . . no. David and I do not have that kind of relationship. We're just buddies. He's my best friend here, which is why it's so cool that you're here now."

"What do you mean?" I asked.

"I may actually get to have a girlfriend," Danielle said sheepishly.

Oh, wow. That would've been pathetic if it weren't so earnest.

She checked her watch. "David's actually going to be here any second to go down to dinner. You can come with us!" she said brightly.

She was so **jubilant** at the prospect of dinner, I nearly laughed out loud. Then it hit me that we were standing here talking about someone who had the very same first name as one of my suspects. Could I possibly be that lucky?

I pulled out a Hereford student directory that Ms. Bean had given me.

"What's David's last name?" I asked. I flipped open the directory as if I were just run-of-the-mill curious to see what he looked like.

"Rand. David Rand," Danielle clarified. "He's the best. You're going to *love* him."

I couldn't believe it. My roommate was BFF (best friends forever) with one of my **prime** suspects! How perfect was this? I was so caught up in the **felicitous** turn of events that I barely even noticed the fact that Danielle was acting like she already knew me and could tell what kind of people I was going to *love*.

There was a knock at the door, and my stomach lurched. This was it. The investigation was *on*.

"Hey!" Danielle said, opening the door for a guy who was, without a doubt, suspect number one—David Rand. His hair was cropped a

---

forlorn: sad or unhappy **prime:** major or foremost **felicitous:** fortunate
jubilant: joyful

bit closer than it had been in the picture, and he was shorter than I expected, but it was him—my little hacker.

"Hey. Ready for some grub?" David asked, rubbing his hands together. Then he noticed me, and his eyes did that kind of flicking thing they do when you see someone you find attractive. Whatever David saw in me, he obviously liked it. I wasn't sure whether to feel flattered or scared. I mean, he *was* a suspect, and from the sound of his file, he was also kind of a nut job.

"And you are?" he asked, sidling over to me. He didn't lack confidence, that was for sure.

"David, this is Kim, my new roommate," Danielle said with that giddy smile. "Kim, meet David Rand."

"Hey," I said. "Nice to meet you."

"The pleasure is mine," David said with that broad smile he'd **evinced** in his picture. "Shall we?" he asked, glancing at Danielle.

"We shall," she joked back with a formal nod.

She grabbed her keys, and we all headed out for the dining hall together. David and Danielle walked ahead of me as I closed the door, and I couldn't help saying a little thank-you to the gods. I was already in with my first suspect, and I'd only been at Hereford for half an hour.

This case was going to be cake.

---

evinced: displayed

"So, Kim, you ready for your first class with **Nefarious** Nitkin?" Danielle asked the following morning as she, David, and I made our **descent** to the basement classroom where senior History class was held. At dinner the night before they had given me a rundown of all my teachers, but no one had mentioned this guy.

"Nefarious Nitkin?" I asked, raising my eyebrows.

"Danielle came up with that one," David said with a laugh. "It's so perfect."

"What? Is he really evil or something?"

"You'll see. I would have told you about him, but no one could ever do Nitkin justice," Danielle told me, tucking her hair behind her ear.

Within seconds I understood why. Mr. Nitkin was a skinny little man with **angular** features and a dark mustache that gave him a serious Hitleresque vibe. Judging by the pursed expression on his face as he watched us fill the room, he also had a **distinct** dislike of all teenagers. When I approached him with my schedule, he eyed me with **disdain** and gave me a **curt** welcome.

"Take any empty chair," he said, waving his arm about. That was when I caught a whiff of his cologne or aftershave or whatever it was. It was so **noisome** I almost heaved up my nutritious Hereford breakfast.

That was one thing I had to give this place. My first teacher may have been **odious**, but so far the food was beyond **reproach**. After that morning's yummy oatmeal, fresh fruit, and endless supply of OJ, I actually couldn't wait to see what the chefs whipped up for lunch.

---

nefarious: evil or wicked
descent: move downward
angular: lean or bony
distinct: clear

disdain: disrespect or ill will
curt: abrupt or rude
noisome: harmful or nasty

odious: horrible
reproach: criticism

Danielle and David both took seats at the front of the room, saving an empty desk for me right between them. No good. If I sat up front I'd never be able to scan the rest of the classroom and see if either of the other suspects was there. Unfortunately, Danielle was waving at me giddily, and I couldn't ignore her. She was so obviously **ecstatic** to have someone new to sit with. Poor kid. I sighed, **resigning** myself to a class period with nothing to absorb except historical facts. Ones I probably already knew.

"Good luck. You're probably gonna need it," David said, leaning toward me.

"What, you think I can't handle this class?" I asked.

"It's not a commentary on you," he said with a grin. "*None* of us can handle this class."

I smiled. After spending dinner and breakfast with David, I was having a hard time believing this kid could be a drug dealer. He was just so sweet and funny and smart. He couldn't be the type of person who would get involved with something like that. Could he?

"Did you hear about Cora Klein?" a girl behind me whispered to her friend. "Her parents are sending her off to some school in France."

"That's what happens when you flunk the urine test," the other girl said, snorting a laugh.

Danielle and David exchanged a loaded look. "Who's Cora Klein?" I asked innocently.

"Just some moron who got busted for E," David replied as he opened a notebook. "There were, like, five kids booted from here last week. If you get a Big Brother vibe around here, it's probably because everyone's watching us like hawks now."

Interesting. Would David talk about the situation so easily if *he* were the drug dealer?

"Bet your parents wouldn't have sent you here if they knew it was

---

ecstatic: delighted or overjoyed

resigning: giving up or yielding

Ecstasy central," the girl behind me said snottily.

On the contrary, I thought. *That's* why *I* was sent here.

"All right, class!" Mr. Nitkin slapped his hands together the moment the bell rang, and everyone fell into their seats. "Let's see who among you has actually done the reading."

A **general** groan went up among the students, and I felt a little wave of nerves run through me. A pop quiz? But I wasn't prepared!

Then I realized that it didn't matter if I wasn't prepared. I wasn't a student here. I no longer had to **maintain** my straight-A average. Kim Stratford had never failed a quiz in her life, but maybe Kim Sharpe did it all the time!

Or not, I thought, the very idea of Fs causing goosebumps to pop out all over my skin. I mean, a person couldn't go from perfectionist to **delinquent** *that* fast. It could give you whiplash.

All my **obsessing** turned out to be pointless anyway. Nefarious Nitkin wasn't handing out papers. He was simply standing at the front of the classroom eyeing us like we were the slush he'd kicked off his boots. Meanwhile, all the kids around me were practically trembling.

"Revere!" Nitkin barked, causing an **obese** kid to my left to **flinch**. "In what year was the Battle of the Bulge fought?"

Revere, whose first name I later was to learn was actually Paul— cruel parents—**blanched**. "Uh . . . end of 1944 into 1945?"

"That is correct," Mr. Nitkin said, making a mark in his leather-bound notebook. "Although you should know by now that I do not award full points to a person who begins his answer with '*uh.*' "

Paul sank a bit lower in his seat as Nitkin paced the front of the room.

"Fisher!" he blurted. I was happy to see that Danielle was not intimidated. She stared back at him, her hands folded on her desk, her expression **impassive**. "Who was the Allied General in charge of the Normandy Campaign?"

---

general: common or universal
maintain: keep up

delinquent: careless or irresponsible
obsessing: worrying or fixating

obese: fat or overweight
flinch: cringe or start
blanched: grew pale
impassive: emotionless

"General Dwight D. Eisenhower, Mr. Nitkin," Danielle replied **nonchalantly**.

"Very good," Nitkin said with a smirk. I could tell he liked Danielle, but I wasn't sure if that was a good thing or a bad thing. If someone clearly evil likes you, there must be something wrong.

Just kidding.

"Cone!"

Everyone turned around as my heart leaped into my throat. Marshall Cone, suspect number two, was sitting at the back of the classroom, his chair tipped onto its back legs and his arms draped over two more chairs that he had pulled closer to him. He lifted his chin at Nitkin and smiled the same cocky smile I'd noticed in his picture. Unlike most of the kids in the room, he was **unabashed** by Nitkin's attack.

I instantly disliked him and all his little friends. They reminded me all too much of the so-called "popular kids" at my high school—the ones who thought they were so cool and that everyone loved them, even though everyone hated them for being such egotistical jerks. **Ironic** how the kids who are called "popular" are usually only friends with a very small group of people.

"Cone, name the United States' primary Allies in World War II," Nitkin said.

Easy question.

"Iraq and Iran?" Marshall said, his grin widening. A group of kids around him laughed and slapped hands, and a pretty but way-too-dolled-up girl in front of him rolled her eyes and smiled.

Nitkin's face hardened. "I suppose you think you're funny, Mr. Cone," he said. "But you get zero points for the day." He made a note in his book and resumed with the **rapacious** questioning. I continued to stare at Marshall for as long as I could without drawing attention to myself. He wasn't even remotely **ruffled** by the zero he'd just earned. As an overachiever by nature, I just couldn't

---

nonchalantly: casually or coolly
unabashed: unembarrassed or unashamed

ironic: opposite to what was expected
rapacious: aggressive or predatory

ruffled: bothered or intimidated

understand people like that. Besides, wasn't this kid on scholarship? How could he afford to pull a stunt like that?

The class period dragged on endlessly. Nitkin spent the entire hour quizzing us **incessantly**. He even threw a couple of **queries** my way, but I answered them both correctly, much to his obvious **exasperation**. He seemed determined to prove that wherever I had come from, my education had been substandard. But I like to think I **debunked** that theory. Still, by the end of the class I was exhausted from trying to remember all the facts I'd learned the year before. And then Nitkin assigned a ten-page paper. I couldn't believe it. In all my excitement to go undercover, I'd neglected to realize that this job was going to require actual homework of the precollege variety.

Now I had yet another **motivation** to solve this case quickly. I had to get the heck out of here before that paper was due!

Even though Marshall and his friends were sitting at the back of the room, they were the first ones out the door when the bell rang. I grabbed my stuff and raced after them, hoping David and Danielle wouldn't want to chat and **detain** me from my mission. I was too fast for them, though, and the second I hit the hallway, I called out Marshall's name.

Every single person in our vicinity stopped and gaped at me. Not that I could blame them. How dare the new girl deign to speak to this **exalted** popular one?

I have to admit, I felt pretty cool. If this were last year I probably would have been intimidated by this crowd, but it was like my mission had sparked some kind of previously untapped well of audacity within me.

I turned beet red as Marshall turned to face me, a question in his eyes. He really was gorgeous. **Arrogant**, but gorgeous.

My heart pounded nervously and I hated it. This kid wasn't supposed to be able to make me nervous! He was in high school!

---

incessantly: continually or relentlessly
queries: questions
exasperation: frustration or annoyance

debunked: exposed as untrue
motivation: reason or incentive

detain: delay or hold back
exalted: lofty or high-ranking
arrogant: proud or conceited

"Who're you?" he asked, shoving one hand into the front pocket of his jeans and squaring his shoulders, a maneuver that only made him seem more imposing. The pretty girl from class reached out and **clasped** his free hand, glaring at me as I approached.

Jeez. Possessive, aren't we?

"Don't worry, I'm not after your boyfriend," I heard myself say.

The girl pressed her high-gloss lips together. "Like I'm threatened," she said with an **indifferent** scoff. (She clearly was.)

"Cheryl, I'm telling you, I don't even know this girl," Marshall said.

"No, you don't," I said. "I'm Kim Sharpe. I hear you're the person to talk to about the karate program."

Marshall and the guys that hovered around him laughed, but Cheryl's face took on a wicked gleam.

"Oh, you're the poor thing who got stuck rooming with Danielle, aren't you?" she said with **calculated** fake sympathy. She made a face as if the name tasted **rancid** on her tongue. "I feel sorry for you."

"Well, don't," I said. I had to bite the inside of my cheek to keep from lashing out with the rest of the **caustic** comebacks that were bouncing around inside my head. If I was going to investigate Marshall, I had to **infiltrate** this crowd. The last thing I needed was to **implant** myself at the top of his girlfriend's list of enemies.

"Sorry, new girl," Marshall said with a sneer. "We don't have chicks on our team."

Ugh! He was so **puerile**, I was surprised he wasn't sporting Pampers. He started to turn away, but now he had me fuming, and I refused to be **rebuffed**. I stepped in front of him and glared right into his eyes.

"You do now," I said.

Marshall paused and looked me up and down, clearly impressed by my attitude but trying not to show it. Cheryl's grip on his hand tightened, but he didn't seem to notice.

---

clasped: held or grasped
indifferent: uncaring or unconcerned
calculated: deliberate or plotted

rancid: rotten
caustic: sharp or bitter
infiltrate: break into
implant: insert or place

puerile: childish
rebuffed: rejected or snubbed

"All right, new girl," Marshall said finally. "You wanna get your ass kicked after classes today, then show up at the gym at five o'clock."

"I'll be there."

Marshall and his followers moved away, muttering and laughing. Freakin' popular kids. I couldn't stand them. Who did they think they were, anyway? A few of Marshall's friends cast wondering looks back at me and shook their heads as if they thought I was doomed.

They obviously had no idea who they were dealing with.

* * * * *

"Yeah, Cheryl pretty much **detests** me," Danielle said over lunch that afternoon.

I placed my tray of food at a table near the wall and dropped my books on an empty chair. The **aroma** coming from the kitchen caused my stomach to grumble **inaudibly**. I was still in shock over the fact that the lunch lady had grilled my hamburger right in front of me, making sure it was medium rare the way I'd ordered it. This wasn't a school lunch. It was fine American **cuisine**.

"Why?" I asked, dumbfounded. Who could hate such a sweet, **innocuous** person like Danielle? I mean, the girl had given up half of her closet for my clothing overflow. She was a saint.

"Cheryl was **biased** before she ever even met Danielle," David explained, shoveling French fries into his mouth. "All she had to hear was that we had a new **genius** on our hands, and she was ready to hate whoever it was."

"Oh, so you're a genius?" I teased.

Danielle flushed and looked down at her hands. "I'm probably going to be valedictorian," she said, her smile **abject**. "Apparently Cheryl was the **forerunner**, and then I got here . . . ."

"So you **surpassed** the princess, and she couldn't handle it," I

---

detests: hates	**innocuous:** harmless	**abject:** miserable
aroma: smell	**biased:** unfair or prejudiced	**forerunner:** predecessor
inaudibly: faintly	**genius:** brilliant person or	**surpassed:** beat or outdid
cuisine: cooking	mastermind	

said, glancing across the room at Marshall and his **raucous** friends. Cheryl was gabbing with a **bevy** of impeccably dressed girls, casting **scathing** looks in my direction every few seconds. They were probably making some **obnoxious assessments** about me and my wardrobe. "You gotta love it when people are that predictable."

"Amen," David said with a laugh. "I think surprises are highly **overestimated**."

At first this statement caught me off guard. David seemed to have exactly the kind of fun-loving personality that would **thrive** on surprises. But then I remembered his file, and it actually made sense. A guy who broke into houses to see if he could **bilk** the alarm system? Someone who hacked into the school's computers to keep watch over his classmates? That, my friends, is a control freak.

"Well, it's not my fault I'm here. I didn't even *want* to come. My parents only sent me because they thought I would have a better chance of getting into Harvard if I had a Hereford diploma," Danielle said. She glanced across the room at Cheryl. "I wish they would move on already and stop directing their **animosity** at me."

"They?" I asked.

"It's not just Cheryl, it's her friends," David explained, rolling his eyes. "That whole crowd. They're total lemmings. Going against Cheryl and Marshall is like . . . **blasphemy** around here."

I raised my eyebrows. "Well, then, no offense, Danielle, but David, why did you rise above the crowd?"

They both laughed, and I was glad Danielle didn't seem to take **umbrage** to my question. David shrugged, smiling across the table at her.

"What can I say? I took the time to actually know the girl, and I like her," he said. "Except she has this *nasty* tooth-picking habit."

"David! I do not!" Danielle said, tossing a crumpled napkin at him.

I smiled and dug into my lunch. If I had been at Hereford to

raucous: wild or rowdy	**assessments:** judgments or opinions	**bilk:** trick
bevy: crowd	**overestimated:** overrated or hyped	**animosity:** hostility or ill will
scathing: mocking or wounding	**thrive:** prosper or blossom	**blasphemy:** serious disrespect to beliefs
obnoxious: annoying or intolerable		**umbrage:** offense

make friends for life, I had definitely landed the right roommate. Danielle and David were clearly two of the more **congenial** people at this school.

Except he's still a suspect, Kim. It could just be a **façade**, I told myself. *You can't get sucked in.*

Unfortunately, it sounded like being friends with them was going to **hinder** any strides I might otherwise make with the cream of the crop, so to speak. If Marshall and Cheryl really hated Danielle, then the more I hung out with Danielle and David, the slimmer my chances of being accepted into Marshall's crowd. And I had to be accepted. The investigation depended on it.

"So why were you talking to Marshall Cone, anyway?" David asked.

"Oh, I want to join the karate team," I replied, eyeing Marshall as he wolfed down his second burger.

"Really? You do karate? That's **astonishing**," Danielle said, her eyes wide. "Are you any good?"

"Hey, you're talking to the girl who won the Connecticut State Tournament last year," I replied.

The second the words had left my mouth, my stomach was in upheaval. Kim Sharpe was supposed to be from *California*, not Connecticut.

"I thought you just moved here," Danielle said, not missing a beat.

Oh, God. They knew I was a **fraud**! I hadn't even lasted a full day before blowing my cover. Why couldn't I **refrain** from listing my many accomplishments? Was my ego that **inflated**?

"Oh, I meant the California State Tournament," I said with an embarrassed laugh. "Connecticut . . . California . . . I guess I just have Connecticut on the brain."

"California, huh? You don't seem like a California girl," David said. I was so happy that he'd moved on I could have screamed.

---

congenial: friendly	**astonishing:** incredible or	**refrain:** avoid
façade: false appearance	unbelievable	**inflated:** puffed up or
hinder: get in the way of	**fraud:** fake or phony	overblown

"That's why they **ostracized** me," I replied lightly, even though my heart was still pounding. "I think it was the brown hair that pushed them over the edge."

Danielle and David laughed, easing my nerves even further. "Where did you go to school?" Danielle asked.

"Stanford Prep," I said. My mother had decided it would behoove all of us if we set Kim Sharpe's past in a place I was familiar with so that I could talk freely. So Northern California and the Stanford area it was. If only I could manage to *remember* that in casual conversation!

"Why did you transfer?" David asked. "I mean, you could have stayed even if your parents moved, right?"

"Yeah, but my mom didn't like the idea of being so far away from me, so . . ."

"**Overbearing** parents," Danielle said. "I can relate."

"Well, good luck with Marshall," David told me. "He's a little **intense**."

Oooh. I could tell a spillage of inside info was **imminent**. Maybe I could make up for my earlier flub. "How so?" I asked. *Leading questions . . .*

David smiled **conspiratorially**. "Want a little known fact about Marshall?" he said, leaning across the table. I leaned in as well. "He's here on scholarship."

I made my mouth drop open. "Really?" I said. Like I didn't already know this. I was *so* **duplicitous**.

"Yep. For sports," David told me, nodding. "He's gotta produce on the field *and* keep his GPA up, or he's outta here."

"Yeah? Well, he didn't seem too intense in history today," I pointed out.

"It's a **ruse**," David told me. "He does that for his groupies, but he'll probably write an extra few pages on the paper to make up for it. Does it all the time."

---

ostracized: disliked or did not accept
overbearing: bossy or domineering

intense: forceful or extreme
imminent: coming up
conspiratorially: sneakily or secretively

duplicitous: two-faced or dishonest
ruse: trick or hoax

"How do you know all this?" I asked. "Are you **clairvoyant** or something?"

Danielle and David exchanged a knowing look. "I have my ways," David said.

Yeah. You hacked into the school's central computer, I thought, resisting the urge to call him out. My brain was dancing around to the tune of "I know something you don't know! *Na-na-na-na-na.*"

Sometimes my brain can be *so* **callow**.

I was about to ask him to elaborate when I saw someone emerge from the lunch line out of the corner of my eye. It struck me as **incongruous** because most of the students had gotten their food and sat down by now. I felt all the blood rush to my head as I realized I was looking at my third suspect.

Jon Wisnewski was slouching his way across the cafeteria with a heaping tray of food. He kept his eyes trained straight ahead and down toward the floor. His jacket was so big for his thin frame that it **billowed** out behind him as he walked. He shoved through the metal door at the top of the room and trudged outside where he took a seat at one of the picnic tables in the quad.

Even though it was about ten degrees outside, he proceeded to sit there and eat his lunch, his breath making mist clouds in the **frigid** air. He was even hotter in person—in that moody, scowling way.

"Kim? What're you staring at?" Danielle asked.

"Sorry," I said. "Guess I zoned out for a second there. See? I *am* a California girl."

My joke earned a couple of smiles, and then they thankfully moved on to the subject of Nitkin's assignment, leaving me free to watch Jon for a few more minutes. Anyone who would choose to sit outside alone in the freezing cold rather that eat lunch among his classmates was either a total **outcast** or an avowed **introvert**. There was something about Jon that made me think it was the latter—he

---

clairvoyant: psychic or mind-reading
callow: immature

incongruous: strange or out of place
billowed: fluttered or waved

frigid: freezing
outcast: outsider
introvert: shy person

was **solo** by choice. I had a feeling Jon Wisnewski was going to be a tough nut to crack.

* * * * *

After lunch, the students at Hereford got a half-hour break that was **akin** to recess. I hadn't had recess since the fourth grade. And they called this place a prep school.

"We go outside when it's nice out, but on days like this we just hang out here or in the library," Danielle told me, leaning back in her chair. Behind her I saw Jon get up from his picnic table and toss his garbage in a nearby **receptacle**. I held my breath as he walked back into the cafeteria, then headed for the door at the far end of the room.

Follow him, a little voice in my head told me. *You have thirty free minutes. You should be doing* something *productive.*

I jumped up from my seat so fast I slammed my knee into the table, causing all the trays to jump. My knee throbbed, but I tried to **repress** any visceral reaction.

"Are you okay? Where are you going?" David asked.

"I just realized I forgot my French book in the room," I told them, rubbing at my knee. "I'll . . . see you guys later."

I scurried along the wall as fast as I could without looking suspicious. Jon pushed through the swinging door that led to the main hallway, and I took a deep breath and followed. I had to get more info on this guy, and if I had to do it **surreptitiously**, then so be it.

Jon walked at a fast pace down the center of the hall, shaking his hair back from his face every so often. At first I had to remind myself to breathe. I kept remembering random things Tad had said about him—that he was constantly looking over his shoulder (he hadn't done that once) and that he hung out with the only rough

---

solo: alone
akin: similar

receptacle: container
repress: hold back or keep inside

surreptitiously: sneakily or secretly

crowd at Hereford (I'd yet to see anyone that looked rougher than the kids from *Smallville*).

But if he caught me following him, what was I going to say?

Hey, you have just as much of a right to be in this hallway as he does, I told myself.

So I **endeavored** to look like just another student out for a casual stroll, but luckily he never noticed I was there. His black boots made so much racket there was no way he could hear my tip-toeing Adidases.

He took a left at the end of the hall, and I pressed my back against the wall and waited for a count of ten, then followed. The doorway to the stairwell at the end of the hall was just swinging shut. I could hear laughter and voices echoing up and out into the hall from below, followed by the acrid **scent** of cigarette smoke.

Interesting. It seemed that Jon was joining in on some secret meeting. Whoever was back in that darkened stairwell, they had played hooky from lunch. Perhaps this was Jon's little "rough crowd." It was all I could do to keep from slapping myself on the back. I'd found out where Jon and his friends secretly **convened**! Go, me!

I stepped away from the wall and was just about to head into the stairwell to introduce myself and let the chips fall where they may, when a hand closed around my upper arm. I gasped, my heart seizing up, and turned to find a pair of flared nostrils right in my face. It was Headmaster Cox, the man who **reigned** over Hereford. I'd met him the day before when my mother had brought me in, but he'd barely even looked at me during our brief meeting.

"Ms. *Sharpe*," he said, his beady eyes narrowing. "Will you please come with me?"

I cast a longing look over my shoulder as he basically dragged me back in the direction from which I'd come. Who did this guy think he was? This could have been a **pivotal** moment in my

---

endeavored: tried   **convened:** met or gathered   **pivotal:** important or crucial
scent: smell   **reigned:** ruled

investigation. I was about to lay into him for interfering, but when we came out into the main hall there was a group of teachers chatting near the door to their lounge. I couldn't openly **defy** the headmaster without blowing my cover to bits. It looked as if Jon Wisnewski had **eluded** my grasp. For now.

Two minutes later I found myself sitting across a huge oak desk from the hulking headmaster, and I was seething. Where did this guy get off **foiling** my mission? Wasn't he the one who'd called the police, railing about the **exigent** drug situation at his school?

"You're **impeding** a police investigation by bringing me here," I said, my jaw set.

"While you're a guest at my school you will treat me with respect," he snapped back.

"Sorry. You're impeding a police investigation by bringing me here, *sir*," I replied, refusing to be **daunted** by him. The students here may have lived in fear of this guy, but that didn't mean I had to. It was important that I maintain an air of authority. After all, I *was* in charge of the investigation here at the school.

How cool was that?

"I suppose you think you're clever," he said, leaning his beefy arms into the edge of his desk. "But let me tell you something, missy. I don't **approve** of having a mole in my school. I don't like lying to my kids."

"Then why did you ask for our help?" I asked.

"When I requested the assistance of the local police department I did not expect espionage," he replied, his voice approaching a growl. He pushed himself out of his leather chair, which squeaked in seeming relief, and walked around the desk so that he could get right in my face again. "If I sense that you are violating the rights of any of my students, you will be out of here so fast your head will spin."

I stood up and kept my eyes locked on his, never **wavering**.

---

defy: disobey or challenge
eluded: escaped from
foiling: blocking or thwarting
exigent: difficult or tricky

impeding: getting in the way of
daunted: frightened or intimidated

approve: agree with or support
wavering: shaking or trembling

I didn't even back up the slightest bit. This guy was a jerk. And jerks didn't impress me.

"Well, sir, it's nice to know I have such **vociferous** support from the front office," I told him, my eyes flashing.

Then I turned and strode from the room, already looking forward to my nightly call with Chief Stratford. I was sure she would be interested to know that the headmaster was trying to **trammel** the investigation. As far as I was concerned, *that* was suspicious behavior. Maybe we should add another name to our suspect list.

Just for fun.

vociferous: vocal or enthusiastic

trammel: get in the way of

By the time classes were dismissed that evening, I was more than ready for a good **therapeutic** karate match. Each teacher at Hereford was more **dour** than the last, and they all seemed to think that the only way to get through to the students was by **inundating** us with homework. I had more assignments in one day than I had been given in my first week at Stanford. That's a top-ten college, people!

I ran to my room and changed into my karate robe, then headed for the gym. I hadn't set eyes on the place yet, and I ended up getting completely turned around in the **labyrinth** of the school's hallways. I was just about to give up on the whole thing and consider Marshall a lost cause when I finally heard the distant sounds of shouting male voices, followed by a smattering of applause. I followed the sounds, and eventually the hallway opened up onto a small lobby with the gym just beyond. I paused in the doorway of the **cavernous** room, taking it all in. So *this* was where all the school's money went.

Toto, we're not in Morrison High anymore.

This place was double the size of my old gym. The ceilings were so high it was like a cathedral, and the hardwood floors gleamed under the fluorescent lights. The bleachers were state-of-the-art—metal with cushioned seats—and obviously just recently installed. Burgundy-and-gold championship banners for **myriad** sports covered the walls. Apparently Hereford had won its division in every sport imaginable for the past three years.

"Impressed?" Marshall asked, breaking away from the rest of the team. He **loomed** over me.

---

therapeutic: healthy   **labyrinth:** maze   **loomed:** appeared or
dour: stern or unfriendly   **cavernous:** huge or vast   rose up
inundating: overwhelming   **myriad:** countless

"The **accolades abound**," I said **facetiously**. "Let me guess. You're responsible for all of these," I added, glancing up at the banners.

"Not all of them," Marshall said with a shrug. "The chicks won theirs on their own."

I made a noise in the back of my throat. I was *so* going to enjoy **vanquishing** this guy.

"You sure you want to do this?" Marshall asked, looking me up and down derisively. Not that I could blame him. My karate robes only **accentuated** my petite size.

All the better to fool you with, my dear.

"Oh, yeah. Bring it on," I said.

"Your funeral."

Marshall led me over to the mats where the rest of the team was sparring. Even if I wasn't impressed by the **multifarious** championship wins, I *was* pleasantly surprised at the number of guys on the team. Not to mention their **agility**. The two kids who were battling were fast, smart, and displayed some sophisticated moves. Still, I had a feeling I could take them.

I was, after all, a karate goddess.

As we watched, the tall blond guy flipped the shorter, less-blond guy over his shoulder and pinned him with a foot to the chest. Everyone cheered. Match over.

"All right, guys!" Marshall shouted, then whistled with both fingers in his mouth—a skill I had always wanted to master. "This is Kim. She thinks she can fight." A few of the guys laughed. "Tom, why don't you show her what the Hereford karate team is all about?"

I blinked, surprised. "Why don't you show me yourself?" I asked Marshall, as Tom, a rather **gaunt** guy, descended from the bleachers. A bunch of the guys "ooohed" predictably at my challenge.

Marshall laughed. "Trust me. You don't want that."

---

accolades: praise or compliments
abound: are plentiful
facetiously: jokingly

vanquishing: defeating or crushing
accentuated: drew attention to

multifarious: various
agility: swiftness or dexterity
gaunt: thin or bony

"Try me."

I could practically see the gears in Marshall's head working. I was calling him out, and if he ignored the challenge of a girl, he was going to look like a complete coward. His immature friends would never let him live it down.

"All right, fine," he said, adjusting his belt. Tom sat down again. "Your funeral."

"You said that already."

As we took our places on opposite sides of the sparring circle, Marshall **glowered** at me, his nostrils flaring. I was probably a total **aberration** to him. Marshall was the kind of guy that people didn't talk back to or **denigrate** in any way.

One of the guys I'd seen hanging out with Marshall at lunch blew a whistle, and I bowed to my opponent. Marshall barely tipped his head forward. Then the whistle sounded again, and the fight was on.

After eleven years of karate lessons and matches, I can tell when a guy is **discomfited** by the idea of fighting a girl. And I know how to use it to my advantage. Marshall was one of those guys. Instead of coming out no-holds-barred, he circled me **tentatively** for a few moments, unsure of what to make of me.

So I surprised him with a roundhouse kick to his upper chest. He was completely taken off guard and didn't even get his hands up. When he stumbled back, the guys in the crowd groaned. In a formal match, a shot like that would've earned me a point. In this match, it just made me grin.

But after that, Marshall didn't hold back.

He came at me with a one-two punch, and I dodged right, then left, so he caught only air. While he was off balance, I dropped to the ground and swept his feet out from under him. The bigger they are, the harder they—you know. And Marshall was definitely one of the bigger. There was an **audible** intake of breath as he went **horizontal**,

---

glowered: looked angrily
aberration: irregularity or freak
denigrate: talk down to

discomfited: uncomfortable
tentatively: cautiously or hesitantly

audible: capable of being heard
horizontal: parallel to the ground

hitting the ground with a thud. The rest of the team was clearly **disheartened** by their bumbling leader.

But Marshall wasn't one to stay down for long. He popped to his feet and **buffeted** me with a flurry of frustrated punches. I backed up quickly, so most of them just glanced off my shoulders and chest, but he was fast for his size, and one finally hit home with full force, right in my ribs. The pain was mind-blowing, and I gasped for air. This guy was powerful.

He backed up, waiting for me to catch my breath, and I knew I couldn't let him get in another shot like that or I was done for. This thing was going to have to end *now*.

I was about to do him in with my patented Kim Stratford jumping-kick-and-elbow-jab combination when something in his belligerent face triggered a realization within me and made me sick to my stomach.

I had to let him win.

This was a guy's guy—the campus stud—captain of three championship teams in three different sports. Getting beaten by a girl would probably be the single most **ignominious** thing that could happen to a guy like that. How was I supposed to investigate him if he was reminded of his **infamous** defeat every time I stepped into a room? If I beat him, he'd never speak to me again.

I was going to have to throw the fight—something I'd never done in my life.

Damn. And I had *so* wanted to **belittle** Mr. Cocky. Oh, well.

It was **heinous**, it was **reprehensible**, but I took a dive. I left my right side wide open, and Marshall landed a chop across the back of my neck that took me right down. I could've gotten up again, but I didn't. Instead I did my best **dramatic** rendition of a person too weak to go on, pushing myself up and then stumbling down again. Marshall's friends went wild, and soon he was offering his hand to help me to my feet.

---

disheartened: discouraged or dispirited
buffeted: beat or battered
ignominious: humiliating

infamous: well-known or legendary
belittle: put down
heinous: terrible or offensive

reprehensible: wrong or blameworthy
dramatic: staged or theatrical

I was flushed from **exertion**, but it was **compounded** by my frustration over what I'd just done and the fact that the guys were now **jovially** jeering at me. Oh, how I wished I could take every last one of them on in a match.

"All right, guys, that's enough for tonight!" Marshall dismissed them, smiling triumphantly.

I hung back while the rest of the team filed past me, some of the more human members shooting me **awed** glances. I had, after all, **dominated** for most of our time on the mat.

"Nice fighting," a kid with curly blond hair said. He was hanging back with Marshall, and they both seemed to be looking me over.

"So, am I on the team?" I asked.

"Well, I'm definitely impressed," he said. "I gotta admit, you had me there for a while."

I had you there 'til the end, I thought.

"We do need a replacement for Dumbo," the blond kid said.

"Dumbo?" I asked.

"This kid Danny Dumbrowski," Blondie replied. "He got kicked outta school last week because he got caught with drugs."

"So we've been calling him Dumbo ever since," Marshall put in, wiping his face with a towel.

"Wow. That's the second person I heard about getting booted," I said. "Is this a school or a crack house?"

Marshall and Blondie both laughed. "The moral of the story is, don't get caught," Blondie said cryptically.

I wanted to punch him in the face. So typical. A bunch of his friends get expelled from school for drugs, and he still thinks it's okay to do them as long as you don't get caught. You'd think he'd learn something from his friends' lives being ruined.

"Okay, I guess you can work out with us," Marshall said finally. "You're pretty cool, New Girl. It takes guts to do what you just did."

---

exertion: physical effort   **jovially:** merrily or gleefully   **dominated:** been in control
compounded: made worse   **awed:** impressed

I couldn't believe he was actually **conceding** to my worth. Maybe he wasn't so bad. Unless, of course, he was the dealer. "Thanks," I said, shoving my feet into my sneakers. "And my name is Kim."

"You know, you should ditch those losers you've been hanging out with and have lunch with me and mine tomorrow," Marshall said.

Okay, scratch that. He is so bad.

"Omigod, you are such a—"

Marshall's face darkened.

Dammit, Kim! Bite your tongue!

"Such a *saint*!" I **improvised**, smiling. "I would *love* to sit with you guys."

"Cool," Marshall said.

"Cool," Blondie repeated.

As we walked across the gym together, I swallowed back the **impertinent** remarks that kept creeping their way into my mouth. I had to be nice to Marshall—it was one of the requirements of the job. But when all this was over, I really wanted to get him back on that mat. Big time.

*   *   *   *   *

"So, what's so great about David's room?" I asked as Danielle and I climbed the stairs into the guys' dormitory that night. After dinner, David had suggested we chill with him at his digs, and Danielle had taken him up on it before I'd even had a chance. She really was making my job easier.

"David is a total technophile," Danielle explained, swinging her long hair back. "He's got a flat screen, surround sound, a stereo most guys would kill for. It's, like, entertainment central."

"His roommate must *love* that."

---

conceding: admitting

improvised: made up or ad-libbed

impertinent: impolite or disrespectful

"Oh, he does," Danielle said. "Christian owns more DVDs than God. These two only leave their room when it's absolutely **imperative**."

I was pretty sure that God wasn't a big DVD collector, but I kept my mouth shut as Danielle rapped on the door for room 209. I was just happy to have the opportunity to check out the **domicile** of one of my suspects.

Keep your eyes peeled and say as little as possible, I reminded myself.

The door was flung open and David stood there, grinning, wearing the most **ostentatious** Hawaiian shirt I've ever seen. The theme to *Star Wars* blasted through the door at a decibel level formerly reserved for fire sirens.

"Welcome to my **humble abode**!" David announced, throwing his arms wide.

It was like stepping into a funhouse. A huge flat-screen TV hung from the far wall between the two windows with the *Star Wars* opening story scrolling up it. A computer monitor in the corner flashed David's name rapidly like a strobe light, changing the font and color each time. Attached to the computer was every accessory known to man, from an electric piano keyboard to speakers and microphones and something that looked suspiciously like a police scanner. The bass lights on the keyboard jumped up and down with some random beat that was pumping through the speakers, adding to the **cacophony**. On one of the two beds, a scrawny, pasty-faced kid was lying prone on a **drab** gray comforter, busily pounding away at his GameBoy.

"Christian, this is Kim," David said, closing the door behind him.

"Hey!" I said brightly.

Christian grunted in response.

"Not exactly the **garrulous** type, huh?" I said under my breath.

"You can't talk to him when he's in the zone," David explained.

---

imperative: necessary   **humble:** modest or lowly   **drab:** dull or dingy
domicile: dwelling or home   **abode:** dwelling or home   **garrulous:** talkative
ostentatious: showy or flamboyant   **cacophony:** harsh noise

I decided to attempt it anyway. Christian was David's roommate. If I could befriend him and then **isolate** him at some point, I might be able to **garner** some useful information and start **compiling** my David Rand file. I perched on the edge of his bed near his feet.

"Whatcha playing?" I asked.

Christian sighed, hit pause, and fixed me with a glare. His eyes were glassy from hours of playing, and his angular features were screwed up in a scowl.

"Do you *know* anything about video games?" he asked.

"I **dabble**," I said with a shrug. It was a total lie. As far as I was concerned, video games were a huge waste of time, but I was bent on being as charming as humanly possible. Christian's face, however, was full of **scorn**.

"I don't have time for this. I have a level to clear." He pushed himself off the bed, taking his GameBoy with him, and stormed out of the room, slamming the door behind him.

"**Surly**, isn't he?" I said, deflated.

"Sorry. I should've warned you," David said, picking up the remote and mercifully muting the television just as Darth and the Stormtroopers were boarding Leia's ship. (I'm as much of a *Star Wars* **fanatic** as the next person. I just never felt the need to be deafened by it.) "He's been like that lately. That new Dragon Ball Z game is driving him over the edge."

"Whatever. He's always like that," Danielle said.

"So, what do you guys want to do?" David asked.

I got up and walked nonchalantly over to his computer, **feigning** interest in his many gadgets and peripherals.

"This thing is state-of-the-art," I said, hitting a key to make the screensaver dissolve. David had SpongeBob SquarePants wallpaper. I wasn't sure whether that was cute or disturbing.

"Wanna see something cool?" David asked, slipping in front of

---

isolate: separate
garner: gain or collect
compiling: putting together
dabble: mess around

scorn: ridicule or annoyance
surly: rude or abrupt
fanatic: enthusiast or maniac

feigning: faking or simulating

me, **ostensibly** to open up some program. I had a feeling he just wanted to **thwart** my attempts to get to his computer. **Paranoid** much?

But then, I guess he had a right to be. I *was* spying on him.

David punched away at his keyboard and pulled up what looked like a list of student names, each with a file icon next to it.

"I can tell you anything you want to know about any student in this place," David said, suddenly quite the **braggart**.

"Seriously?" I said, pretending to be shocked. "How?"

"I hacked into the school's mainframe," David said matter-of-factly. He didn't seem to have any problem talking about his questionable **ethics** with near-strangers. Not exactly the cautious behavior you'd expect from the guilty. Maybe David wasn't our dealer. He just seemed too . . . upfront.

"Wait . . . is that what you meant at lunch about having your ways?" I asked.

"Hey, you've gotta know who you're dealing with, right?" David said with a Cheshire-cat grin. "And it's not like the **administration** will **divulge** all our dirty little secrets. You wouldn't believe how many people at this place have checkered pasts," he added, glancing at Danielle.

"You have some serious issues, Mr. Rand," Danielle said with a smirk.

"I'm just taking care of me and mine," David replied, grinning.

Meanwhile, I was practically salivating to see what he had on his computer. "Come on. You can't have everyone's info on there," I prodded.

"You don't believe me?" David said, returning his attention to me. "Name one student, and I'll tell you everything about him . . . or her."

I could've kissed the kid right then and there. Little did he know he was basically offering to **facilitate** my investigation.

---

ostensibly: supposedly
thwart: block
paranoid: unreasonably suspicious

braggart: someone who brags or boasts
ethics: morals or principles

administration: officials
divulge: make known
facilitate: make easier

"Okay, how about Jon Wisnewski?" I asked. He was the one person I had yet to make contact with, and I still knew very little about him, "He seems like an interesting guy."

"Oh, he is," David said, the grin widening. I thought he would click Jon's file on his computer, but he simply **reclined** in his chair and rubbed his hands together. "Jon Wisnewski. A-minus grade point average, plays the drums, leaves campus every weekend in his 2001 Jeep Wrangler to head up to Evergreen Ski Lodge to snowboard. And get this—he's not allowed to have anything stronger than Tylenol because he got hooked on painkillers a couple years ago after he was in a serious boarding accident."

David leaned back even further, **basking** in the glow of his **omnipotence**. It was kind of cute but at the same time rather disturbing. Where did he get off nosing around in people's private business?

Then again, that was what I was doing—kind of. But it was my job! I had to stop obsessing.

"Wow," I said. "You do know everything."

Got hooked on painkillers, huh? I thought, trying to focus on the **pertinent** matter at hand. *Now there was incriminating evidence—something Tad hadn't even known about. Maybe Jon was a* **legitimate** *suspect.*

"Anyone else you want to know about?" David prompted. There was a **mischievous** spark behind his eyes now as he looked at me—like he was looking right into my soul.

Suddenly it was like my blood was freezing up in my veins. *Oh my God. He'd tried to look me up, hadn't he?*, I thought. What did my computer file say about me? Was I even *in* the Hereford computer system?

We couldn't have one of our main suspects suspecting *me.* I took a deep breath in an attempt to soothe my freshly frayed nerves. *Please let Mom have thought of this,* I begged silently, my palms

---

reclined: sat back or lay back
basking: reveling or indulging

omnipotence: power
pertinent: important or relevant
legitimate: valid or genuine

mischievous: naughty or playful

starting to sweat. *Please, please, please.*

I had a sudden mental image of me stepping into a cab to make my way home, my mission having failed on the very first day.

"What did you find out about me?" I asked finally, biting the **proverbial** bullet.

David flushed slightly. "Nothing. I wouldn't invade your privacy like that." He averted his eyes and toyed with a Slinky he had next to his cable modem. Not a good liar. If David *was* the perp, this case was going to be way too easy to solve.

"Why not? You do everyone else's," Danielle piped up. She was sacked out on Christian's bed staring at the muted television.

"Come on, David. I know I'm not **immune**. You've got every kid in this place on that list."

Please let there be something in there. Something that doesn't say I went to Morrison High and graduated last year.

"All right, all right," David said, sitting up and planting his feet on the floor. He pulled his chair toward the desk and tapped a few things into the computer. Instantly my picture and fake name appeared at the top of the page, followed by a transcript from Stanford Prep and a list of extracurricular activities.

I felt the oxygen whoosh back into my lungs. It was all I could do to **abstain** from jumping up and down in glee.

Instead, I leaned forward, intrigued. My mom had given me straight As, made me captain of the debate team and a member of the track and karate teams, just like I'd been in high school. I'd apparently **amassed** a total of three detentions in my **fictional** time at Stanford Prep and been suspended once for cutting school to go to the beach.

Damn, my mom was thorough. I felt as if I'd just dodged a speeding train.

"Not really the rebel, are ya?" David joked.

"Yeah. You can just call me goody-goody Kim," I replied, giggling

---

proverbial: well-known or commonly spoken of

immune: untouchable or exempt

abstain: refrain or avoid

amassed: collected or accumulated

fictional: imaginary

uncharacteristically. I guess that's what seeing your life flash before your eyes will do to you.

*   *   *   *   *

"See you tomorrow!" I said to David as I left his room later that night. Danielle had already bailed an hour ago to get some studying done, and Christian had never returned. David had **theorized** that his roomie was in the ancient-history section of the library, tearing his hair out over his video game.

I'd spent the last hour chatting with David about *Star Wars* (he knows *everything*), school, and his social life—or lack thereof. Like Danielle, David seemed to be a bit of an outcast, which was probably why they clung to each other's side. Even though David was such a **gregarious** guy around Danielle and me, I wasn't surprised that he wasn't rolling in friends. He was suspicious of everyone around him, and that could be a bit off-putting. I had a feeling the only reason he trusted me so much was because he was attracted to me—which only made me feel all the more **compunction** for messing with his head.

I sighed and trudged down the hall. This undercover gig was tough on the conscience.

As I rounded the corner toward the stairs, I slammed right into someone and had to hold onto the wall to catch my balance. Imagine my shock when I realized I was looking down at the battered boots of none other than Jon Wisnewski.

"Sorry," I said, looking up into his deep green eyes.

He held my gaze for a split second, then sidestepped around me and yanked his keys out of his pocket.

"I guess I'm kind of a klutz tonight," I said, attempting to get him to respond. Nothing. I stared at his back as he worked the lock on room 225.

---

theorized: guessed or speculated

gregarious: social or talkative

compunction: guilt

Sheesh. Give a girl a break.

Say something! You know about him now! Mention the drums! Or snowboarding!

But I couldn't. I wasn't supposed to know that stuff about him, and if I just blurted it out, he was definitely going to think it was **absurd**.

"Uh—"

But it was too late. Jon slipped into his room and shut the door in my face.

"I guess Hereford doesn't have a class in **courtesy**," I muttered, turning away.

At that point it was easy to **surmise** that earning Jon's trust was going to be the most **arduous** part of my job. I was going to have to get creative with that one. But I could **ponder** that later, in bed, where I did my best thinking. (I always keep a pad by my bed to jot down my middle-of-the-night brainstorms, and last semester I'd written an entire paper between the hours of 2 and 5 A.M. My room-mate, Cathy, had been slightly **perturbed**.) For now, I had to get to my dorm, grab my cell, and find a quiet spot from which to call my mom. She would worry if I didn't check in soon.

"Ms. *Sharpe!*"

Headmaster Cox's barrel of a chest greeted me at the bottom of the stairs. How did someone with such **brawn** end up being a head-master? Shouldn't he be chopping logs somewhere?

"Headmaster *Cox!*" I shot back, **mimicking** his emphasis.

His jaw clenched at my **irreverence**. "It is after 10 P.M."

This meant nothing to me, so I just stared back at him.

"Female students are not allowed in the boys' dormitory past 10 P.M. and vice versa," he told me. "While you are a student here I expect you to follow the rules of our institution."

I took a deep breath and let it out slowly. "Of course," I said. "No problem."

---

absurd: strange or ridiculous
courtesy: good manners
surmise: guess
arduous: difficult or tiring

ponder: think or meditate about
perturbed: bothered or disturbed

brawn: strength or brute force
mimicking: imitating
irreverence: sassiness or cheekiness

Then I walked around him and sauntered down the hallway, trying to show him how little an effect he had on me.

What is that guy's deal? I wondered. *Doesn't he* want *me to solve this case?*

I waited until I heard Danielle's breathing slow to a nice, rhythmic pace before stealing out into the hallway with my cell phone. On the way back from the guys' dormitory, I'd noticed three old telephone booths built into the wall near the lounge. They looked like they hadn't been used in a **decade**, probably because every kid at Hereford had been given a cell phone as soon as they'd said their first word. I **deemed** it the perfect place for my midnight phone call.

I ducked into the booth closest to the lounge and farthest from any dorm rooms. Sure enough, the inside walls were peppered with graffiti like "S.G. Class of '91" and "New Kids Rule!" It seemed the phone booths were the one area that had escaped the recent **refurbishment** that had left all of Hereford smelling of paint and new carpet.

I closed the glass door behind me. It let out a loud creak that **reverberated** through the silent dorm, causing my heart to hit my throat. I waited for a moment, holding my breath, but no one seemed interested in checking out the noise.

Sitting back against the hard wooden wall, I hit the speed-dial number for my house. My mother picked up on the first ring.

"Chief Stratford."

"Hey, Mom," I said. "It's me, calling with my **quotidian** update."

"Kim! How's it going up there?" my mother asked. "Are you doing all right?"

"Well, I've talked to all three of the suspects, although one of them didn't actually talk back," I said, **cringing** slightly as I recalled the **encounter** with Jon. "David **corroborated** the fact that Marshall is here on scholarship, but I haven't learned anything

---

decade: ten years
deemed: judged or considered
refurbishment: restoration or renovation

reverberated: echoed or boomed
quotidian: daily
cringing: wincing or flinching

encounter: meeting
corroborated: confirmed

new—yet. Oh! Except that Jon Wisnewski was addicted to painkillers a couple of years back. That's incriminating, right?"

I waited for my mother to convey her thoughts, wondering whether she'd be proud of the tidbit I'd managed to unearth or irritated that I hadn't gotten very far.

"That's great, Kim, but I was more concerned about you," my mother said. "How are the people up there? How's your roommate? What are they feeding you?"

For a moment I just sat there, rendered speechless by surprise. I had expected my mother to **interrogate** me—to be all business. This was, after all, an important investigation. What did she care if my roommate was cool or not?

"Mom? Are you okay?"

"What, I can't be concerned about my daughter?" she shot back.

Suddenly I couldn't help smiling. I **relished** the rare moments when my mother dropped her hard-ass persona and became motherly.

"My roommate is great," I told her. "But the teachers suck. **Mediocre** at best. I definitely got a better education at Morrison High. This place is a **flagrant** ripoff."

"I had a feeling," my mother said.

"Except for the food. Mom," I added, experiencing a sudden **craving** for the chocolate chip cookies they'd served up after dinner. "I swear they should open a restaurant up here."

"Well, that's good, at least," my mother replied. "So listen, you said you talked to all the suspects. Do you think any of them has **deduced** why you're there?"

"Nah. I'm definitely not impressed by their collective intelligence," I told her, adjusting my butt on the rock-hard seat. "David's the only one who seems **incisive** enough to figure it out, but I don't think he will."

"Why not?"

---

interrogate: interview or cross-examine	**mediocre:** average or second-rate	**craving:** hunger or desire
relished: enjoyed	**flagrant:** obvious or glaring	**deduced:** figured out
		incisive: sharp or perceptive

"I think he's kind of **enamored** of me," I said, flushing.

"Kimberly Stratford, you are not there to make friends!"

Finally! A **reprimand**! Now *that* sounded more like the mother I know, love, and sometimes fear.

"I know, Mom. Don't worry. It's not like I'm going to start dating him!" I said. "All I'm trying to say is no one suspects a thing."

"Well, if they start to question you or make you feel at all uncomfortable, I can bring you home at any time," she told me.

"I know, Mom, but I'm not leaving here until I **prevail**," I told her, twisting the silver cord of the **obsolete** phone in my hand. "I feel like this is something I have to do."

My mother sighed. "Kim, we didn't really talk about this before you left, but if this is about Corinne—"

"It's not," I lied, **truncating** her speech. I didn't want to have all that baggage dragged out right before bed. It had already caused enough **insomnia** over the past few months, and I had to be alert tomorrow. "I just want to help. That's all. Besides, I was going out of my mind sitting at home. This is *much* more interesting."

"If you say so," she said.

"I do," I replied with a nod. "I'll call you tomorrow. I'm having lunch with Marshall, and I'm hoping to get in with Jon as well."

"Okay, but honey . . . just be careful."

My heart warmed. My mother had never called me *honey* in my life. Taking on this case may have been the greatest decision I'd ever made.

"Don't worry, Mom," I told her. "I will."

*　*　*　*　*

By the time I emerged from the lunch line the next afternoon, I was all nerves. I was about to sit with Marshall and his obnoxious, **vain**, **fatuous** friends—a prospect that made me **queasy** for three reasons.

---

enamored: in love with
reprimand: scolding or lecture
prevail: win or succeed

obsolete: outdated
truncating: cutting short
insomnia: sleeplessness

vain: proud or conceited
fatuous: stupid or childish
queasy: sick or uneasy

First, I knew that David and Danielle were going to be completely thrown and would probably **excise** me from their lives forever. Second, I was going to have to maintain complete **focus**—not one of my **attributes**—and be careful about everything I said. After my flub yesterday at lunch, I realized that social situations could be **hazardous** to my cover. Apparently when I got too comfortable I got careless. Of course, comfort probably wasn't going to be an issue, because third and most difficult to admit, I also was nervous because I was about to have lunch with the cool kids.

Big confession time. I, Kim Stratford, had **heretofore** never hung out with the cool kids. At least not until I got to college and nobody knew that in high school I was barely a blip on the social radar. I never really wanted to hang with them because they were all elitists, but that didn't mean they weren't intimidating. I had *always* found them intimidating.

So there I was, a high school graduate, a college student from Stanford University, *and* a policewoman, and I was **cowed** by a bunch of kids wearing Tommy Hilfiger and laughing over the latest episode of *The Jamie Kennedy Experiment*. Not my proudest moment.

Here goes nothing, I thought.

Marshall waved to me from across the cafeteria, as if I could miss him and his **obstreperous** friends even in all the **chaos**. Their table stood out like a cruise ship in the middle of a sailboat race—big and long and packed with **boisterous** people. Cheryl turned to see what he was waving at and her face grew **livid** the moment she laid eyes on me. Wow. This girl was seriously jealous. I had a feeling she was going to tear me down the first chance she got. It was so unfair. I couldn't have been less interested in her potential drug-dealer boyfriend.

You can deal with her, I told myself. *Whatever she attempts to throw at you, just make sure her efforts are* **futile**. *You're older, you're cooler, and you have way-better hair.*

---

excise: cut out
focus: concentration
attributes: traits
hazardous: dangerous
heretofore: up to this point

cowed: scared or intimidated
obstreperous: loudmouthed or unruly

chaos: commotion or madness
boisterous: lively or noisy
livid: furious
futile: useless or unsuccessful

I knew it would be easier said than done, but my internal pep talk calmed me a bit. Keeping my chin up, I **gamely** walked along the wall until I reached the packed table. Each guy was sporting more hair gel than the one next to him, and the **commingled** scents of the many products the girls were currently abusing created a **noxious** cloud over the table.

"Everyone, this is Kim," Marshall said, looking proud that he'd remembered my name. "She's cool."

The few people who **acknowledged** my presence seemed unimpressed. A couple of girls gave me the once-over and then looked away, returning to a heated debate over the benefits of thongs versus tangas.

I was in hell. I mean, how **banal** could they be?

You have to be **tolerant** *here,* I told myself, sliding into an empty seat next to Marshall. *They can't be* all *bad.*

I hazarded a glance toward the table where I'd sat yesterday with Danielle and David. They were both staring at me, and their pain was almost **palpable**, even from across the room. I hated that I was the one who had made them feel that way. I smiled at them **obsequiously**, but they both turned away. My stomach contracted.

This is your job, I reminded myself. *You can't worry about Danielle's and David's feelings. You're gonna have to* **ingratiate** *yourself with these people, and you're gonna have to do it fast.*

"Hi," I said, smiling at the most welcoming-looking person there—a cute guy with shaggy red hair who sat across from me.

"Hey. I'm Curtis," he replied, extending his hand to me from across the table. The headphones of his iPod dangled from his neck as he rose from his seat. I was impressed that he was actually shaking hands with me. Not something most teenage guys bothered to do.

"Nice to meet you," I said.

"What do you think of Hereford?" Marshall asked as he shoved a fistful of fries into his mouth.

---

gamely: eagerly or cheerfully
commingled: mixed or blended

noxious: poisonous or harmful
acknowledged: recognized or accepted
banal: ordinary or predictable

tolerant: open-minded
palpable: physical or solid
obsequiously: in an overly flattering or polite manner
ingratiate: suck up to

"It's okay," I replied, pushing my fork around in my spaghetti and meatballs. I was too tense to eat just yet. "Some of your teachers are tough, though," I added, hoping to get a conversation started. If there was one thing I remembered about being a high school senior, it was how much we enjoyed **lamenting** our lot in life.

"What did you expect, **remedial** classes?" Cheryl said, looking down her nose at me. "Hereford is a **reputable** school. You can't just coast here."

"Who said anything about coasting?" I shot back immediately. "I go to Stanford. I've never coasted in my life."

"What do you mean you *go* to Stanford?" Cheryl asked.

Damn. There I go again. Apparently I wasn't only in danger of blowing my cover when I was too comfortable. It was also going to happen whenever I was **heckled**. *Good job, Deputy Moron.*

"I mean I *went* to Stanford Prep," I explained, proud of the smooth save. "The teachers were actually tougher there, but I didn't want to make you guys feel **inferior**."

"Whatever," Cheryl said, rolling her eyes and returning her attention to her girlfriends.

Marshall, Curtis, and a couple of other guys chuckled to themselves.

"What?" I asked.

"Cat fights. Gotta love it," the blond kid from karate practice said.

I had a feeling I wasn't going to be having any **scholarly** debates with these guys during my days at Hereford. I decided to cut to the chase.

"So, what do you do for fun around here?" I asked, raising my eyebrows.

Marshall exchanged cautious glances with his buddies as if he were debating whether he should let me in on something. I felt my pulse start to race. Was I already on to something **disreputable**?

---

lamenting: crying about	**reputable:** highly regarded	**inferior:** lesser or worse
remedial: meant for slower learners	**heckled:** harassed or jeered at	**scholarly:** intellectual
		disreputable: dishonest

"She seems cool," Curtis said finally, lifting one shoulder.

"Like I said," Marshall replied firmly, as if he wanted to make sure he was **credited** with being the first person to say I was cool.

"So tell her," some meathead suggested.

I saw Cheryl shoot Marshall a warning glance, but he was either **oblivious** or decided to ignore her.

"We have this secret party every month in the gym," Marshall explained through a full mouth. "It's totally **exclusive**. Just us and some of the cooler juniors and sophomores."

I could tell that his "us" didn't apply to all seniors, just the ones at this table—the Hereford **regime**. I held my breath as Marshall's eyes flicked over me. Would I be included as one of "us"? I had an **inkling** my investigation depended on it. An underground monthly party sounded like the perfectly **unwholesome** venue for some serious drug use.

Instantly my mind turned to Corinne, and I felt my blood start to boil. I shoved the thoughts away. I couldn't go there now. Otherwise I'd be blaming *these* kids for what happened to her, and they never even knew the girl.

"You can come if you want," Marshall said.

At that moment Cheryl shoved her chair back from the table in an **intemperate** manner, making far more noise than was absolutely necessary, and stalked through the cafeteria toward the bathroom.

"Don't mind her. She's on the rag," Marshall said, causing Meathead to guffaw.

Ugh! He was so **uncouth**!

"So, you in?" Curtis asked me.

"Sure. When is it?"

"Next Friday," Curtis replied. "We meet in the gym at midnight."

"How do you guys get away with it every month?" I asked. "I mean, doesn't the Hereford administration sort of frown on this kind of thing?"

---

credited: given recognition
oblivious: unaware
exclusive: private or restricted

regime: rulers or commanders
inkling: hunch or idea
unwholesome: dishonest or indecent

intemperate: hotheaded
uncouth: crude or offensive

"They turn a blind eye cuz it's us," Marshall said, reaching out to slap hands with his friends. "Gotta love it."

"It's gonna be wicked this month," Chris said with a grin. "Marshall is DJ-ing with his new speakers."

"I'm making some killer mixes, man," Marshall said, nodding his big head. "Wait'll you hear what I got in store."

Suddenly, in a flash of brilliance, I saw my opening. A **feasible** way to **insinuate** myself into Marshall's good graces.

"I have a ton of new CDs if you want to borrow some," I said, munching casually on my roll. "A lot of West-Coast stuff you may not have."

This was actually true. My friend P.K. back at Stanford had a brother who worked for Universal Records, and he was constantly sending us new albums by up-and-coming DJs and bands. Some of it was **vapid** crap, but most of it was kicking party music.

"Good deal," Marshall said. "Bring 'em by my room tonight. I'm in 315."

Yay! Progress!

"I'm there," I said, relaxing. Now that things with Marshall were settled, I was finally able to dig into my lunch, but I **devoured** it quickly—before Cheryl could come back and turn my stomach to knots all over again.

*   *   *   *   *

As soon as lunch was over, I found myself in the **deserted** hallway once more, following Jon Wisnewski back to his stairwell. I was feeling a little more daring after my success with Marshall, and I must admit, I wasn't quite as **stealthy** this time. My sneakers made **sporadic** squeaking noises, and with each one I expected Jon to turn around and **confront** me, but he didn't. He was either deaf or didn't care that he was being tailed.

---

feasible: possible
insinuate: weasel a way into
vapid: dull or bland

devoured: ate quickly
deserted: empty or isolated
stealthy: quiet or sneaky

sporadic: occasional or intermittent
confront: challenge or face

Okay, I'll just tell them I'm lost or something, I thought as Jon shoved through the swinging doors that led to the stairwell. Once again, voices, laughter, and smoke wafted out into the hallway. *Or maybe I'll try to bum a smoke . . . and make a complete idiot of myself when I choke all over them.*

I was still **contemplating** these options when I pushed open the door, and it was grabbed by Jon himself. I stopped, my breath catching in my throat. His face was inches from mine.

"Why are you following me?" he demanded.

So much for not caring about being tailed.

contemplating: considering or thinking over

"I . . . uh . . ."

Hadn't I just had some **plausible** excuses lined up? My mind was completely **devoid** of words. No **poise** under pressure—not a good quality in a cop.

"I just . . . lost!" I exclaimed, completely unintelligible.

"You just lost," he said, his brow **furrowing** over his seriously piercing green eyes. Somehow they made my heart pound even more furiously. "How caveman of you."

"Look . . . I'm new around here," I explained. "And I just . . . I'm trying to make friends, and to be honest, you seemed . . . interesting."

What the hell was I *saying*?

"Really?" he said, ushering me back out into the hallway. It seemed he didn't want whomever was down below doing the **cavorting** and the smoking to overhear us. "I thought I just saw you eating lunch with the Conenites. You seem pretty much **acclimated** to the situation around here."

"Um . . . Conenites?"

"Marshall Cone and his friends?" Jon said like I was some sort of doofus for not having **inherent** knowledge of his nickname for them.

"Right. Well, they're okay, but—"

"No, they're not. But that's not exactly the point. The point is, you don't hang out with the Conenites and find *me* interesting. The two things don't mesh." His face was growing hard as he spoke and took a **menacing** step closer to me. I felt my pulse speed up. Was this kid dangerous? I mean, I could definitely take him, but the last

---

plausible: possible or believable	**poise:** self-assurance or composure	**acclimated:** adjusted
devoid: empty	**furrowing:** creasing or wrinkling	**inherent:** natural or inborn
	cavorting: horsing around	**menacing:** threatening

thing I wanted was to get **embroiled** in a sparring match in the middle of the hallway—especially not with Cox potentially lurking around here somewhere.

"So I repeat," Jon said. "Why were you following me?"

"You know what? I don't have to stand here and take this kind of **invective** from you," I said, deciding to cut my losses. We were in a deserted hallway, and his behavior was getting more and more **disquieting**. "We could have been friends. And who knows, you may have found *me* very interesting. But now we'll never know."

"Gee. I'm real broken up about it," Jon said, narrowing his eyes.

"Fine," I said.

"Fine," he replied, shoving through the door again.

I stormed away, fuming, my face so hot it felt as if my makeup was going to melt right off. Jon Wisnewski was infuriating.

So why was my brain imagining what it might be like to run back there, grab him, and kiss him? Ugh! I needed to see a shrink, stat.

*   *   *   *   *

"I can't believe you were hanging out with Marshall Cone!" Danielle seemed **anguished** by the new development as she paced our room later that day. "Actually, wait. I can believe it." She paused and looked at me. I was sitting on my bed with my tail between my legs. "Don't you hate it when people say they can't believe something that's totally believable?" she asked.

She sat down right across from me and sighed. She looked so **distraught**, I felt the need to beg for **absolution**. But what was I going to say?

"*Gee, sorry, Danielle, but I have to hang out with Marshall, because he could be a drug dealer and I might have to bring him in?*"

---

embroiled: involved
invective: criticism or attack
disquieting: disturbing or unsettling

anguished: pained or agonized

distraught: upset
absolution: forgiveness

Not likely.

"I'm sorry," I began, feeling like evil **incarnate**. This was insane. I'd come here to solve a case, not break the heart of some poor **vulnerable** girl. I was suddenly **acutely** aware of just how much Danielle needed me. And she'd known me for only two days! What was she going to do when I up and *left*?

Okay, don't think about that right now. You're not responsible for this girl's social life. Still, she was so disappointed, I felt the need to explain.

"He asked me yesterday at karate, and I just thought . . . you know . . . it would be good to get to know some other . . . people," I told her.

Oh, God. I was **faltering** here. I sounded like a totally insensitive social-climber. I would hate me if I were her.

"Don't worry about it," she said finally. "I completely understand. If Marshall asked you to sit with them, then you have to sit with them. Only the strong survive around here."

She looked up at me, her eyes sad. "We're still gonna be friends, right?" she **beseeched** me. "I mean, if you don't want to talk to me in front of them, I totally get it. Just don't start ignoring me when we're here. I don't think I could handle that."

"Of course we're still going to be friends!" I protested, getting up and plopping down next to her. "Look, I have never let any clique define who I am and I'm not gonna start now."

"Really? Cuz I haven't had a real girlfriend in so long . . ."

My heart went out to Danielle. She was such a cool, sweet, smart girl. Why did everyone have to treat her like a **pariah** just because she excelled in her classes? Didn't everyone around here excel in their classes? Who cared who was **paramount** among them? They were all going to get into Ivy League schools anyway.

"I promise I am not going to change just because I'm hanging out with Marshall," I told her firmly.

---

incarnate: in material form
vulnerable: weak or defenseless
acutely: sharply or intensely

faltering: weakening or hesitating
beseeched: begged or pleaded

pariah: outsider or reject
paramount: of greatest importance

Danielle smiled, finally accepting my **assertions**. "Cool," she said, bouncing up from her bed. "So, I was going to go to the library to work on history. Do you want to come?"

She sorted through her books, **painstakingly** organizing each subject's notes and texts on her desk. My heart tightened as I watched her. In that moment, she reminded me so much of Corinne that I was **consumed** by **nostalgia** and sadness. Corinne had been **slovenly** in every **facet** of her life, but when it came to school, she was more uptight than a Republican touring the Playboy Mansion.

There were actually a lot of **parallels** between Corinne Ryan and Danielle Fisher. They were both **diffident**, yet funny when you got to know them. Both **self-deprecating** in public but privately aware of their worth. Corinne had even been just as distrustful of the popular crowd at Morrison High as Danielle was at Hereford.

And **justifiably** *so, as it turned out,* I thought, my mouth set in a line.

Thinking of Corinne **catalyzed** me into action. I had to solve this case, and I had to do it fast. There was no way I was going to let what had happened to Corinne happen to Danielle. No way in hell.

"Actually, I told Marshall I'd lend him some of my CDs," I said, crossing over to the **bulky** box that held all my music. It still was sitting on the floor next to my bed because I figured I'd probably never have to unpack it. I planned to solve this case and be out of here before I needed to really set up shop.

Danielle shot me a look, and I smiled.

"I'm just gonna drop them off, and then I'll meet you in the library," I **assured** her. "I swear I am not up and joining the Conenites."

"The Conenites?" she asked with a laugh. "I like it."

I flushed. "Yeah. I don't know where that came from."

"Okay, but just keep an eye out for Cheryl," Danielle warned me. "If she finds you in his room, she'll kill ya. She'll kill ya dead."

---

assertions: statements or claims
painstakingly: carefully or meticulously
consumed: overwhelmed
nostalgia: longing for the past

slovenly: sloppy or messy
facet: aspect or part
parallels: similarities
diffident: hesitant or timid
self-deprecating: self-critical
justifiably: rightly or understandably

catalyzed: inspired or incited
bulky: large or massive
assured: promised

"I appreciate your **candor**," I said, laughing.

I gathered my favorite albums and headed for the door. The phone rang as I walked out, and Danielle lunged for it.

"Hello?" she said. Her entire face lit up, **elated**. "Hey, honey!" she exclaimed, her eyes flicking toward the framed photo on her dresser. Clearly it was her boyfriend—someone she'd yet to confide in me about. I had, however, checked out his picture. He was tall, broad, and a little scruffy with a mischievous smile. Another bad boy—something else Danielle and I had in common. I closed the door behind me, happy that Danielle had someone who could so instantly **alleviate** all her loneliness.

It kinda took the pressure off.

*   *   *   *   *

As I was coming around the corner into Marshall's hall, I heard a door swing open. I paused, then ducked back behind the wall. I don't know if it was detective's **intuition** that made me do it, but I was instantly glad I did. When I peeked around the corner, I saw none other than Jon Wisnewski slinking out of Marshall's room. He didn't **loiter** either—he was out of there faster than you could say "suspicious."

What was Jon Wisnewski doing hanging out in Marshall Cone's room? Hadn't he insulted him and his friends to me that very afternoon? Or was that just something I had **inferred** from his use of the word "Conenites"? No. There was no way these two were friends.

I was going to have to ponder this one later. I waited until Jon was long gone—didn't want to be accused of stalking him again—then knocked on Marshall's door.

The first thing I noticed when he welcomed me into his room was the smell. He must have been showering himself with **gratuitous**

---

candor: openness or honesty
elated: excited or overjoyed

alleviate: lessen
intuition: instinct
loiter: hang around
inferred: assumed

gratuitous: unnecessary or unreasonable

amounts of CK Be about five seconds before I got there. In seconds I was dizzy from **deprivation** of oxygen.

"What do you think?" Marshall asked, tipping his head back slightly as if he wanted to impress me with the **girth** of his neck. It took me a second to realize he was asking what I thought of the room.

The place was a **bastion** of **materialism**. There was a state-of-the-art twenty-disc changer on top of his desk, hooked up to **authentic** surround-sound Bose speakers that were suspended from each corner of the ceiling. His computer was a seventeen-inch PowerBook, and his iPod was hooked up to it, downloading songs. A pair of brand-new skis **jutted** out from behind his bed, and a home theater system—even better than David's—was showing *Old School*. Every inch of wall was covered in posters of **voluptuous** women in **scant** clothing who seemed to be lusting over the red sports cars they were posed on.

Testosterone city.

"It's . . . nice?" I said.

"Nice? Me and Rob have the sickest setup at this school!" Marshall was offended. He certainly liked to put himself up on a **pedestal**. I placed my CDs near his stereo and caught a glimpse of his BlackBerry sitting in the center of his desk.

"What's this?" I asked, picking it up on **impulse**.

Marshall grabbed it out of my hand swiftly, but not before I saw a reminder that read: "1/9 Delivery." A reminder he obviously didn't want me to see. Yet another tidbit to file away.

"It's a BlackBerry," he said, his expression **patronizing**. "Where're you from? Idaho?"

Sheesh. Did anything intelligent ever **issue** from this guy's mouth?

"Not exactly," I said. "But I'm sure all Idahoans would be happy to know that you think they're too **naïve** to recognize a BlackBerry."

deprivation: lack	**jutted:** stuck out	**patronizing:**
girth: size or thickness	**voluptuous:** sexy or sensual	condescending or belittling
bastion: stronghold	**scant:** tiny or minimal	**issue:** emerge
materialism: love of luxury	**pedestal:** high position	**naïve:** gullible or simple
items	**impulse:** sudden urge or	
authentic: genuine	whim	

"Well, you didn't," he said.

"I just hadn't seen that model before," I shot back. Then, in an effort to **retain** his respect for my coolness factor, I ran my hand down one of his Salomon skis. As far as I knew, they were the most expensive ones on the market. "These are sleek," I said. "I bet you get some serious speed with those."

Marshall seemed surprised by my knowledge, but then covered it well. "Gotta love it," he said. This seemed to be his favorite phrase. "Check it out. I got a pair of Ray-Ban goggles too—UV-protected, glare-resistant, and damn if I don't look *fine*."

He held them up to his face, and I gave him the expected impressed frown and nod. I barely even noticed how he looked, however. I was too busy taking in the **opulent** designer wardrobe, including a **preponderance** of suede jackets and leather boots, in the closet behind him. There was no way this kid was here on scholarship. His room was more **lavish** than the latest *Real World* house.

"So, whaddaya got for me?" Marshall asked, flipping through my CDs.

"Most of that stuff is pretty **obscure**, but it's good. Trust me," I said, trying to take in more **notable** details of his room. Unfortunately there wasn't much out of the ordinary—for a millionaire. Then I noticed a stack of **correspondence** on his desk, which upon further **scrutiny** turned out to be college applications—exactly the institutions you'd expect for a Hereford student—Yale, Princeton, Duke, Dartmouth.

"You know where you want to go to school yet?" I asked **cavalierly**.

Marshall glanced at the apps and shrugged. "Eh, they're all after me, but I'm going to Duke."

"I admire your **optimism**," I said.

"What?" He seemed a little **riled** by my comment.

"I mean you seem fairly confident you're going to get in."

---

retain: preserve or maintain
opulent: fancy or extravagant
preponderance: excess or surplus
lavish: fancy or extravagant

obscure: little-known
notable: prominent or noticeable
correspondence: mail or communication
scrutiny: study or inspection

cavalierly: casually or offhandedly
optimism: confidence or hopefulness
riled: angered or annoyed

Marshall scoffed and looked at me as if it was just too obvious *why* he should be so confident about that. Somehow I **squelched** the desire to smack him in the head. He acted like he was **heir** to the throne.

"Duke's an expensive school," I said, trying to do the leading thing Tad had taught me.

"Money's not an **impediment** for me," he said, still rifling through my CDs.

He didn't blink or clear his throat or touch his face or anything. If the kid was lying, he was doing a bang-up job.

"How?" I wanted to scream. *"According to your record, you are* **currency deficient**. *How are you affording all this stuff?"*

I paced across the room, picking up a watch here, glancing at a stack of old Post-its there. I examined a shelf full of Twinkies and Doritos and cans of Red Bull. There was nothing to **implicate** him. Unless you were looking for a **hedonist**.

"So . . . are you and Jon Wisnewski friends?" I asked.

I heard my CDs clatter to the desk. "That loser? Why would you ask me that?"

My heart pounded with **anticipation**. I was *so* onto something.

"I just saw him in the hall, and it looked like he was coming from your room," I mentioned **blithely**. "Just curious."

"Well, he wasn't. Coming from my room, I mean," Marshall said, his face set like stone.

You're so busted! I thought. Though busted on what, I had no idea.

"Thanks for the CDs. I'm gonna get to work on the mixes," Marshall said, slipping right by me and opening the door. Not too obvious an **ejection**.

"No problem," I said as I stepped out of the room. "I'll just get them back from you later in the week?"

"Yeah. Whatever," Marshall said. And he closed the door in my face.

---

squelched: suppressed or held back
heir: successor or inheritor
impediment: obstacle or barrier

currency: money
deficient: poor or lacking
implicate: point the finger at
hedonist: someone who seeks pleasure

anticipation: expectation
blithely: casually
ejection: kicking out

You mention Jon Wisnewski to Marshall, you get booted, I thought. *Interesting.*

I wasn't sure if it meant anything to the case, but my curiosity was **piqued**. What was going on between Mr. **Peevish** and the biggest of the Big Men on Campus?

piqued: awakened or aroused

peevish: cranky or irritable

Chapter Seven

The following day after classes I accompanied Danielle to the student post office to drop off a birthday present she was sending to her sister. The box was wrapped in plain brown paper **embellished** with glittering flowers Danielle had spent half the night working on. She was so proud of it, she'd showed it to me first thing that morning. (She was already at her computer emailing Tag, her boyfriend, when I'd woken up.) Still, she seemed **listless** as we made our way along the pathways that **meandered** through Hereford's **extensive** grounds. Something was up.

"Why aren't you going home for your sister's birthday?" I asked, pulling my coat closer to me to guard against an **eddy** of wind.

"I wanted to, but my parents didn't think it was worth the money," Danielle replied with a shrug. She attempted a carefree smile, but I could tell she was **disconsolate**. "I was just there for Christmas . . ."

"Well, I'm sure she's going to like the present. I mean, a twelve-year-old and a complete makeup kit? It doesn't get any better than that," I told her, attempting **levity**.

Danielle's smile seemed to brighten a bit. "Thanks. This is it."

She paused in front of a short wooden door in a stone wall that was covered in ivy. The whole building looked like something from a bygone **era** with its round windows and its turrets. A metal sign with the letters "S.P.O." stamped on it hung above the door, but the letters had been almost entirely **obliterated** by the elements.

"State-of-the-art, huh?" I said.

"Yeah. We don't need **newfangled** things around here. Like, oh, **legible** signage," she replied, opening the door for me.

---

embellished: decorated
listless: limp or lacking energy
meandered: wandered or zigzagged

extensive: large or far-reaching
eddy: gust or current
disconsolate: depressed or sad
levity: humor

era: time period
obliterated: wiped out
newfangled: new or original
legible: readable

I laughed as I stepped into a long room, the left wall of which housed at least three hundred tiny mailboxes, each with its own keyhole. There was a window cut out of the wall to the right, behind which a **wizened**, **stern**-looking old man stood, sifting through a stack of mail. Behind *him* was a system of wooden slots for sorting letters, and who should be **haphazardly** stacking packages in front of it but Jon Wisnewski?

I swear, sometimes I'm just so **hapless** I can hardly believe it. How many times could I bump into the guy?

Okay, but he didn't see you last night, so he only knows about two of the three times, I thought, although it didn't make me feel any better.

"Hey, Mr. Smoot!" Danielle said, sliding her package across the counter. The old man's face lit up when he saw Danielle. I was starting to notice this was sort of a trend with her. People just took to Danielle. Adult people, anyway.

"This is going to your sister, huh?" Mr. Smoot asked **genially**.

"Yep."

"Got anything else for me today?"

"Nope. Not today," Danielle replied. "Just this."

When Danielle spoke, Jon looked up and noticed me standing there.

"Stalker," he said, **dispassionately**.

I graced him with my most **saccharine** smile. "I'm with her," I told him as Danielle fed instructions for shipping to Mr. Smoot. "I swear I didn't even know you worked here."

"Whatever," Jon said. He turned and tossed a package marked "**fragile**" halfway across the room. I couldn't help thinking that his working here was just a little too perfect. He was the **epitome** of a **disgruntled** postal worker.

"Do you find it **hampers** your job performance to ignore the warnings on the packages?" I asked.

---

wizened: wrinkled or aged	**genially:** in a friendly manner	**fragile:** delicate
stern: harsh or serious		**epitome:** ultimate example
haphazardly: randomly or messily	**dispassionately:** without emotion	**disgruntled:** irritated or discontented
hapless: unlucky	**saccharine:** overly and falsely sweet	**hampers:** gets in the way of

From the **mutinous** look on his face I had a feeling the next box would have a direct **trajectory** for my nose. But he simply turned his back on me and continued to stumble about his job.

"So, how long have you worked here?" I asked the back of his head.

"Why do you care?" he shot back.

What was the point of trying to **initiate** a conversation with this person?

Because you have to. It's your job, I reminded myself, **bolstering** myself for another try.

"Do they pay well?" I asked.

Ever **taciturn**, Jon snorted in response and tossed another package on the pile. I watched as he picked up a small box and read the address. Unlike the others, this one he placed carefully on a high shelf. Huh. What was the **import** here? Why did it merit such **distinction**?

And then it hit me. Maybe the package was for Jon himself. And *maybe*, just maybe it was a shipment for his little underground drug enterprise. Of course! What better way to smuggle drugs into Hereford than to **ensconce** yourself in a job at the **antiquated** post office? They had no computer system to log who received what and when, and Jon probably handled every package that came through here!

"Do you have some kind of staring *problem*?" Jon suddenly snapped.

That was when I realized I had been gaping at him, **enthralled**, while my Nancy Drew brain worked its wonders.

"You know, it's always *so* great talking to you," I said **mordantly** as Danielle finished her transaction. I followed her over to her mailbox, my **turbulent** thoughts muddling my brain. This was it. A real lead. I had to tell my mother about this, and I had to step up my attempts to whittle my way into Jon's life. But how? The kid clearly thought I was **deranged**. Whenever I was around him, I became

---

mutinous: defiant
trajectory: route or flight path
initiate: start
bolstering: giving a boost to
taciturn: quiet or distant

import: importance
distinction: honor or worth
ensconce: install
antiquated: old-fashioned or outdated

enthralled: fascinated or gripped
mordantly: bitingly or sarcastically
turbulent: chaotic or restless
deranged: crazy or insane

either **inarticulate** or totally shrill. And at this point, I was having a hard time masking *my* **contempt** for *him*.

I shot a glance over my shoulder at Jon, just in time to see him bump a shelving unit with his elbow and cause an **avalanche** of letters to rain down on his head. Ha! Served him right. Dealing drugs out of a school post office. Could there be anything more **sinister**? I was going to lock him up and throw away the key.

"Kim? Are you okay?" Danielle asked, looking from me to Jon and back again. She raised her eyebrows in a surprised, leading way as if she thought I was checking Jon out—as a **potential** date, not as a potential criminal.

I flushed. "I'm fine. It's just . . . what is that guy's *deal*?" I said as Danielle unlocked her box. "Is he that **boorish** to everybody?"

"Are you kidding? You got him to say two words to you," Danielle replied, her eyes wide. "That's **tantamount** to a miracle."

"Seriously?"

"I don't think I've ever even heard his voice before," Danielle said, shoving a bunch of envelopes into her bag. "He and his little snowboard buddies only hang out in deserted areas or in each other's rooms, and he even **snubs** the teachers. According to David, if Jon weren't **irreproachable** on paper, he wouldn't even be here."

"Is he really that smart?"

"The only other **contender** for Cheryl's throne before I got here, apparently," Danielle said. "Trust me. If I thought Jon was capable of liking anybody, I'd say you were it."

She slammed the door of her post office box, and we headed out. As we walked by the window again, I eyed Jon's tanned face. Was it **remotely** possible that Danielle was right? Could the fact that Jon even **grudgingly** acknowledged my existence mean that he didn't detest me as much as he detested the rest of the student body? It seemed **improbable**. Unless, of course, he *liked* his girls inarticulate and shrill.

---

inarticulate: speechless or incoherent
contempt: dislike
avalanche: landslide
sinister: menacing or creepy
potential: possible

boorish: rude
tantamount: roughly the same as
snubs: ignores or rejects
irreproachable: perfect

contender: candidate or rival
remotely: the least bit
grudgingly: unwillingly
improbable: unlikely

Just as we were about to leave, Jon looked up and caught me staring—again. I didn't look away and neither did he. A slight shiver of attraction ran through me, but I squelched it. I was not going to be attracted to a drug dealer! I did have a chance to notice that there was the faintest **discrepancy** between the color of the skin around his eyes and the color of the skin on his face—sun-goggle tan.

He and his little snowboard buddies . . .

Suddenly I was struck with one of my **brilliant** ideas. Maybe there *was* a way to break through to Jon Wisnewski.

* * * * *

"Kim, this is all very good work," my mother told me after I explained the Jon situation to her. At first she had been upset that I hadn't waited until midnight to call her. (I was so excited about the suspicious behavior I'd witnessed at the post office, I'd run off with my cell the second I returned from dinner.) There wasn't much my mother hated more than a break in procedure. But she forgave my **lapse** the moment she heard about Jon and the mysterious box.

"So, you'll send it?" I prompted.

"Absolutely," she replied. "I think it's an **astute** plan of action."

I grinned. My mother was **lauding** my plan of action. How cool was that?

"Great. I'll keep an eye out for it. Thanks, Mom," I said, trying not to let my voice **betray** my giddiness. But I couldn't help it. I couldn't wait to get started on this new **aspect** of my **probe**.

"No problem. And Kim?" she said. "Be safe."

* * * * *

---

discrepancy: difference
brilliant: clever or inspired
lapse: error

astute: smart or clever
lauding: praising
betray: give away

aspect: part or phase
probe: search or investigation

That night, I sat in David's room, propped up on Christian's pillow, watching a particularly **poignant** episode of *Buffy the Vampire Slayer* (he had every available episode on DVD) and waiting to put my **premeditated** plan into action. Even though I was practically ready to **convict** Jon, I had to try to stay **objective** in this investigation, and that meant finding out everything I could about each of the suspects. I was going to **abolish** this drug problem no matter who I had to take down in the process. Luckily, once I had made my breakthrough with Jon, brilliant plans seemed to be coming to me **spontaneously**.

Tonight I was going to work my magic on David.

Unwary, David was over in the corner—a small area he called his "culinary **nook**"—making grilled cheese sandwiches on his hotplate. He kept telling me he was starving, which seemed impossible considering the amount of food he'd **consumed** at dinner. But I guess it wasn't *that* surprising. I've never known a teenage guy to be **abstemious**. Besides, his snack-time jones was perfect for me, since my eating something was **integral** to my plan.

"Voila!" David said, **ceremoniously** presenting me with my first David Rand Special—a grilled cheese accompanied by barbecued potato chips and, I was sorry to see, a glass of iced tea. I glanced at the bottle on his desk. Empty. Thank goodness.

"Thanks," I said, taking the plate from him. "You definitely know how to **regale** your guests."

"Your wish is my command," David said with a tiny bow.

We laughed, and I leaned back again. I took a few bites of the sandwich, which was, by the way, the best I'd ever had. Then I decided it was as good a time as any to put my plan into action.

I swallowed a wad of sandwich, and then I started to choke. David looked up from the hotplate, his face concerned, as I tipped over my plate and dropped my glass to the floor, shattering it and spilling iced tea everywhere. I stood up, coughing my little heart

---

poignant: moving or touching	**abolish:** put a stop to	**consumed:** eaten
premeditated: thought out beforehand	**spontaneously:** suddenly or without thought	**abstemious:** self-denying
convict: find guilty	**unwary:** innocent or unsuspecting	**integral:** essential
objective: neutral	**nook:** corner	**ceremoniously:** formally or properly
		regale: entertain or please

out, and held my hands to my neck in the **universal** sign for choking.

My high school drama teacher would have been so proud.

"Are you all right?" David asked.

I shook my head, coughing all the way.

David's face went ashen. He ran over and started pounding me on the back—hard.

"Water . . . ," I rasped. "Soda . . . I need—"

David nodded and ran from the room, **unwittingly** playing into my hands. I felt guilty for a split second—he looked so **overwrought**. But my fake choking display was a mere **peccadillo** compared to the sin I was about to **commit**.

The second he was gone I sat down in front of his computer and opened up his personal files. Tad had coached me to look for anything that sounded **inordinately** innocent or harmless. He wasn't going to label his drug-dealing records "Drug-dealing records." It would probably be something more like "Term Papers" or "Family Tree" or—

"Poetry," I said aloud, clicking on the folder. There were probably a lot of kids at this school who considered themselves to be oppressed artists, but David did not seem like the type.

My heart pounded as the file opened, and I kept one ear on the hallway for rapid footsteps. I knew, however, that David would have to go all the way downstairs and through the lobby to get me a soda from the first-floor lounge. I had about five minutes.

I gasped when I saw the file open in front of me. "Got it in one," I said, suddenly feeling **morose**. There was a list of students' names— at least thirty of them—with dollar amounts next to them. Some kind of **pecuniary** record. It was all very incriminating.

But David's a technology freak. Wouldn't he have **encrypted** *a file with a list of drug monies owed?* I thought, my mind trying to find a way to **absolve** him. I realized suddenly that I had hoped David

---

universal: common or widespread
unwittingly: unknowingly
overwrought: emotional or overexcited

peccadillo: small crime or wrongdoing
commit: perform or do
inordinately: overly or excessively

morose: gloomy or glum
pecuniary: financial
encrypted: protected or hidden with a secret code
absolve: pardon

would turn out to be innocent. I really liked the guy. And maybe he *was* innocent. After all, I had expected a lot more resistance from his computer than I'd faced. Maybe David had just lent out a lot of money and this was a list of his debtors.

Of course, if this list *was* a rundown of his drug customers, it probably wouldn't hold up in a court of law, and David had to know that. It wasn't labeled, and there was no way to **verify** that it had anything to do with drugs. Plus, keeping it semi-exposed actually made him look more innocent by default. The more hidden it was, the more incriminating it would be if someone did hack in and find it. The kid was good.

I heard footsteps pounding down the hall, and there was an actual **tremor** in the floor, **heralding** David's approach. I hit the command button to bring up the screensaver again and flew across the room to sit down on Christian's bed. When David entered the room, he was panting, and he practically fell to the floor at my knees. I had resumed coughing, but I wasn't hamming it up quite so much.

"Thanks," I said, making my voice all gravelly. "It went down the wrong pipe."

He opened the soda can for me and handed it over. "I'm just glad you're all right," he said, catching his breath. His eyes were wide and worried. "You scared the crap outta me."

My heart hurt over his concern for me, but I managed to smile slightly and slugged at the soda. I wished I'd found something that would allow me to grant David **clemency**, rather than another clue to heighten suspicion against him. He was such a sweetie. Could he really be a drug dealer?

---

verify: prove or confirm   **heralding:** signaling   **clemency:** forgiveness
tremor: vibration or tremble

The very next day, I received a yellow slip informing me that I had a package waiting for me at the student post office. I was so psyched, I didn't even give myself time to **deliberate** about what I was going to say. I grabbed my coat and ran for the post office, giddy over my **impending** success. The plan, I believed, was totally foolproof.

Of course, minutes later, I realized my **folly**. As soon as I was face-to-face with Jon, I was reminded once again of just how much he **loathed** me. He handed over my package with a sneer.

"Do I have to sign for it or anything?" I asked.

Jon merely grunted and rolled his eyes, then went about his business.

My self-assurance plummeted. Danielle must have been insane to think that he had anything other than **hostile** feelings toward me. What was I thinking? This was never going to work.

Still, I was there, so I figured I may as well give it the old college try.

"I've been waiting for this for *days*," I said to the nearly empty post office.

Mr. Smoot glanced at me without much interest, and even Jon didn't give me *that* much. I tore open the white FedEx box right there and made a big show of **extracting** my snowboard, pretending it was harder to free than it was. I made so much noise that it **whetted** Jon's curiosity, and he grudgingly turned around.

Perfect timing. I saw his eyes widen as the bubble wrap fell away and I produced one of my most prized possessions—my Burton snowboard, light blue with swirls of purple and dark blue along the edges.

---

deliberate: think or ponder
impending: coming up soon
folly: foolishness

loathed: hated
hostile: unfriendly or resentful

extracting: pulling out
whetted: awakened or aroused

"Wow," Jon said, and then he blushed. He had clearly spoken **inadvertently**.

"Nice, isn't it?" I said.

Jon hesitated before answering, then took a step closer to the window. "Is that a Custom?" he asked, eyeing my board in an almost **covetous** manner.

"Nope, it's a Feelgood. I've taken this thing all over the place with me—Tahoe . . . Denver . . . Aspen . . ."

Of course, I hadn't actually boarded at all those slopes, but I had to **fabricate** an impressive boarding history. It was **crucial** to my plan that he know I wasn't just some **neophyte** boarder—that I was the real deal.

"How nice for you," Jon said, the sneer returning. Then he turned his back on me yet again. My confidence **deflated** slightly. That was it? That was all he was going to give me?

"I take it you board?" I asked, leaning my Burton against the counter.

"Some," he replied.

God! Cut me some slack, would ya?

"Any good slopes around here?" I asked.

"Some," he replied again.

Ugh! I was so totally going to knock this kid's block off. I had two choices. I could throw myself at his mercy and **implore** him to show me where the slopes were, then hope that he would hang out with me long enough to make some inroads with him. Or I could do what an actual normal person would do if they were being treated in such a **repugnant** way—walk out.

I **mused** on the matter for a moment, then decided that a guy like Jon, if he was going to respond at all, would respond to the latter course of action.

"Great. Thanks for all your help," I said sarcastically. I gathered up my stuff and walked out as slowly as I could without arousing

---

inadvertently: by accident	**crucial:** essential or	**implore:** plead
covetous: jealous	important	**repugnant:** disgusting
fabricate: make up	**neophyte:** beginner	**mused:** thought
	deflated: lessened in size	

suspicion. I was just about to cut my losses and push through the door when Jon's voice stopped me.

"Hold up," he said.

I grinned. Maybe there *was* a **gullible** bone in his body. Before turning around, I made sure to rearrange my face into a bored, annoyed mask quite like the one he was sporting.

"What?" I asked.

Jon came around the counter and approached me, still eyeing my board in a semi-**daze**. It was almost as if he thought the very idea of my being a snowboarder was **preposterous**—he looked that surprised. As **exultant** as I had been on Christmas morning last year when my mother had given me the snowboard, I was even happier now. Thank God she had dipped into the savings and bought the high-end deck. It was clearly having a **profound** effect on Jon.

I also noticed that he was even cuter when he forgot to scowl.

He took a deep breath before jumping in. "Look, me and a couple of guys go up to this mountain on the weekends to get in a few hours," he said, eyeing me as if he still were unsure about whether he should say what he was about to say. "You can come if you want. I mean, if you're any good."

I had a feeling that Jon inviting anyone to do anything was a totally **unprecedented** occurrence. If Danielle were with me, she would have been saying, "See? I told you so!"

Still, I had to **perpetuate** the persona I had **assumed** in the last couple of minutes—that I was impatient and as rude as he was, and that I found his behavior totally irritating. It wasn't that difficult to pull off.

"Wow! I am totally blown away by your **largesse**," I said, dropping my jaw for good measure. "Thank you *so* much for deeming me worthy enough to board with you and your pals!"

"Hey. I was just trying to be nice."

"A little late, don't you think?"

---

gullible: easy to fool
daze: fog or haze
preposterous: ridiculous or unbelievable

exultant: thrilled or overjoyed
profound: intense or overwhelming

unprecedented: first-time or extraordinary
perpetuate: keep up
assumed: taken on
largesse: generosity

Then I turned and pushed the door open so hard it swung out and slammed back against the outside wall. I think I even knocked a couple of rocks free from the **corroding** façade. Oops.

Storming away was risky, I know. He could easily have **rescinded** the invitation, but I had a feeling my new attitude would prove too intriguing to him. I was right.

"We meet in the parking lot Saturday morning at eight if you change your mind!" he called after me before the door slammed in his face.

I couldn't help grinning as I trudged through the slush and snow back toward my dorm, **gratified** by my performance. If only my mother could see me now.

* * * * *

That evening I was getting ready for my **inaugural** karate match when I heard a burst of laughter from the hallway, followed by a string of **incoherent** jeers. I quickly tied the belt on my robe and stuck my head out into the corridor. What I saw made my stomach clench.

Just outside the stairwell, Danielle was sprawled on the floor with a dozen library books scattered around her. Cheryl and her **unscrupulous** friends hovered over her, laughing. It was easy to **decipher** what had happened. Incredibly mature girl that she was, Cheryl had obviously tripped Danielle on her way up the stairs.

Incensed, I stormed past the other onlookers and helped a trembling Danielle to her feet.

"Are you okay?" I asked as she dusted herself off.

"I'm fine," Danielle replied, her face an embarrassed red.

I shot Cheryl a **withering** glance as I helped Danielle gather her books.

"I've got it," Danielle told me, even as I piled half the heavy volumes into the crook of my arm.

---

corroding: crumbling or decaying
rescinded: taken back
gratified: satisfied
inaugural: first

incoherent: jumbled or garbled
unscrupulous: immoral or wicked
decipher: figure out

incensed: angry or furious
withering: sneering or hateful

"Can't you find somebody else to **persecute**?" I demanded, glaring at Cheryl.

"Oh, but Danielle just makes it so much fun!" Cheryl said, causing another round of laughter.

Danielle turned on her heel and ran down the hall, slamming our door behind her.

"Congratulations, Cheryl. I think you just beat the all-time record for **infantility**," I told her. "How old do you feel right now? About five? Six?"

Cheryl clenched her jaw and stared at me with her piercing eyes. "You'd better watch what you say, New Girl. Maybe I'll find someone else to pick on."

"Oooh! **Ominous**!" I said facetiously. Then I turned and tromped down the hall, back to our dorm room.

I found Danielle sitting on her bed, her arms crossed over her chest and her legs crossed at the ankles. She stared resolutely at the ceiling, trying not to cry, and didn't even acknowledge me when I walked in.

"I'll just put these over here," I said, stacking her books on her desk.

"Thanks so much for your help," she said flatly. "I can take care of myself."

I blinked, taken aback. "I . . . I know you can," I said quickly. "I just didn't want to leave you alone out there. Cheryl has backup. So should you."

"Yeah, well, I just looked like a total wuss."

"Danielle, I'm sorry," I said, sitting down on the edge of my bed. "I was just trying to help." I felt as if a huge **gulf** had opened up between us. I had no idea that I was **perpetrating** an insult by defending her. Who knew Danielle **harbored** so much pride?

"Don't be mad," I told her. "Next time I won't **intervene**. I swear."

---

persecute: bully or harass
infantility: immaturity or childishness

ominous: threatening
gulf: gap

perpetrating: committing
harbored: hid or guarded
intervene: get involved

Danielle let out a sigh and sat up a bit. "I just . . . I **despise** this place," she said, pulling at the fraying edge of an old, gray throw she had on her bed. "Why did my parents have to send me here?"

It was a rhetorical question, so I remained silent. Outside the door a few girls giggled, and I imagined that the story of what had just occurred was making its way through the dorm like a **contagion**. Girls really can be so **crass** sometimes.

"Just forget about Cheryl," I told Danielle. "She's an idiot and so are her friends."

"At least she *has* friends," Danielle said, her **desolate** eyes filled with tears.

My heart went out to her. It must have been totally awful, being sent away against her will and then, to add insult to injury, the entire student body turning around and deciding to hate her.

"I'm your friend," I said. "And so is David. And I don't know about you, but I think we're **superb**. Especially compared to Cheryl's entourage."

Finally, Danielle **relented**. She cracked a smile and rolled her eyes in my direction. "I'm sorry I snapped at you," she said. "I'm just so sick of them."

"Me too. And I haven't even been here a week," I told her, **reciprocating** the smile.

"You know what I'd like?" Danielle said, sitting up and throwing her legs over the side of the bed. "Let's do something chill tomorrow. We could take the bus to the mall and hang out and be total **gluttons** at the food court."

It sounded like a great plan to me, but I was swept through with an acidic sense of guilt. I wasn't exactly free tomorrow. And after what had just happened to Danielle, I could **foresee** that she wasn't going to react well to what I was about to tell her.

"Actually, I already have plans for tomorrow," I said.

"Really?" Danielle asked. "What?"

---

despise: hate	**desolate:** unhappy or depressed	**reciprocating:** returning
contagion: virus		**gluttons:** people who overeat or eat greedily
crass: rude or insensitive	**superb:** wonderful	**foresee:** predict
	relented: gave in	

"I'm kind of going snowboarding with Jon Wisnewski," I told her. Danielle looked **befuddled**. "You're kidding."

"Well . . . he asked, and I haven't been boarding in forever so—"

"Fine. Go," Danielle said, lying back down again.

"Can we **defer** the mall thing until Sunday?" I asked, standing up. "Or . . . maybe you can come with us! Do you ski at all?"

Danielle scoffed. "Oh, yeah. Me hanging out with Jon Wisnewski and his friends. Sure."

"Why not? I haven't even met his friends, and I'm going," I said. "It could be fun."

"Please! They'd laugh me right off the slopes," Danielle said. "Look, obviously you're just better at making friends than I ever was. You should enjoy it."

Her words were kind, but her voice was still **brittle**. On some level, I understood where she was coming from. She'd been here all year and had only David to talk to. I'd been here a couple of days, and it seemed like I was turning into Miss Popularity. Still, she didn't have to take it out on me. If only she knew the real reason I was hanging out with these guys.

For a split second, I entertained the urge to tell her. To let her in. It would make her feel so much better, and I would have someone to discuss the investigation with—a **confidant**. But then, her best friend was one of the potential **culprits**. I couldn't count on her silence. And if David was tipped off, it would be **devastating** to the whole operation.

"Well, I'll be back tomorrow night," I said, **fidgeting** with the end of my belt. "We can hang out then."

"How **charitable** of you," Danielle said.

Then she turned and faced the wall, **shunning** any further advances I might have made. I tried not to roll my eyes. I had really liked Danielle in the beginning, but she was turning out to be almost as immature as Cheryl. She was sweet and all, and I did feel sorry

---

befuddled: confused
defer: postpone
brittle: fragile or dry

confidant: someone to talk to
culprits: criminals
devastating: damaging

fidgeting: playing with nervously
charitable: generous
shunning: rejecting

for her situation, but I had just gotten here and she was **bemoaning** my other friendships as if I were **betraying** her trust.

Well, there was no way I was going to stand there and try to **coddle** her. I grabbed my keys and gym bag and headed out the door, thankful that I had a karate match to go to. In the past five minutes, I had built up some serious **aggression** that was in desperate need of release.

* * * * *

"Point, Sharpe! Match, Sharpe!"

The referee grabbed my wrist and pulled it into the air, declaring me the winner of the **penultimate** fight in the match. I grinned as I fought for breath, but instead of the round of cheers and applause I was expecting, I was **accosted** by shouts, jeers, and boos. Apparently, the Hereford and Coakley Academy karate fans had yet to be ushered into the twenty-first century. Girls weren't supposed to beat guys twice their size. To them, it was **unfathomable**.

I glanced at my opponent, and he bowed to me quickly, but I could tell he was **abased**. He ran back to the bench, head down, and I knew he felt that by losing to me he had been permanently cast in a **pejorative** light. Guys have such **frail** egos.

Oh, well. I thought he was an **adroit** and **nimble** fighter. If that wasn't enough for him, that was his problem.

I headed back to the bench, and Marshall reached out to slap hands with me as he got up to take the mat. It was an unexpected gesture, and it buoyed me a bit as I took a seat next to my teammates. The crowd exploded with shouts of **adulation** as Marshall readied himself for his fight.

"Nice work," Curtis said. He held a washcloth against a **laceration** over his eyebrow, but still managed to grin as he congratulated me.

---

bemoaning: complaining about
betraying: being disloyal or treacherous to
coddle: overprotect or fuss over

aggression: anger or violence
penultimate: second-to-last
accosted: confronted or attacked
unfathomable: unbelievable
abased: humiliated

pejorative: negative or uncomplimentary
frail: fragile
adroit: skillful
nimble: quick or agile
adulation: admiration
laceration: cut or gash

"Is it any better?" I asked him. He'd suffered the injury in the first round and had been bleeding ever since.

"Eh. It'll be fine," Curtis said. "I almost hope it scars. Girls think scars are sexy."

"If you say so," I replied with a laugh. At least someone around here still knew how to laugh. Between Cheryl, Danielle, Jon, Marshall, and the ever **sober** faculty, I'd been starting to think there was some kind of mystical **pall** over this school making everyone miserable.

The whistle blew, and down on the mat, Marshall **assailed** his opponent with a series of **deft** blows. The guy retreated right out of the circle, and Marshall was awarded a point.

"This should take about five seconds," Curtis said under his breath.

But it wasn't over so quickly. After the first setback, Marshall's opponent **retaliated** with **frenzied** and strong blows, raining slices, chops, and kicks on Marshall like a man possessed. Marshall **balked** at a few but took the brunt of most of them. Everyone in the crowd **recoiled** every time Marshall got hit, and Curtis appeared to be **baffled** by his friend's **lackluster** performance. Clearly this was not Marshall's finest hour.

Still, after about ten minutes the points were even. Marshall still had a shot, but he appeared to be winded. He even made the mistake of bracing his hands on his knees during a quick time-out. If there was one thing I knew was a bad idea, it was showing your weakness. I was taught to do everything I could to appear at the **pinnacle** of strength, even if I felt like I was about to keel over.

The whistle blew again, and Marshall met his man in the middle of the circle. I gasped as I saw the uppercut coming, but Marshall was looking the other way. The guy's hand collided with Marshall's chin, and there was a **resounding** *crack* as Marshall

---

sober: serious or dreary
pall: gloom
assailed: beat or attacked
deft: nimble or quick

retaliated: struck back
frenzied: wild or furious
balked: blocked
recoiled: shrank away
baffled: puzzled

lackluster: lifeless or mediocre
pinnacle: height or peak
resounding: echoing or booming

was taken off his feet. He slammed into the ground, and the ref called the fight. Marshall was down—points to Leffers. Match, Leffers.

From the reaction on the Hereford side of the bleachers as the ref raised this Leffers kid's arm into the air, you'd think Marshall's loss was a **calamity**. There was booing, the ref was cursed out of the gym, and half the school was **clamoring** to see whether Marshall was okay. This guy really was like a **deity** around here.

Marshall waved off his concerned citizens, and gradually the spectators began to **disperse**. Some of them crowded around the bench to congratulate us. (Even with Marshall's loss, we had won the match.) I saw Marshall heading for the locker room and excused myself from the crowd, wanting to keep an eye on him.

I climbed the bleachers, trying not to be too **conspicuous**, and pretended to busy myself with packing up my bag. It wasn't as if I expected him to do anything right at that moment, but I figured I should watch him when I had the chance. Just before he got to the locker-room door, David Rand broke away from a crowd that was hanging out beneath the raised basketball net and walked over to Marshall.

I froze. I couldn't help it. I thought David hated Marshall, but the two of them bent their heads together in **dialogue** as if they had something pressing and quite secret to talk about.

Then—and I know I didn't imagine this—the two guys slapped hands, and in the process, Marshall passed a few bills over to David, and David quickly pocketed them. Then David strolled back to his friends as if nothing out of the ordinary had happened.

Suddenly, I felt as if I had hit the **nadir** of my existence. What did *this* mean? Was Marshall buying drugs from David? How else could a **circumspect** transaction like that be **construed**? If only I'd had more time to study that list on David's computer. I couldn't recall whether Marshall's name had been on it or not.

---

calamity: disaster
clamoring: shouting or crying out
deity: god

disperse: scatter
conspicuous: noticeable
dialogue: conversation
nadir: lowest point

circumspect: cautious or guarded
construed: interpreted

Okay, David has a list of students with dollar amounts next to them, and now Marshall is paying him off. This obviously looks very bad for David.

So did this mean Jon was innocent? And if so, what was that box he was so careful to conceal in the post office? Plus Jon and Marshall had had a **clandestine** meeting the other night, and Marshall had been tense when I asked him about it. Was Marshall somehow the **linchpin** in all this? Were all *three* of the suspects involved?

I sat down hard on the bleachers, my mind **oscillating** from one guy to the next. Each second I was convinced another one of them was guilty. One thing was for sure, though—I was dealing with three equally **mendacious** people. How was I ever going to get to the truth if I couldn't trust anything any of them said?

"Come on, Ronnie, get your stuff and let's go," I heard a woman's voice behind me. "I told Donny we'd call him and let him know how you did."

I glanced over my shoulder and instantly recognized Mrs. Burke, the mother of Donny Burke, a karate badass who'd taken the trophy in his division in every championship I'd been to in the last three years. I had never met her, but we all knew who she was. She was infamous for fighting with officials and coaches—a total stage mom. She was talking to a freshman who had to be Donny's little brother. My heart dropped into my sneakers. Had she seen me fight? Had she recognized me?

I saw David break away from the group again and head in my direction. I shoved my feet into my sneakers and stood up without tying them. If Mrs. Burke talked to me while David was there, I was dead.

"Hey!" David said as I half-tripped down the stairs. "Nice match! If I ever need a bodyguard I'm calling you."

"Great. I'm there," I said, my heart pounding. I refused to look

---

clandestine: secret
linchpin: key player

oscillating: moving back and forth

mendacious: dishonest or misleading

behind me. "I'm starved. How about another grilled cheese?" I asked, grabbing his arm and spinning him toward the door.

"You okay?" David asked as we hustled across the gym.

"Yeah, just *really* hungry," I said.

A group of kids from Coakley were gabbing in the doorway, blocking our progress. Didn't they know this was a matter of life or death?

"Excuse me!" I said, trying to wedge my way out of the gym. "Coming through!"

I tried to step over someone's leg, and my sneaker got caught and came off. Before I could stop myself, I went flying forward and sprawled out on the floor of the hallway. My knee exploded with pain. All the Coakley kids cracked up laughing as they finally moved on from the door.

"Kim! Are you okay?" David asked, dropping down at my side.

At that moment, Mrs. Burke and her son Ronnie stepped through the door and noticed me. Mrs. Burke did a double-take. I closed my eyes and moaned. I was done for.

"Oh . . . hello," she said. She still looked confused, like she couldn't place me. If I could just get out of here before she figured it out . . . I struggled to my feet, my knee protesting with freshly bruised pain.

"Uh, hi. I gotta go put some ice on this." I started to turn away.

"I'm sorry, but you just look so familiar to me," Mrs. Burke said, stopping me in my tracks. My stomach turned. "Have I seen you compete before?"

David was supporting me with one arm, looking back and forth between me and Mrs. Burke with interest. I wanted to hurl. This **scenario** could be devastating.

"I don't think so. I just moved here from California," I said.

"Really?" The woman wasn't about to give up so easily. "I was at the county finals last year with my elder son, Donny Burke. He's at UConn now, but I could have sworn I saw you fight there."

---

scenario: situation

"Mom? Can we go?" Ronnie semi-whined at her side.

Yes! Thank you, Ronnie! Get the hell out of here!

"There were a few girls who participated," the woman continued. "Ronald, doesn't this girl look like the one from the county championships last year?"

Ronald glanced at me. "I don't know, Ma. I wasn't there, remember? I was getting my braces."

"Well, it wasn't me," I said. "There are a lot of girls in the martial arts these days. It must've just been someone who looks like me."

I had to concentrate to keep from looking at David to see if he was digesting all of this. Of all people to question my identity in front of, it had to be the most suspicious guy in the Western Hemisphere.

"I suppose you're right," the woman said. "I wasn't wearing my glasses that day . . ."

"See? There you go!" I said, adjusting the strap of my bag on my shoulder. "Well, nice meeting you!"

Then I turned around, grabbed David's arm, and steered him around the corner.

Saturday morning, Jon and I hopped onto the chairlift and pulled the protective bar down, then sat in comfortable silence as we were whisked to the top of the mountain.

Comfortable silence. Even I can't believe it. But one day of snow-boarding and something **fundamental** between us had shifted. Jon was awesome on his board, **lithe** and skilled—the kind of boarder who **mesmerized** everyone on the slopes. And I had impressed him as well, I think. He hadn't overtly complimented me, but his jaw had dropped on my last jump. I had a feeling Jon was seeing me in a whole new light, just as I was him.

He hadn't even said one rude word to me all day and, much to my surprise, he *had* said "please" and "thank you" at all the appropriate times. He was like a different person once he let you get close.

Of course, there's a one-in-three chance that he's a drug dealer, Kimbo, I reminded myself. Sheesh. I really had to get a grip here.

I looked down at the skiers below, the **variegated** colors of their gear dotting the slopes, and took in the **tranquil** atmosphere. My face was warm from exertion, and the cool air felt **invigorating** against my skin. Last night, I had lain awake in bed, fretting over what David might have been thinking about the conversation between me and Donny Burke's mother, but he had said nothing to me about it this morning. So I had decided to let myself have some fun—while working on Jon, of course. I would deal with David if and when I had to.

Jon's friends Tek and Michael shouted and whooped from the chair behind us, and Jon and I turned around to roll our eyes at them.

---

fundamental: important or deep
lithe: flexible or graceful

mesmerized: captivated or entranced
variegated: multicolored or flecked

tranquil: peaceful or calm
invigorating: energizing or refreshing

"They're a couple of meatheads," Jon said, by way of apology.

"I like them," I answered honestly. "They're definitely different from anyone else at Hereford."

Unsure of what to expect in Jon's "rough crowd" friends, I had **resolved** to go into this day **unbiased**, and I hadn't been disappointed. Tek and Michael may have been **inane**, but they were **hilarious** and very sweet. They definitely balanced out Jon's characteristic **melancholy**. If this was what the Hereford administration considered to be a rough crowd, I shuddered to think what they would do if they were dropped in the middle of an inner-city school.

Probably run screaming.

"Yeah. That's why I like them too," Jon said, gazing off toward the horizon.

"This place is totally **unaltered** from the last time I was here," I said lightly.

"I thought you'd never been here," Jon said, eyeing me.

My face burned with embarrassment. Snagged again! Damn that comfortable tongue of mine! When was I going to learn?

"Oh . . . well . . . I thought I hadn't, but now I think this might have been the place my dad took me when I was little," I babbled. "I know we went skiing out here at least once . . ."

"Oh, well, then he definitely would've brought you here," Jon said. "If you're gonna ski in Connecticut, this is the place."

He had that right. I had spent every other weekend on this mountain for the past five years, and **dedicated** skiers made the **pilgrimage** here from all over the Northeast.

I let out a relieved sigh. Another flub covered well.

A few minutes later we hit the top of the slope and slid away from the lift. Tek and Michael came up behind us.

"Ready for another run?" Michael asked, pulling his goggles over his eyes.

---

resolved: determined
unbiased: neutral or open-minded
inane: silly or stupid

hilarious: very funny
melancholy: gloom or sadness
unaltered: unchanged

dedicated: enthusiastic or devoted
pilgrimage: journey

I glanced over my shoulder at the lodge. A plume of smoke rose into the air from the chimney, **dissipating** into the blue sky. It looked mighty welcoming.

"I think I'm gonna go for some hot chocolate," I said, hoping Jon would surprise me and come with. "I'm sort of beat."

"Dude, you can't quit now. This is the single most beautiful day in the history of Evergreen Mountain," Tek said. One thing I'd learned about him on the ride up here—Tek was definitely given to **hyperbole**. It was a beautiful day, but the most beautiful day in history? That was **overstating** it a bit.

"Nah, you guys go," Jon said. "We'll meet you up there."

I blinked, **incredulous**. Jon was coming with me! Yay! This would be the perfect opportunity to pump him for more info, gain a little **insight** into who he really was. I unstrapped my board, and we started on the **trek** up to the lodge. Unfortunately, I couldn't think of a thing to ask without **inciting** his temper. Jon was, as I originally predicted, a tough nut to crack. He'd been so cool and uncharacteristically **benevolent** all day, I was **apprehensive** about saying anything that might cause him to **bridle** again.

We were silent until we got to the snack bar in the lodge and ordered our hot chocolate. The lodge was nothing **luxurious**—just a simple wooden floor and scattered sofas, chairs, and tables here and there, but it was definitely cozy. We found an empty couch near the fireplace and staked our claim.

I sat back in the comfy cushions and sipped at my cocoa, wondering what to talk about. I felt like such an **ingénue**. What kind of detective was I if I couldn't even **initiate** a conversation with my suspect?

"So, listen, I wanted to apologize for being such an asshole the first time we met," Jon said **unflinchingly**.

I was so surprised that my cocoa almost went down the wrong pipe—for real this time. "The first *few* times, you mean."

---

dissipating: dissolving or fading
hyperbole: exaggeration
overstating: exaggerating
incredulous: amazed or disbelieving
insight: knowledge

trek: hike
inciting: provoking or stirring up
benevolent: kind or generous
apprehensive: worried or nervous

bridle: get angry or annoyed
luxurious: fancy or deluxe
ingénue: naïve or inexperienced girl
initiate: start
unflinchingly: fearlessly or determinedly

He scoffed. "Yeah, well. I guess I misjudged you."

"Misjudged?" I asked. "Why? What did you think when you first met me?"

"I just figured you were another one of those Hereford girls," he said with a shrug. "**Conceited, condescending.** But you're not."

"God, I hope not," I said.

"Yeah, well, I figured you must be different if you were actually trying to be friends with *me*. That doesn't happen very often," Jon said. "But I guess I just have a problem with trusting people. I don't know. Maybe people sense that."

Wow. He was very **forthright** once he got talking.

"Are you **implying** that I'm untrustworthy?" I asked, raising my eyebrows and feeling sort of **hypocritical**. I *was* untrustworthy after all. He didn't even know who I really was.

"No. Not at all," he said simply. "I'm just not a people person."

"Color me shocked," I said with a smile.

Omigod, I was flirting! How had I gotten around to flirting?
Drug dealer, drug dealer, drug dealer, I reminded myself.

I cleared my throat and tried to get back to business. "Anyway, I accept your apology," I said, feeling **magnanimous.** He *had* been a serious jerk.

"Good," Jon replied.

"So . . . how long have you been going to Hereford?" I asked.

"Forever," he replied, sitting back with a sigh. "When I first got there in seventh grade I used to pretend I was just **transient**—just passing through. You should see my journal from back then. I was totally **delusional**—coming up with escape plans and all this stuff. What a moron."

I stared at him. A journal? The word "transient"? Who knew the gruff exterior was hiding a **latent intellectual**?

Drug dealer, drug dealer, drug dealer . . .

"What?" he said, looking skittish.

---

conceited: vain or stuck-up	**implying:** suggesting	**transient:** temporary
condescending: snobby or superior	**hypocritical:** two-faced or deceitful	**delusional:** crazy or hallucinating
forthright: direct or upfront	**magnanimous:** generous or noble	**latent:** hidden or buried
		intellectual: thinker or scholar

"I've just never heard you string so many words together at once," I replied.

"Won't happen again." He laughed, and his smile **illuminated** his face. I felt my heart thump in response, and I looked away. What was I doing? I could not develop a crush on a suspect. Especially not such a sketchy one as Jon Wisnewski.

Drug dealer, drug dealer, drug dealer!

"So, if you're so transient, where do you want to be?" I asked.

Back home running your drug cartel? I wondered, wishing it would be that easy—that someone would just come right out and confess.

"I just want to get to college," Jon replied, sitting forward. "I'm applying everywhere."

"What do you think you'll major in?" I asked.

Economics of drug dealing?

"Literature," he replied.

"That's my major!" I blurted. He looked at me, his brow furrowed. "I mean, that's what I'm going to major in."

I swear I have total foot-in-mouth disease.

But Jon seemed to accept my explanation and sat back again. Over the next hour or so, as the sunlight began to wane, we relaxed by the fire and talked about school and the writers we liked and the books we'd read. The longer we talked, the more smitten I became. Jon was not just an intellectual, but also he was sensitive, funny, and **intuitive**. Suddenly I found myself imagining again what it would be like to kiss him. This was not good.

Then we began discussing the social structure at Hereford, which brought me back to stark reality. Jon, as it turned out, had been friends with Marshall back in freshman year but dumped him when his head got too big for his shoulders.

Of course, this made me wonder anew—if Jon had dumped Marshall way back when, then why was he chilling in his room late at night?

---

illuminated: lit up

intuitive: sensitive or perceptive

"So you guys don't hang out at all now?" I asked.

"Please. Neither one of us would be caught dead talking to the other," Jon said.

You've already been caught, not-dead, I thought, hating that he was lying to me yet again. I had thought we had made a break-through and that he was starting to trust me as a friend. But the second Marshall came up, he started lying all over again. What had I been thinking?

You just can't let yourself get sucked in, Kim, I scolded myself **internally**. *Not by David, not by Jon, not by any of them.*

Jon leaned forward and grabbed my empty cocoa mug, shooting me a lopsided smile that made my heart flip.

"I'll go get us some refills," he said.

I'd been at Stanford for months and not a single person had made my heart flip like that. I'd forgotten what it felt like.

Okay. At least don't get sucked in until you know he's innocent, I amended, my face warming. *Then maybe you can kiss him.*

*   *   *   *   *

On the way back to Hereford, I sat in the passenger seat of Jon's Jeep Wrangler. Tek and Michael had passed out in the back and were snoring up a storm. Every once in a while one of them would let out a particularly loud snort, and Jon and I would exchange an amused glance. I couldn't seem to **curb** the urge to smile. We were acting as if we were old friends.

Unfortunately, I wasn't there to make friends, and I'd been an **ineffectual** detective all day. I'd yet to **extricate** one piece of useful information from Jon, and we were only about ten minutes from campus. If I was ever going to act, the time was now.

"So, what's it like working in the post office?" I asked, breaking the relative silence.

---

internally: on the insid   **ineffectual:** useless or weak   **extricate:** pull out or extract
curb: hold back

"It's okay."

He was back to talking in phrases.

"It must be pretty cool, I mean, seeing what everyone's getting before they do," I said. "Knowing who's sending them mail and packages . . ."

Jon gave me a look that caused my mouth to snap shut. I had never known anyone so **accomplished** in the art of **tacit** messages.

"What?" I asked innocently, trying to keep the mood light.

"I'm not really interested in other people's business," he said flatly.

Abort *mission! Abort mission!* my mind screamed. I felt like he was scolding me. Had he realized I was fishing for information? Was I that **transparent**? If so, this was definitely not the job for me.

"Sorry," I said. But I could tell it was too little too late. I watched him **transmute** into his old, closed-off self. I tried to put my finger on my **transgression**, but it wasn't easy. All I'd done was asked about his job. Why was that such a problem?

It's obviously a sore point with him, I thought, looking out the window as the scenery flew by. *You suspected that something was going on there, and now you know for sure.*

After a few minutes of silence, we arrived at the school. Jon brought the Jeep to a screeching stop in front of the girl's dormitory and waited for me to get out.

"Do you need help?" he asked.

"No, thanks," I said as I unbuckled my seatbelt. "Listen, I'm sorry if I said something wrong . . ."

I was desperate to make **amends**, feeling that if I didn't do it now, I would **efface** all the progress we'd made today. To my relief, he cracked a small smile. "No. It's okay. I'm just . . . tired. I want to get back to the dorm."

"Okay. Well, thanks for including me. It was fun," I said as I

---

accomplished: talented or skillful
tacit: unspoken or implied
abort: stop or terminate

transparent: obvious or see-through
transmute: change
transgression: wrongdoing or intrusion

amends: peace or compensation
efface: erase or wipe out

stepped out of the car. I pulled my snowboard from the back of the Jeep and walked around to the window.

"See you around," I said.

"Yeah. See ya." Then he peeled out, kicking up snow and slush in his wake.

*   *   *   *   *

Instead of heading into the dorm, I walked across the quad, my snowboard stuffed under my arm. The boys' dorm was **accessible** through a back door, which I wasn't surprised to find unlocked. For a school so concerned about crime, they were certainly **lax** when it came to security.

I closed the door quietly behind me and **lumbered** up the stairs toward Marshall's floor. I was **despondent** after the **abysmal** work I'd done that day. The one question I'd asked that even remotely **pertained** to the investigation had caused my suspect to clam up completely. I had to do something to make myself feel better.

Marshall had told me he would return my CDs later in the week, and now seemed like a perfect time to stop by and pay him a little visit. If I played my cards right, maybe I could find out where he was getting the money for all the swag he had in his room.

I shifted my snowboard from one arm to the other and knocked on Marshall's door. As he answered, he was pulling on his jacket as if he were heading out. Judging from the **lush** cashmere sweater he was wearing and the **pungent** scent of cologne, I **assumed** he was going on a date with Cheryl.

"Hey," I said. "Just wanted to pick up those CDs."

"They're right here," Marshall said, grabbing up the stack and attempting to hand them to me. They balanced **precariously** in my free hand, and I looked at Marshall, **blatantly perplexed**. What did he expect me to do?

---

accessible: reachable	**abysmal:** very bad	**assumed:** supposed or took
lax: careless	**pertained:** related	for granted
lumbered: walked heavily	**lush:** luxuriant	**precariously:** unsteadily
despondent: miserable or	**pungent:** sharp or strong	**blatantly:** obviously
pessimistic		**perplexed:** confused

"Got a bag or something?"

Marshall sighed loudly just to let me know that I was **imposing** upon him, then made a big dramatic show of looking around for a bag as if it were a serious **undertaking**. I couldn't believe it. Here was the guy the rest of the school **idolized**, acting like a big **querulous** baby. Finally, he dropped to the floor and yanked out a leather backpack with the Tommy Hilfiger flag **emblazoned** on the flap.

I smiled. Little did he know he'd given me the perfect opening.

"Wow. This is nice," I said as he held it open so I could dump the CDs inside. "Where did you get it?"

"It was a gift," Marshall said, pulling on the cord to tighten the closure.

Oh, great. Was he going to go all **laconic** on me, too?

"Actually, I've been meaning to ask you, do you remember where you got your Bose speakers?" I asked, stepping further into the room to prevent him from **prematurely** tossing me out, which he clearly was on the verge of doing. He seemed tense and wasn't going to **tolerate** my presence much longer.

"I got 'em in New York last summer," Marshall said. "Now if we're done with the twenty questions—"

"How much were they?" I blurted. Marshall sighed and rubbed his fingers into his forehead impatiently. "I mean, if you don't mind my asking."

"They were expensive," Marshall said curtly, eyeing me like I was such an obvious **pauper**, I could never hope to afford them. "Now I'm late to meet somebody, so you really have to go." He held the door open and glared daggers at me. Suddenly, I realized that his cheeks were **tinged** with color and his hands were curled into fists. He was definitely more **agitated** than necessary if he was just late for a date.

Huh. Either Cheryl was a real shrew when it came to **punctuality**,

---

imposing: being a burden or annoyance
undertaking: job or task
idolized: worshipped
querulous: grouchy or difficult

emblazoned: inscribed or decorated
laconic: quiet or curt
prematurely: quickly or too early
tolerate: put up with

pauper: poor person
tinged: tinted or shaded
agitated: restless or disturbed
punctuality: being on time

which wouldn't be surprising (she seemed a real shrew in general), or Marshall was meeting somebody else. Maybe even a buyer? Could it be? Was that why he was so **flustered**?

My pulse pounded with excitement. This definitely could be something.

"Right," I said, hoping there was no external evidence of my intrigue. "Well, I hope you liked the CDs."

"Yeah, definitely. Thanks," Marshall said, totally **distracted**. He locked up behind us and headed for the stairs. "See ya."

"Yeah. See ya."

It was all I could do to keep from running right after him. I took a deep breath and held it for a count of twenty, then hustled toward the stairwell. The door on the first level was just slamming. I dropped my stuff, hoping no one would be **petty** enough to steal it, and raced down the stairs.

Marshall was speed-walking toward the parking lot, his hands in his pockets, his head down. Keeping a good distance between us, I followed as quietly as possible, my heart in my throat the whole time.

Who was he meeting? And where? Was I about to witness a transaction right here, right now?

Marshall disappeared around a corner, and when I peeked around it moments later, he was hopping into an idling Ford Focus. I had no idea what to do. The last thing I had expected was that Marshall was going to leave campus. I'd figured he'd be doing his deal with another student at Hereford. That was, after all, the issue, wasn't it?

The car peeled out, and I dove back around the wall, praying he hadn't seen me. I didn't even have time to get a glimpse of the driver or memorize the license plate. Before I even had a chance to think, the car had disappeared down the windy drive.

I leaned my head back into the cold brick wall. My mother was

---

flustered: tense or uncomfortable

distracted: thinking about something else

petty: low or small-minded

going to kill me. Whoever was in that car may have been a buyer or a supplier—or some other brand of **accomplice**. And I'd completely dropped the ball. Obviously I was just going to have to chalk this up to one of those **dismal** days in the life of a detective.

After retrieving my things from the guys' dorm, I headed for my room. Danielle was sitting on her bed reading Jane Austen's *Emma*. She barely looked up when I walked in. Just what I needed. More **fractious** behavior. I wished I could turn back time and go back to the slopes to start my day over from there. I had had so much fun with Jon, Tek and Michael. Where had I gone wrong?

"Hey. How was your day?" I asked Danielle, attempting to **thaw** the freeze-out.

"Fine," she said. "Yours?"

"It was great," I replied. "Mostly."

"Great," she said. "Actually, if you don't mind, I'm at my favorite part, so . . ."

"Right. I'll leave you alone," I said, my heart falling even further.

I put my stuff down and started to peel off my boarding clothes. The longer the silence in the room **endured**, the more I felt as if my brain and heart were in **turmoil**. But this was stupid. I mean, how immature could you be? All I'd done was spent one day hanging out with other people. And I liked the girl, but I had been assigned to be her roommate, not her best friend for life. Sheesh!

I took a deep breath and changed into my pajamas, deciding that I was not going to let these people affect me. I wasn't here to be Miss **Affable**. These people didn't have to like me. I was here to ferret out a drug problem. They could all hate me if they wanted to. From this point on, I was not going to care.

I had a job to do, and starting that second, I was going to do it. Clearly the **subtle** approach wasn't going to work with Jon, Marshall, *or* David. It was time to start tailing them more, start

---

accomplice: partner in crime
dismal: dreary or miserable
fractious: touchy or irritable

thaw: melt or defrost
endured: lasted

turmoil: confusion or chaos
affable: friendly or pleasant
subtle: delicate or restrained

asking questions around campus. I was going to find out who the bad guy was, and I was going to do it stat.

Because, after today, a whole winter break spent **languishing** on the couch was starting to sound pretty darn good.

languishing: wasting away

I spent most of Sunday in the library, pretending to work on my history paper when I was in fact making lists—one for each of my suspects. I made three columns in my notebook and wrote down anything **abstruse** that I had witnessed, hoping the **juxtaposition** would help me to make some **shrewd** deductions, or at least an educated guess. Unfortunately, when I was done, each of the guys still was a suspect. Every one of them came off as **corrupt** in some fashion.

I was still at square one. But not for long. I was going to solve this case if it killed me.

Monday proved to be the warmest day of the winter so far, which I took to be an **auspicious** sign. After classes, I went to the quad to stake out the post office. The facility closed at 5 P.M., and I knew Jon would be working. I had decided to tail him and see if he did anything odd after work. If there was something going on with him, it definitely hinged on the post office. It was the best lead I had.

I sat on a bench alongside the ancient building, a textbook open on my lap. I was hidden from view of the main entrance, but I'd be able to see if anyone walked out. Luckily, there were other kids out and about, so I was able to blend in—just a regular student enjoying the relatively **balmy** day.

At **precisely** 5:03, the door to the post office opened and slammed, and Jon took off across the pathway to the guys' dorm. In the dusk, I could just make out the outline of a package as he shoved it furtively under his jacket. My skin sizzled with excitement—and apprehension. This could be it! Yay! But I so didn't want Jon to be the guilty party. Damn.

---

abstruse: puzzling
juxtaposition: side-by-side comparison
shrewd: sharp or clever

corrupt: shady or dishonest
auspicious: positive or favorable

balmy: mild or pleasant
precisely: exactly

I mean, could I really be attracted to a criminal?

I waited until he was a good twenty yards ahead of me, then tucked my book away and scurried after him. He entered the dorm through the back door, so I waited for a count of thirty (I was getting better at this) and then snuck in. Instead of stopping at his own floor, Jon continued upstairs to the third. After the door closed on the hallway, I jogged up and glanced through the slim window down the hall. Jon was knocking on the door to Marshall's room.

I held my breath. Marshall opened the door, and the two of them exchanged curt greetings. No **camaraderie** between these two, that was for sure. Then, Jon unzipped his jacket and handed over the package to Marshall. My heart felt as if it was pounding in my temples as Marshall slapped a wad of cash into Jon's hand. This was it. Clear evidence. Jon and Marshall obviously were **colluding**.

But was Jon selling Marshall drugs right now, or was he simply delivering the pills to Marshall, who would then sell them to others later? Either way, it was obvious that Jon was **complicit** in the crime. Suddenly I felt as if I needed to sit down. Jon was guilty. How could he be guilty?

Jon did a **cursory** check of the bills in his hand. It didn't seem like an **exorbitant** amount of money to me, but I didn't have time to dwell on what that might mean. Jon didn't **dawdle**. The door closed, and he turned toward me and started back down the hall. My heart hit my throat and I went to run back downstairs, but then realized I'd never make it all the way out without Jon hearing my running footsteps. Thinking fast, I headed upstairs instead, toward the fourth floor. As the door opened, I sat down quietly on the stairs above and pressed myself against the wall, hoping against hope that Jon wouldn't **randomly** decide to go up instead of down.

He didn't. I listened as he descended the stairs. The door to the second floor opened and slammed. I was safe.

---

camaraderie: friendship or brotherhood
colluding: plotting or scheming

complicit: associated with or involved in
cursory: quick or hurried
exorbitant: excessive or outrageous

dawdle: hang around or waste time
randomly: by chance

Impetuously, I jumped up and ran back down to the third floor. Something inside me was telling me that now was the time to catch Marshall red-handed. Chances were he was opening the package and inspecting its contents right then. If I could catch him in the act, I could call in my mother and this could all be over by tonight.

I paused in front of Marshall's door, took a deep breath, and tried the doorknob. It turned and clicked quietly. Locked.

Dammit! There was only one thing left to do. I raised my hand and pounded on the door. There was an instant stream of incoherent mumbling, then the sound of crinkling paper and plastic wrap. I cursed under my breath. Whatever Marshall had received, he was hiding it right then. By the time the door opened, his hairline was dotted with sweat.

He seemed surprised and **bemused** when he saw me standing there, as if my presence were a huge **quandary.** He even stuck his head out into the hallway to look both ways and make sure it was just me. For my part, I felt nothing but **rancor** in his presence. I so wanted Jon to be innocent that in three seconds I had **rashly** decided that Marshall had somehow **coerced** Jon into being his accomplice. The fault, in my mind, rested entirely on Marshall's shoulders. He was, after all, still the biggest ass I'd met on campus. It would be so perfect if I could arrest him and find Jon and David, both of whom I liked, to be blameless.

"Hey!" I said, shoving by him into the room. My eyes did a quick scan of Marshall's side of the place. There was nothing. No box. No wrapping. No pills. Nada.

"Hey. What're you doing here?" Marshall asked, closing the door. His expression was almost **malevolent** as he turned to me. I obviously had interrupted something important. As if I didn't know that. But his behavior only **underscored** that fact.

All I needed to know was, where he had hidden the box.

---

impetuously: suddenly or without planning
bemused: puzzled
quandary: dilemma

rancor: bitterness or resentment
rashly: hastily or without thinking

coerced: tempted or pressured
malevolent: wicked
underscored: emphasized

"Oh . . . I just thought I'd drop by," I said, sitting down on his bed. I bounced a couple of times to see if I could hear any paper crinkling, thinking he may have shoved everything under the mattress. All I heard was the squeaking of the springs.

"Uh huh," Marshall said, hovering over me. He eyed me up and down as if he was trying to figure me out. "What for?"

"Oh, you know, just to say hi," I said with a shrug.

Maybe it was *under* the bed. I yanked my hat off and twirled it around my finger until it flew right off. Marshall and I both hit the ground to retrieve it, and I checked under the bed. There was a ton of crap under there, and it was too dark in the room to tell if any of it was a freshly opened box. This little **excursion** was not going well.

When I stood up again, Marshall handed me back my hat, and there was something completely different in the way he was looking at me. His **irate** frown had turned into a **smug** smile, his eyes were now alight with his usual cockiness, and he was standing way too close to me for comfort.

"Okay, I get it," he said, nodding. "I see why you're here."

"You do?" I asked, **bewildered** by his **mercurial** behavior.

"Don't play **coy**, now," he said. "I don't know why I didn't figure it out before. You come to karate . . . you sit with us at lunch . . . you're all over me about lending me CDs. . . ."

Oh my God. He had to be kidding me. He thought I was *attracted* to him?

And then, before I could even process my disgust, Marshall grabbed the back of my neck and pulled me to him. His lips covered mine, and his grip was like an iron clasp. I reached up with both hands and shoved his chest as hard as I could. Marshall stumbled back, and I wiped my mouth, **aghast**.

"What the hell are you doing?" I demanded. My stomach was having an **adverse** reaction and threatening to bring up my lunch.

---

excursion: outing or detour	**bewildered:** dazed or	**coy:** shy or timid
irate: angry	confused	**aghast:** shocked or stunned
smug: self-satisfied	**mercurial:** changing or	**adverse:** negative or bad
	unpredictable	

"I thought you wanted me to do that!" Marshall protested, looking hurt now.

"You've got to be kidding me!" I shouted. "God! Don't you have a girlfriend?"

"Yeah, but you're not the first new chick to make a play for me," Marshall said. "This kind of stuff happens all the time."

"Omigod, you're such a slimeball," I said, making for the door.

"Kim! Wait!" Marshall said, moving in front of me and blocking my escape. "Don't tell Cheryl about this, okay? She'll kill me."

His eyes were wide and **plaintively** pleading. He was suddenly so **contrite** that he may as well have been on his knees. I already knew there was no way I was going to tell Cheryl. It would just open up a whole can of worms that I did *not* need to deal with. I wasn't here to create high school dramas. But that didn't mean I couldn't have a little fun with Marshall—maybe **chastise** him a bit.

"Why shouldn't I tell her?" I asked, crossing my arms over my chest. "There's a code among women, you know. I'm duty-bound to tell her that her boyfriend's a pig. And you are, my friend. You're a **gross opportunist**."

This insult may have hit home if he had any clue as to what it meant. But Marshall just blinked at me. He was so **obtuse**. How could a guy like this be the one secretly **shilling** the **opiate** of the masses? How had he managed to get away with it before now?

"Come on, Kim. I'm sorry," Marshall said. "I'll do anything. I swear. Just don't tell her."

I'll do anything. . . . Interesting. Would he maybe tell me what was in the package he'd just received? Was there any way to even ask that without totally blowing my cover? There wasn't. At least not that I could see. He'd want to know how I'd known he'd gotten a delivery, and then I'd have to tell him I was spying on him and Jon. How did detectives *do* this stuff?

---

plaintively: sadly
contrite: sorry or ashamed
chastise: yell at
gross: disgusting

opportunist: someone who takes advantage of people or circumstances

obtuse: stupid or simple-minded
shilling: selling or promoting
opiate: drug or narcotic

I sighed, defeated. "Just forget it," I said. "But if you step out of line one more time, I'm going straight to your girlfriend. Got it?"

Marshall rolled his eyes. "Women. The **bane** of my existence."

"Yeah, well. Not if you're careful," I said. Then I swept out of his room, letting the door slam behind me.

*   *   *   *   *

Next I had planned to stop by Michael and Tek's room. I knew it was a **brazen** move—the details of my visit would probably get back to Jon **expeditiously**, but I felt that I was running out of options. And Michael and Tek seemed like the type of guys who would know who was selling and who was buying around this place. They were obvious stoners, and if they smoked pot, they probably at least knew where to get other stuff. All I had to do was act like I was hard up for drugs and get them to **counsel** me about what to do.

As I walked down to the end of the third-floor hallway, a steady **cadence** grew louder and louder, the type of beat that forces you to match your steps to it. I wasn't surprised to find that it was loudest when I was standing directly in front of Michael and Tek's room. I could just imagine them inside, cavorting and dancing and ignoring their homework entirely.

I smiled, filled with sudden **certitude** that I was doing the right thing. These guys were such party animals, they'd probably give up the information—no **deception** needed—just so they'd have someone new to party with.

More confident than I'd felt in days, I knocked on the door.

"Entrez!" Tek's voice shouted.

Of course *these* guys left their door unlocked. I smiled and walked in. Unexpectedly, Michael and Tek were seated at desks on opposites sides of a **capacious** corner room, their heads buried in

bane: curse or great annoyance	**counsel:** advise	**deception:** trickery
brazen: bold or shameless	**cadence:** beat or rhythm	**capacious:** large or roomy
expeditiously: quickly	**certitude:** confidence or certainty	

their books. The music was loud, but it seemed it was simply the soundtrack for studying.

The room itself, however, looked like it had seen plenty of **carousing** in its history. One wall was completely **defaced**. It had been used as the **canvas** for an **iridescent mural** of Jimi Hendrix. The painting had been signed in an **indecipherable** hand, making it impossible to **discern** the artist. But it was pretty darn good. Lining the opposite wall was a long shelf, packed with empty beer bottles of every brand imaginable, **reverently** lined up with their labels facing out. I had no idea how high school students got away with displaying such things, but it **revived** my spirits. These guys were definitely not down with sobriety. There was no doubt they'd know how to help me.

"Kimmy!" Michael exclaimed, looking up from his books. He stood and **enveloped** me in a bear hug. I felt more **devious** than ever, knowing I was about to pump them for information that might lead to the arrest of their best friend. But I couldn't entertain any **qualms** I might have about this. There was a criminal on the loose, and I had to find out who it was.

"Sweet! Kim in her **munificence** has graced our pad with her presence," Tek said, as **animated** as ever. He reached for the mini-fridge next to his desk. "Can I offer you a beverage?"

"No, thanks," I said, impressed by the **cordial** greeting. I decided to go for the **guileless** approach. "Actually, I wanted to ask you guys a question," I said, crossing to the bed near the Jimi painting and taking a seat.

"Shoot," Michael said. He lowered the volume on the music and regarded me with interest.

"Well, I was wondering if you guys might know . . . you know . . . where a person might be able to purchase some recreational . . . chemicals around here." I raised my eyebrows and watched as Michael and Tek exchanged a **sly** look. It was clear that they knew

---

carousing: partying
defaced: vandalized
canvas: background or setting
iridescent: shimmering
mural: wall painting
indecipherable: unreadable

discern: make out
reverently: respectfully
revived: reenergized
enveloped: surrounded or enclosed
devious: tricky or dishonest
qualms: doubts or worries

munificence: kindness or generosity
animated: excited or lively
cordial: warm or friendly
guileless: straightforward or upfront
sly: sneaky or secretive

who I could buy from. The question was whether they were going to tell me.

Michael straightened up, and an instant sense of foreboding **pervaded** the room.

"Why are you asking us?" he asked.

"I don't know. You just seemed like the kind of guys who would be into . . . extracurricular activity," I said.

"Yeah, well, we're not," Tek said innocently. He even added a laugh to try to convince me. Unfortunately for him, it was so fake it did nothing to **extinguish** my suspicion.

"Then what's up with all the beer bottles?" I asked. I knew they knew something, and I was going to show some **forbearance**. I had to get facts out of *someone* around here.

"Eh, that's just beer," Michael said, shrugging it off.

"Come on, you guys," standing up and attempting to **cajole** it out of them. "I just need something to take the edge off. This school is tougher than I thought."

Tek flushed, and I could tell it was becoming difficult for him to stay silent, but he prevailed. Suddenly, he seemed very **preoccupied** by a thread hanging off of his sock. Meanwhile, Michael turned around and flicked through the pages of his binder, pretending to **peruse** his **copious** notes. This was going nowhere fast.

I took a deep breath. "Okay, well, if you guys don't know, then what about Jon? Would he know?"

The second the question was out of my mouth, I regretted asking it. It was way too direct and nonleading. Tad would have whacked me upside the head if he had been there to witness it.

But Michael and Tek both laughed heartily. "You obviously don't know Jon very well," Michael said, **abjuring** the very thought.

"Yeah, he's like the purest of the pure around here," Tek added. "That kid won't even take cough medicine."

Once again, I was presented with a **conundrum**. Was Jon an

---

pervaded: spread through
extinguish: put out or turn off
forbearance: patience

cajole: coax or sweet-talk
preoccupied: worried or fixated
peruse: read carefully

copious: numerous or plentiful
abjuring: rejecting
conundrum: puzzle or mystery

unalloyed innocent, or was he a guy who was delivering **illicit** packages to people he hated for cash? It was like the more I learned, the more confused I became.

"Okay, well, if you guys do happen to hear of anything, let me know," I said, standing. "I could really use something to help me relax, you know?"

Once again, the two guys exchanged a look. "We'd love to help you out, you know. It's just that . . . you're new around here," Tek said.

I narrowed my eyes. What did he mean by that?

"I'm sure you've heard about the mondo expulsion that happened here a coupla weeks ago. We just . . . don't know if we can trust you yet, that's all," Michael said. "Sorry."

Wow. These people were a lot more paranoid—and had greater **acumen**—than I gave them credit for.

"Well, you can," I said, lying to their faces. "Just let me know when you decide to believe me."

Then I stormed out, hoping they'd believe my **indignation**. In fact, I was simply frustrated by the fact that I'd hit yet another wall. Even the obvious stoners wouldn't help me out with this stuff? I thought they were supposed to be all giving and loving. So much for *that* **stereotype**.

When was I going to catch a break around here?

*   *   *   *   *

I returned to my room, **dejected** about what a **fiasco** the investigation had become. Not only had I learned nothing from Michael and Tek, but they obviously were going to tell Jon I'd been sniffing around about drugs. One of my main suspects was going to know I was onto him.

But maybe that's a good thing, I thought. If Michael and Tek told

---

unalloyed: pure or absolute
illicit: illegal

acumen: insight or shrewdness
indignation: anger or annoyance

stereotype: oversimplified belief
dejected: unhappy or depressed
fiasco: disaster or mess

Jon I was a potential buyer, maybe *he* would come to *me* hoping to make a sale. Then I could snag him on the spot.

Of course, that was a doubtful scenario. Jon had already accused me of stalking him. It was much more likely that he would realize I was a cop who had been trailing him from the beginning.

I had totally screwed up.

Danielle was out, so I had the room to myself. I sat down at my desk thinking about the **disparate** images I had of Jon. Michael and Tek thought he was some kind of naïve innocent, but Tad thought he was a **valid** suspect. He had seemed so **disaffected** and rude when I first met him, but then at the ski lodge he'd become talkative and **attentive** and sweet. Which of these **discordant** Jons was the real one?

There was a knock at the door, and I was **dilatory** in responding. I didn't want to lose my train of thought. But the pounding became more and more **ardent**, so I made myself trudge across the room. When I opened the door, I found David standing there, his face hard, his eyes accusatory. Somewhere in the back of my head, my death **knell** sounded. I knew what he was going to say before he said it, and I was **inclined** to **hurdle** him and head for the hills. But it was too late for that.

"Hi, David," I said, **reticent**.

"Hello, Kim *Stratford*."

---

disparate: different or dissimilar
valid: real or legitimate
disaffected: discontented or rebellious
attentive: caring or kind
discordant: conflicting or incompatible
dilatory: slow
ardent: eager or intense
knell: ring or chime
inclined: ready or feeling like
hurdle: jump over
reticent: quiet or reserved

Chapter Eleven

"I think we need to go back to my room and talk," David said.

"I think maybe we should talk right here," I countered, my heart slamming into my ribs.

David didn't even blink. "If you want to talk to me, it's not gonna be here," he said. "And I really think you want to talk to me as much as I want to talk to you."

Okay. Apparently, David had seen one too many episodes of *Law & Order*. He clearly thought my room was bugged. But going back to his room could be the stupidest of stupid cop moves. Who knew what he might have waiting there for me?

"Are you coming?" he asked.

Just tell me, I thought. *Just tell me you're the guy and let's get this over with.* I was dying to know. I was dying to hear him say it.

"Fine," I said, grabbing my jacket. "Let's go."

As David walked me back to his dorm room, my brain flipped into **crisis** mode. A million thoughts crowded my mind. I knew the conversation with Donny Burke's mother, not to mention my Connecticut-California slip at our first lunch, definitely had got him thinking. But how had he found out my real name? And more important, was *he* the dealer? And if so, what was he going to do once he got me alone in his room? A couple of times I thought about bolting—making a run for it and calling my mother—but two things made me **forgo** this course of action.

First, at this point my curiosity was **immeasurable**. If David *was* the bad guy, I needed to know.

Second, if I ran off and called my mommy, I was going to feel like a big, fat baby.

---

crisis: disaster or emergency

forgo: give up

immeasurable: huge

David was silent all the way across the quad and up the stairs of the boys' dorm. It gave me time to come up with a **tactic** for handling the situation. I was not going to **grovel**. I was not going to **reveal** a thing. I had to exercise some **restraint** and let David talk. Once I found out what he was after, I could proceed from there.

We walked into his room, and he shut the door behind us. My heart was pounding with nervousness. From behind his dresser, David pulled out something that looked like a **blunt** sword attached to an electrical cord. It looked like some kind of **medieval** torture device. This was when I started to **fret** that my life might actually be in **jeopardy**.

Okay, you can take him, I told myself. *You're a martial arts expert, he's a computer geek. You do the math.*

David flicked a switch on the handle of the wand and walked over to me. My eyes widened, and I clenched my hands into fists, readying myself for an **assault**. Then he thrust the **implement** in my direction. I was about to disarm him, but at the last second, I realized he was going to miss my body by inches—which he did. Instead of impaling me with the device, David started running it around my body.

"What're you doing?" I couldn't help but ask.

"Checking for bugs," David said matter-of-factly. He then **systematically** checked my legs and arms, then ran the wand over my back.

I had to laugh. Why was I even remotely surprised that David had spy gear like this in his room?

"So, Kim Stratford, you *did* win the Connecticut State Karate Tournament in your weight division last year," he said, laying the device aside finally and glaring into my eyes. "Your mother is the chief of police, right? So what, she found out about my **exploits** and sent you here to spy on me?"

---

tactic: strategy or plan	**medieval:** from the Middle	**implement:** tool or
grovel: beg or plead	Ages (5th–15th centuries	instrument
reveal: tell	A.D.)	**systematically:** thoroughly
restraint: self-control	**fret:** worry	or methodically
blunt: dull	**jeopardy:** danger	**exploits:** deeds or activities
	assault: attack	

I said nothing. It sounded like David might be on the verge of a **revelation**. If he was about to confess, I was just going to let him **prattle** on. The sooner we got this over with, the better. I could practically taste freedom from Hereford on my tongue.

"But you didn't count on the fact that I was prepared, did you?" David continued. He walked over to his computer and smiled at me **complacently**. "You see, Kim, I have a system on my computer that tells me when anyone unauthorized has been using it."

My heart fell. Of course. A guy as paranoid as David would definitely have some kind of anti-hack program on his computer. I knew it had been too easy.

"What is it?" I asked. "Do the keys recognize **alien** fingerprints or something?"

"Not quite," he said. "I have a camera."

He reached out and cupped a little ball on top of his computer screen. A little ball with a lens in it. He adjusted it until it was facing me, and my nose appeared all huge and **distorted** on the monitor. I couldn't believe I had been that **negligent**. The camera was sitting right there!

"You must not be that good at your job," David said, echoing my thoughts. "All you had to do was **tamper** with the wire, and I never would have known you were on here."

"Great, thanks for the tip," I said.

"When I overheard that woman asking you all about the county championships the other day, it got me to thinking about you and a couple of things you've said that didn't add up, so I checked out the roster from last year's competition," David explained. "There was no Kim Sharpe, but there was a Kim Stratford. There was even a picture of you with your trophy on their website. You really should learn to cover your bases."

I took a deep breath and looked away. I was not going to **capitulate** to this guy. Let him show off about how smart he was.

---

revelation: confession or admission
prattle: babble or chatter

complacently: smugly or self-assuredly
alien: foreign or unknown
distorted: misshapen

negligent: careless or inattentive
tamper: tinker or meddle
capitulate: submit or give in

Sooner or later he would get around to the good stuff.

"Of course, then I realized that you had tricked me into leaving you alone in here the other night, so I checked my tape and there you were, searching my files," David continued, shaking his head as if to **chasten** me. He hit a couple of buttons on his computer, and my ID photo from Stanford popped up on the screen. "Look what I found when I ran your real name!" he announced as if it was a big surprise. "You're in the **index** of the freshman class at Stanford University. You're not even in high school."

Again, I said nothing, but the whole situation was **galling**. I had come to Hereford all cocky and **arrogant** and ready to save the world, and now here I was, trapped in a dorm room with a computer geek **illustrating** to me my every mistake. The **gravity** of the situation began to creep up on me. David had blown my cover. I had failed my mother. My presence here was now totally and utterly pointless.

"So, I know you found my list of customers," David said, sitting down in his desk chair and crossing his arms over his chest. "What're you going to do now, report me to Cox?"

I blinked. Didn't he realize the situation was a little more serious than that? Still, I said nothing. Tad would have been so proud. I knew that David liked to talk and *loved* to brag. My silence would most likely **irk** him into saying too much, which he hadn't yet done. He had admitted to having customers, he'd admitted to having exploits, but he'd yet to come right out and say he was a drug dealer. I couldn't leave this room without a confession—if I did I was done for.

As predicted, David started to grow impatient with my silence. I could see him trying to **temper** his internal frustration, but eventually it got the best of him.

"You know, I don't really think that I can be held **liable** for everything, here," David said, standing. He started to pace the room and

---

chasten: scold or punish
index: directory
galling: painful or maddening

arrogant: proud or conceited
illustrating: showing
gravity: seriousness

irk: annoy
temper: control or regulate
liable: legally responsible

ramble, his hands tucked securely under his arms. "I mean, this problem was **rampant** way before I ever came here. I just took it over, you know? Why do I have to be the one to take the fall? And, God, it's just a little innocent fun. What else do they expect us to do around here?"

"Innocent fun?" I blurted. "David, you're hurting people!"

"How? Everyone here has more money than God!" David said, whirling on me. "If they want to gamble it away, isn't that their business?"

I opened my mouth to retort, but the words caught in my throat. Wait a minute—*gamble?*

Suddenly I had a **massive** headache.

"You're running a gambling ring," I stated, my brain struggling to digest this new information. *That* was what the list of dollar amounts represented. Those people owed money for gambling, not drugs.

"We already know this," David said impatiently. "What we don't know is what you're going to do about it."

I wasn't sure whether to feel relieved, angry, or totally disappointed. Part of me was glad that David was innocent—of the drug dealing at least. But if it wasn't him, that meant it had to be Jon or Marshall. And I really didn't want it to be Jon. So that left Marshall. Marshall whom I had seen exchanging money with David last week after the karate match. The karate match in which Marshall had lost.

Wait a second . . .

"Marshall Cone is one of your clients, isn't he?" I asked, sitting down on Chris's bed.

"One of the biggest and best," David said. "Where do you think he gets the money for all that crap he has in his room?"

Oh, God. If Marshall was buying all his stuff with his winnings, then that really only left Jon. I was going to hurl.

---

rampant: widespread   **massive:** huge

Okay, focus, I told myself. *This isn't over yet. Marshall is still getting suspicious packages and sneaking out at night. He's still in the running.*

"So, what? Marshall bets against himself and then throws his matches?" I asked. It seemed **logical**—**insidious**, but logical. Marshall could have totally taken the guy he'd gone up against last week, and we all knew it. I had just thought he was having an off day, but if he'd done it for money, then he was an even bigger jerk than I thought.

"What? No!" David said, **repudiating** my line of thought. "Are you kidding? Marshall's too egotistical to throw his matches. Besides, I don't take bets on high school events. Strictly pro sports and college football. All high-end."

Suddenly David seemed to realize he was giving away too much, and he snapped his mouth shut. I stood up slowly, feeling as if I was drowning in a whole new **quagmire** of issues. David wasn't the drug dealer—that much I knew. But he was participating in illegal gambling. It wasn't as **abominable**, but it still was wrong. And technically I was an officer of the law. What was I supposed to do now?

"Look, I already **deleted** the evidence, and I'll deny everything I've just said," David told me. "You don't have a recording, and it'll be your word against mine."

"Listen, I'm not going to report you," I told him, making an **extemporaneous** decision. I still liked David. And I liked him even more now that I knew he wasn't the source of the drug problem. I was **disinclined** to get him into trouble for something as innocuous as gambling on football games. Especially considering that I myself was in on my floor's NFL pool back at Stanford all semester.

David's entire face lit up, and his hands dropped to his sides. "Seriously?"

"Yeah, seriously," I said. After all, I had not been sent there to **dispose** of a gambling ring. I'd been sent here to investigate a drug

---

logical: rational or reasonable

insidious: sinister

repudiating: rejecting

quagmire: swamp

abominable: terrible

deleted: erased

extemporaneous: sudden or improvised

disinclined: reluctant or hesitant

dispose: destroy or get rid of

problem, and now I was one step closer to doing just that. David had been **exonerated**, and I was down to two suspects.

"Just don't tell anyone who I really am, all right?"

David nodded slowly, mulling the facts over in his mind. I was sure that he was figuring out that I hadn't actually been sent here to stop him. And that if I was still going to stay and keep my cover, I had to be here for some other reason. All I could do was hope that I could trust him. He was either going to keep my secret, or by this time tomorrow everyone at the school would know that I wasn't who I said I was.

"Okay," he said finally. "I'll keep my mouth shut."

I was halfway down the hall when David stuck his head out of his room. "Hey, Kim?" he called out. I turned around, and he smiled his infectious smile. "Thanks," he said.

"No problem," I replied, smiling as well.

Then I sighed and headed back to my room. One down, two to go.

*   *   *   *   *

The next day the unusually warm weather continued. When I saw Jon eating his lunch outside again, alone, I decided to take the **initiative** and join him. Danielle was still being **exaggeratedly** cold toward me, and I had no idea how to act whenever I was around David. I needed a **respite** from both of them, and the last thing I wanted to do was hang out at Marshall's table after he had attacked me the night before. Jon was pretty much all I had left.

He looked up when the door opened and, happily, didn't seem put off by my presence. I sat down across from him and smiled.

"Hey," I said.

"Hey," he responded.

---

exonerated: cleared or acquitted
initiative: lead or control

exaggeratedly: overly or excessively

respite: break

The more time I spent with him, the more **inured** I became to his characteristic silence. I decided that if he wanted to sit there and enjoy the **placid** afternoon, that was fine by me. I wasn't going to try to **elicit** anything from him. I just wanted to have a peaceful, stress-free lunch. This detective was on break.

"I have to ask you something," Jon said, surprising me as I dug into my salad.

"Okay," I said, ignoring my heart, which had skipped a beat when he spoke.

Please don't tell me he's onto me, too!

"How is it that you can sit with David and Danielle one day, the Conenites another day, and then come out here and sit with me?" he asked.

"Is that illegal?" I asked, raising my eyebrows.

Jon shrugged. "Just improbable."

I munched on my quite **palatable** chicken Caesar salad and turned over a response in my mind. "Well, I guess I've never been able to **yoke** myself to one group," I said finally. "It's not that I think I'm above it, it's just that I never totally fit in anywhere."

Jon nodded, and a slight smile played about his quite luscious lips. "Yeah, I can see that," he said.

I felt a skitter run through my heart as he looked at me, and I knew I could take his comment as a compliment.

And just like that, the **vitriolic** Jon was gone again. He made the **metamorphosis** into the Jon from the ski lodge—the open, **solicitous**, even **jolly** Jon that I found it so easy to talk to. This guy was an **enigma**—which was exactly why I liked him.

He also seemed to have forgotten or at least forgiven my questions about his job and was willing to move on—thank goodness.

"So, how're your applications coming?" I asked, zipping up my jacket. It wasn't *that* warm.

---

inured: accustomed	**yoke:** join or attach	**solicitous:** attentive or
placid: calm	**vitriolic:** cruel or spiteful	concerned
elicit: extract or draw out	**metamorphosis:**	**jolly:** cheerful
palatable: tasty or delicious	transformation or change	**enigma:** mystery or puzzle

"Good. I'm sending a bunch of them out today," Jon said. "I'm just psyched to start getting responses."

"You seem **sanguine** about the whole process," I commented.

Jon lifted one shoulder and bit into his hamburger. "I guess I kind of am," he said. "I think I have senioritis. I'm starting to believe that anywhere will be better than here."

"I remember what that's like," I said with a laugh.

Jon's brow furrowed at this comment, and I backtracked. "I mean, I can relate," I said. "Sorry. My brain's a little slow on the uptake today."

"I know the feeling," Jon replied. "I have an English essay due that's kicking my ass. I haven't left the library in days. I just hope all this work is worth it."

"Trust me, it will be," I **asserted**, wishing suddenly that I could talk to Jon without **pretense**. That I could just tell him who I was and talk to him all about Stanford and how **stupendous** it was to be there among all those **revered** professors and **erudite** scholars. I could just see Jon fitting in perfectly on the Stanford campus—on *any* campus. I hated that I couldn't allay his fears.

"You seem pretty sure about that," he said.

"Yeah, well, I can tell you're the collegiate type," I said. "I bet you'll **flourish** wherever you go."

Jon smiled the rare smile, and it sent my heart fluttering inside my chest. Damn, he was cute. And smart. And I swear he was looking at me as if he were thinking the exact same things about me.

*Okay, you've got to **subjugate** your feelings right now,* I thought. *This is an undercover investigation, not The Dating Game.*

The bell rang, ending lunch, and just like that, I was snapped back to my senses. I couldn't **nurture** the **burgeoning** feelings I had for this guy. He was still a suspect—one of only two. What did I think I was doing?

---

sanguine: confident or optimistic
asserted: stated or declared
pretense: deceit or falseness

stupendous: amazing or wonderful
revered: respected
erudite: well-educated
flourish: thrive or prosper

subjugate: overcome or suppress
nurture: encourage or foster
burgeoning: budding or growing

But it's not him. It can't be, I thought as Jon picked up my tray and tossed my trash for me. Once I got to know him, he seemed so **ingenuous**. All he wanted was to get on with his life, just like every other high school senior in the world. I didn't see him messing it all up to make a quick buck selling drugs. In my heart, he definitely was **vindicated**.

Of course, in my *mind*, I knew I couldn't tell my mom he was no longer a suspect. She would ask me why, and then I would have to say it was a gut instinct, and she would know I had a crush on him. That would not go over well. I was going to have to find **irrefutable** proof that Marshall was the dealer. And I was also going to have to prove that, if Jon *was* delivering the goods to Marshall, he was totally unaware of what he was doing.

I had a lot of work to do.

"Where're you headed?" I asked as we walked back into the cafeteria. A few kids were walking outside to enjoy the fresh air, while some still sat at their tables to chat their way through the short break period.

"I was gonna go hang out with Michael and Tek," Jon said, causing my stomach to turn. "Wanna come?"

"Nah," I said, clutching the strap on my backpack. "I'm gonna go to the library and work on my paper."

"Okay," Jon said, smiling before he turned on his heel. "See ya later."

As he walked away, I had to sit down at the nearest table before my knees went out from under me. I had almost forgotten about my conversation with Michael and Tek the night before. Clearly, they had yet to tell Jon that I was asking about him in connection to drugs, or he would have either brought it up or given me the cold shoulder. But they would probably bring it up now. If Jon *was* the dealer (and I was convinced he wasn't), then he would definitely know I was up to something. If he *wasn't* the dealer and he was as

---

ingenuous: innocent or naïve

vindicated: blameless or proven right

irrefutable: unquestionable

clean as Michael and Tek claimed, then he was probably going to be insulted.

Suddenly, I felt as if the world was pressing in on me from all sides. I felt like I was doing everything wrong. It was time to get my **priorities** straight.

Okay, you can't worry about what Jon thinks of you, I told myself, taking a deep breath. *The* **primary** *goal here is to bring the drug dealer to justice. Do that, and then you can worry about your love life.*

I had to figure something out soon before everyone figured out I was a mole.

Luckily, the monthly party in the gym was coming up in a couple of days. All I could do was hope that Marshall wouldn't freeze me out after our little altercation in his room. If there was ever a perfect **forum** for drug dealing, this party was going to be it.

* * * * *

That evening, I followed Jon from the post office to the guys' dorm once again. His backpack was bulging from the weight of something he had concealed inside. He was making another delivery to Marshall. I could feel it.

I hid in the stairwell and watched the transaction take place. This time, the box Jon **extended** to Marshall was much bigger than the last one, which made perfect sense. Clearly, Marshall was stocking up for the party that weekend. I was sure he did a lot more business at the monthly event. He had to be prepared.

As far as I was concerned, at that moment the matter was **decided**. Marshall was the drug dealer, and he was going to be peddling his butt off on Friday night. I wasn't going to **dither** about this anymore. I had to call my mother and tip her off so that we could **forestall** the event.

---

priorities: goals or concerns
primary: main or most important

forum: environment
extended: gave or offered
decided: definite or certain

dither: hesitate or waste time
forestall: prevent

I waited for Jon to return to his floor and then hustled back to my room. Danielle was sitting at her computer, emailing yet again, and she looked up when I ran in and grabbed my cell phone.

"What's up?" she asked, breaking her silence for the first time in days. She appeared concerned, and I realized I must have looked like I was in a panic, my hair wild and my face flushed from running outside.

"Nothing. Just need to make a private call," I told her, flashing my cell phone.

She shrugged, and I headed to the **defunct** phone booths. My mother picked up on the first ring.

"Hey, Mom," I said. "I think I have your dealer."

"You have **compelling** evidence against one of our suspects?" she asked. I could tell she was practically salivating to resolve this case.

"Yep. Marshall Cone has been getting secret deliveries from the post office," I explained. "They're always wrapped in plain brown paper, and he's very careful about hiding them. The whole thing makes him totally nervous."

"What else?" my mother asked.

"Well, he hosts this secret party once a month in the school gym, and it's going to happen this Friday night," I explained. "And he just got this box that's at least twice the size of all the others. I saw it with my own eyes."

"So he could be getting ready for big sales at this party," my mother said.

"Exactly," I said, my skin sizzling with excitement. "Look, I know it's not **concrete**, but I think you guys should stake out the campus on Friday. That way if I see anything go down, I can call you in. We need to **maximize** our chances of catching the guy."

"I **concur**," my mother said. "Here's what we're going to do . . ."

---

defunct: no longer functioning

compelling: convincing or forceful

concrete: rock-solid or tangible

maximize: increase as much as possible

concur: agree

Chapter Twelve

On Friday night, I sat with Jon at dinner—inside this time. A **blustery** snow shower earlier in the day had given way to a cold, still evening, and the new drifts gleamed white outside the windows. It would've been romantic—if we weren't surrounded by hundreds of cavorting kids, and if I weren't more nervous than a hen in a fox's den.

Oh, and then there was that small possibility that Jon could still be the bad guy.

The big sting was going to go down that night, provided I could catch Marshall dealing at the party. I felt like I was hovering on the **brink** of something huge. Tonight was my night. I was either going to fall flat on my face or go home a hero. I just hoped it would be the latter.

"So, what're you gonna do tonight?" Jon asked, pushing his empty plate away.

My heart thumped. Was he asking because he wanted to do something with me? If so, life was really, really **iniquitous**.

"Why?" I asked, delaying the **inevitable**. How was I going to explain to Jon that I was going to be living large with a group of people he couldn't stand? I had a feeling I was in for an earful.

"My dad sent me a couple of new DVDs. I thought you could come by. If you want," Jon said as if it were no big deal that he was asking me to hang out alone in his room on a Friday night. Probably in the dark . . .

Ugh! That sounded soooooo good!

---

blustery: windy
brink: edge

iniquitous: evil or unfair

inevitable: certain or unavoidable

"And I've been **hoarding** those chocolate chip cookies they've been giving us for dessert. I've got a couple dozen stashed in my refrigerator," Jon added.

Wow. He really knew the way to a girl's heart. Those cookies were like heaven on a baking sheet.

I took a deep breath. Jon wasn't going to like what I was about to say, but I had to be **candid** with him. What was the point of lying? This time tomorrow, I was out of here anyway.

And you're never going to see this guy again, I thought, feeling lower than low.

"Actually, I was going to go to that party in the gym," I said, averting my eyes.

Jon snorted a laugh and looked at me like he was waiting for the punch line. I watched his face change as he realized I was telling the truth.

"Wait. You're serious? Why the hell would you want to go to that?" he asked **vehemently**.

I blinked. I knew he didn't like Marshall, but I thought he would throw a few **gibes** my way, not get all worked up. I didn't believe my announcement **constituted** such a terrible offense.

"It sounds like fun," I said, lifting one shoulder and hoping my **mellow** attitude would **mollify** him. "You should come with."

"Yeah, like that's ever going to happen," Jon said, sitting back hard in his seat. "Those guys are **superficial**, idiotic losers with nothing better to do on a Friday night than get drunk and talk about how cool they think they are for getting away with it."

"They can't all be that bad," I said. "Why do you have to be so **hidebound** about them?"

"I'm not being hidebound. They *are* all that bad," Jon said, scowling. "Trust me. You haven't been here as long as I have. And the more you hang out with them, the more likely it is that you'll turn into one of them. Everyone else has."

---

hoarding: saving or stockpiling
candid: open or honest
vehemently: heatedly or intensely

gibes: taunts or jokes
constituted: amounted to
mellow: calm or laid-back
mollify: calm or pacify

superficial: shallow or insincere
hidebound: narrow-minded

Well, *that* was a **disconcerting** thing to say.

"Wow. I'm glad you have so much confidence in my character," I said, crossing my arms over my chest.

"Whatever, if you'd rather hang out with them, I can't stop you," Jon said, getting up from the table.

Suddenly, I realized that he wasn't so much upset that I was hanging out with Marshall and his friends, but that I *wasn't* hanging out with *him*. I couldn't believe it. Our feelings were **mutual**. Jon liked me! He really liked me!

Giddy with glee, I got up and followed Jon out of the room, wanting to **reassure** him that if I had my own way, I would be hanging out with him in his room every damn night of the week. But how could I? What was my excuse going to be? It wasn't as if I could tell him the truth.

Jon shoved through the door of the cafeteria, and I heard myself shout his name. He stopped, sighed, and turned around, fixing me with his piercing green eyes.

Okay . . . now what?

"Um . . . listen," I said, stepping closer to him. "How about a **compromise**? I'll go to the party for an hour or two, and then we can watch the movies."

"We're **banned** from each other's rooms after eleven on weekends," Jon said. As if either one of us cared about rules. I could tell I had already **conciliated** him. Now he was just trying to be difficult.

"I don't think I'm supposed to be in the gym at midnight either," I reminded him.

Jon sighed again and eyed me like he was trying to decide whether my desire to be with him was genuine. It was. It *so* was.

Of course, the only problem was there was a good possibility that I wouldn't be able to come to his room that night because I'd be **enmeshed** in police business. There was also a distinct possibility

---

disconcerting: upsetting or disturbing
mutual: common or shared

reassure: encourage or give confidence
compromise: middle ground
banned: barred

conciliated: made peace with
enmeshed: trapped or tangled

that my mother might show up at his room tonight instead of me, to question him about his deliveries.

But at that moment, I chose to ignore those possibilities. I chose to believe in the **illusion** of me and Jon, alone in his room potentially sitting side by side on his bed while the TV screen flickered in front of us. As long as that was possible, there was also the possibility of a kiss.

What can I say? My hormones got the best of me. It was impossible to be **rational** with him looking at me like that.

Besides, maybe it would all work out. Maybe everything would go smoothly, Jon would be exonerated when Marshall confessed to everything, and I could still squeeze in a date before breakfast.

Yeah, right.

"Okay," he said finally, cracking a smile. "I'll try to stay awake for you."

"Thanks," I said. "And I'll get there as early as I can."

*　*　*　*　*

The music was audible from halfway across campus, and it felt like the bass beat was **resonating** in my heart, **intensifying** the tangle of emotions that had already taken me over. I was nervous, that much was obvious. But I was also excited. After all, if everything went well, tomorrow I would go down as the girl who cleaned up the Hereford Academy Ecstasy problem. Part of me was psyched to get the heck out of the staid school, but part of me was also sad about the prospect of leaving—saying goodbye to Jon and even David and Danielle.

Just call me a sentimental softy.

With all these **contradictory** thoughts in my mind, I was a totally confused mess as I entered the gym, but I had to focus on the task at hand. Tonight I had to be all about business.

---

illusion: fantasy or daydream

rational: sensible or reasonable
resonating: echoing or booming

intensifying: increasing or deepening
contradictory: conflicting

Any **preconceived** notions I might have had about a lame party with a keg in the corner and a bag of greasy potato chips were **eradicated** the second I walked through the door of the gym that evening. The **garish** lights of the gym had been extinguished to make way for dozens of strings of white Christmas lights that were draped all over the room. A disco ball rotated in the center of the ceiling, and the music pounded **unremittingly**. A group of girls on the dance floor attempted to **emulate** Beyoncé's latest video for a crowd of cheering onlookers. Against the far wall was a snack table filled with hot **hors d'oeuvres** and mini-pizzas, and I saw Curtis **dispensing** beer from not one but *three* different kegs—one **domestic**, one imported, and one light. This was totally crazy. How the hell did they get away with it?

I **circumvented** the crowd and made my way over to Curtis as I scanned the room for Marshall.

"**Quench** your thirst at the watering hole!" Curtis called out as I approached. His grin was huge, and he already looked as if he had imbibed one too many of his own beers. "What's your pleasure?" he asked me. "You look **parched**." He waggled his eyebrows in a **droll** manner, and I laughed.

"Nothing for me, thanks," I said.

"If you're worried about the calories, I've got some of the lighter but harder stuff right here," Curtis said, pulling a flask from his cargo pants. He waved it in the air as if to **entice** me.

"You think I should be worried about calories?" I asked, pretending to be miffed in an attempt to **divert** his attention from the alcohol at hand.

As expected, Curtis turned beet red with embarrassment. "No! Of course not! You got nothing to be worried about. The first day you got here, I told Marshall you had the sweetest ass in school. If you don't believe me, ask him!"

I stared at Curtis, dumbfounded by his rambling, and he seemed

---

preconceived: existing beforehand
eradicated: wiped out
garish: bright or gaudy
unremittingly: endlessly or relentlessly

emulate: imitate
hors d'oeuvres: appetizers
dispensing: giving out
domestic: made in this country
circumvented: dodged or sidestepped

quench: satisfy
parched: very thirsty
droll: funny or entertaining
entice: tempt
divert: distract

to realize he'd said too much. He snapped his mouth shut and pressed his lips together.

"Where *is* Marshall anyway?" I asked as if nothing odd had been said.

Curtis was so relieved he almost fell over. Or maybe he was just so drunk he almost fell over.

"He's over at the stereo DJ-ing!" Curtis said, pointing across the room.

I caught a glimpse of Marshall ducking away from the **elaborate** audio equipment. As I watched, he glanced around quickly, then slipped out the back door of the gym. My heart hit my throat. He was sneaking out! This could be it!

I started across the room quickly, dodging dancers and chuggers and one girl who was just twirling nonstop. The second I got to Marshall's exit door, I lifted the cuff of my shirt to my mouth. Tonight my mother had insisted I use the wire Tad had given me at the beginning of all this. It made me feel very official.

"Suspect exited through the north door. Stand by," I said into the tiny mic. Then I pushed the door open as quietly as possible and **embarked** on my mission.

"All units stand by," my mother's voice echoed in my ear.

It was a cold, pitch-black night, and my breath made white clouds in the air. The area behind the gym was covered in thick drifts of gleaming white snow. It was so dark it seemed like it'd be impossible to find anybody back there, but then I saw footprints in the snow along the wall of the building. Rather large footprints with **intricate** treads. A pair of Marshall's expensive designer boots, no doubt. They continued along the gym and disappeared around the corner.

"Proceeding along the north wall," I said into my wrist.

I walked quickly and quietly and paused at the corner to peek around. My heart caught in my throat. Marshall was a few yards

---

elaborate: complex or complicated

embarked: began or started

intricate: elaborate or fancy

away, standing near a circle of benches that surrounded a fountain that was probably functional in warmer weather. He was talking to someone, but his **immense** frame **obstructed** my view. I could tell the conversation was heated by the way Marshall's head kept jerking as if he was arguing. I thought he might be **negotiating** a sale. And then I saw it. The box. It was lying close by on one of the cleared-off benches. This was it! Marshall was making a deal!

But I had yet to hear them say anything incriminating—their voices were hushed, and the words were **garbled** by the music coming from inside. All of this was **incidental** unless I could get close enough to record the transaction on my hidden mic, or at the very least get my hands on that box. Carefully, I took a few steps closer. My pulse pounded through my veins. At any second, one or both of them could turn and spot me.

" . . . thought you loved me," a girl's voice said.

I paused. Was it Cheryl? It didn't sound like her. The voice was too high-pitched.

"I do . . . it's just . . . we never see each other," Marshall replied. "I thought we agreed we could see other people."

"We never *agreed*. We just talked about it. Besides, you're the one who—"

Wait a second. This wasn't a drug deal. It was a lover's quarrel! But that wasn't Cheryl. For a second I was frozen with **indecision**. What should I do? Call their attention to my presence? Run? Hide? As the argument escalated and I had more time to think, my situation was **elucidated**. I had to get the heck out of there. If I *was* going to catch Marshall dealing later, he couldn't catch me spying on him now.

I turned to head back around the corner, and my boot made a squeaking noise against the trodden snow. I **winced**. They fell silent.

"Is that *her*?" The girl's voice shouted.

"Kim? What the hell are you doing?" Marshall demanded.

---

immense: enormous	**garbled:** muddled or	**indecision:** uncertainty
obstructed: blocked	inaudible	**elucidated:** made clear
negotiating: discussing or	**incidental:** beside the point	**winced:** flinched or cringed
bargaining		

Dammit. Dammit dammit dammit.

Slowly, I turned to face them, trying to **concoct** a plausible story. The girl was short like me, African American, and drop-dead gorgeous. Her curly dark hair cascaded over her shoulders as she stood there fuming at me. I could tell just by looking at her that she was too good for the **inconstant charlatan** she was dating.

"Are you her? Are you the girl who's screwing my Marshall?" she demanded.

And she didn't mince words either.

"Um . . . no," I said calmly. "I promise you, I am not the girl who is screwing your Marshall."

"She's nothing. She's no one," Marshall said, dismissing me with a wave of his hand.

My blood boiled. Who did he think he was talking about?"

"But he *did* try to molest me in his room the other night," I stated, narrowing my eyes at him.

"*What?*"

I closed my eyes. It seemed, at that perfect moment, Cheryl had decided to come looking for her man. She stormed past me, almost knocking me into a snowbank, and got right in Marshall's face as if she didn't even notice the girl standing across from him.

"Marshall, tell me she's lying! Tell me you didn't actually cheat on me with . . . *that*," Cheryl said, casting a scathing look in my direction.

The other girl's mouth dropped open behind Cheryl's back, and Marshall tipped his head forward. Things were about to get a lot more **melodramatic**. I smiled, **savoring** the moment. Marshall was *so* snagged.

"Cheat on *you*? Who the hell are *you*?" The girl grabbed Cheryl by the shoulder and spun her around. Cheryl seemed **appalled** that anyone would dare to touch her. She flicked her eyes over the

---

concoct: make up
inconstant: unreliable or unpredictable

charlatan: fraud or faker
melodramatic: sensational or dramatic

savoring: enjoying
appalled: shocked or horrified

gorgeous girl, **appraising** her **rival**, and didn't seem as impressed as I had been. She looked pretty disgusted, actually.

"*I* am Marshall's girlfriend!" Cheryl shouted.

"Sorry, honey. *I* am Marshall's girlfriend," the new girl said, wrapping her arm around Marshall's back. He looked like he was about to be sick.

I felt somewhere in my conscience that I should walk away, but I couldn't seem to make my feet move. It was like watching a car wreck. Except it was actually entertaining.

"Marshall, who the hell does this girl think she is? Tell her! Tell her we've been together for three years!" Cheryl **ranted**.

"Three years?" the other girl shouted. "You only brought up the seeing-other-people thing on Saturday!"

Suddenly it hit me. Saturday. That was why Marshall had seemed so tense on Saturday when I dropped by his room. He wasn't meeting a buyer! He was meeting up with this girl to tell her he wanted to see other people. She must have been the driver of the Ford Focus.

"Now, ladies . . . please," Marshall said calmly. I was momentarily impressed with his **mettle**. Most men would've run for the hills in the face of two such angry and **volatile** women. "There's enough of me to go around." He laughed, trying to lighten the situation. Big mistake.

Both girls started to shout at once, yelling both at Marshall and at each other in a sudden **frenzy** of curse words and insults. Marshall finally seemed to realize he was in trouble and **meekly** began to back away, but that didn't **inhibit** the girls—it only seemed to make them angrier.

"You think you're all that! Well, let me tell you, Marshall Cone, you just lost the best thing that ever happened to you!" the new girl shouted, advancing on him.

"*Both* the best things that ever happened to you," Cheryl added.

---

appraising: judging or evaluating
rival: competitor or challenger

ranted: shouted or raged
mettle: nerve or guts
volatile: unstable or explosive

frenzy: flurry or storm
meekly: timidly or tamely
inhibit: stop or discourage

It seemed I'd been forgotten in all the insanity. As Marshall attempted to **palliate** his sins and **pacify** the girls, I took the opportunity to sneak past the **mayhem** and check out the package they'd left on the bench. If it was the drugs, at the very least I could call in my mother, and she could **impound** the box as evidence.

The package had been ripped open, but the return address was still legible. It had been sent by Tashana Bennett from Newark, New Jersey. My hands shook as I pulled aside the brown paper, expecting to see those tiny Ziploc baggies of pills you always see in the movies and on TV. What I found inside caused me to let out an **aggrieved** groan: candy bars, a mix tape, a few articles about the New York Giants from a local paper, and one very **lurid** picture of the beautiful girl who was now attempting to shove Marshall into the gymnasium wall.

It was a care package. Jon had been secretly delivering Tashana's care packages to Marshall so that Cheryl, who undoubtedly had Marshall on a short leash, wouldn't find out.

I had been totally and utterly wrong. I was an **incompetent** fool.

And this left only one possibility. Only one suspect left on the list. Jon Wisnewski.

*   *   *   *   *

After calling off my mother and telling her to wait for me to contact her, I stormed through the gym and out the door that led to the main hallway. I was upset, confused, and totally disillusioned after the **debacle** with Marshall. I couldn't believe it. It was Jon. Jon was the bad guy. And he had made me fall for him! I felt as if my heart was **deteriorating** inside my chest. I had to confront him, and I had to do it now. I was about to slam through the front door to take a shortcut across the main parking lot when a deep voice stopped me short.

---

palliate: excuse or cover for by apologizing
pacify: calm
mayhem: confusion or chaos

impound: seize
aggrieved: distressed
lurid: racy or explicit
incompetent: useless or bungling

debacle: incident
deteriorating: decaying or falling apart

"Ms. Sharpe."

I closed my eyes. *Not now. Please not now.*

When I turned around, I fully expected Headmaster Cox to be standing there with a triumphant smirk on his face, ready to **harass** me. After all, he'd caught me breaking the rules yet again—out of my room after midnight. But much to my surprise, the headmaster appeared nervous—even scared.

"All right, you've got me," he said, spreading his arms out. "I suppose you're horrified, appalled."

My brow furrowed as he took a few steps closer to me. What the hell was this guy talking about?

"Well, let me tell you something, missy. If you think that running a school like this is easy, you've got another thing coming," he said, his jowls shaking. "At least I *try* to understand these kids. At least I pay attention. You should have seen my **predecessor**. She was totally clueless. Thought she could control them. Well, I'm here to tell you it's just not possible. It may seem like a **radical** idea to you, but you've got to let kids let off steam. Otherwise, they just run all over you."

"Ooooookay," I said. "Look, Headmaster Cox, as much as I'd love to stand here and listen to you **pontificate** about your job, I kind of have somewhere I need to be."

"Going to tell your mommy, are you? Going to report about our monthly **soiree**?" He was growing red in the face. And suddenly, *finally* it hit me. He *did* know about the monthly party, and he *did* turn a blind eye. And he was standing here, delaying me, because he was worried that I was going to tattle on him. No wonder he hadn't wanted a spy installed at Hereford. He feared for his job.

"You know what, Headmaster? If you want to allow your students to get trashed every month and risk their lives and your position here, that's your **prerogative**," I told him. "Right now, I have a job to do."

harass: bother or pester	**radical:** extreme or	**soiree:** evening party
predecessor: person who	revolutionary	**prerogative:** choice or right
held the job previously	**pontificate:** preach	

I turned and walked out into the cold again, leaving him flabbergasted behind me. Somewhere in the back of my mind, I made a mental note to tell my mother all about Cox and his exploits. It would be my pleasure to get him fired.

*   *   *   *   *

Five minutes later, I burst into Jon's room, ready to tear into him, but the second I saw Jon lying there on his bed, my hurt was **eclipsed** by my disappointment in myself. *I* was the one in the wrong. I had done what I had promised myself all along I would never do—I had let myself get sucked in by Jon's **chicanery**. That's what it had to be, right? He'd fooled me into thinking he liked me just to throw me off his scent.

Jon stood up from his bed and rubbed at his eyes in a drowsy way. Clearly he hadn't been able to stay awake long enough for our little **rendezvous**. As if that mattered.

"You're early," he said with a smile as he woke himself up.

"Jon, do you know where I can score some E?" I blurted out. I couldn't help it. There was no **cunning** left in me. I was going for broke.

Jon's handsome face seemed to go flat. He muted the television and dropped the remote on the bed, then shoved his hands deep into the pockets of his jeans and looked away. The body language of the guilty. I knew it! He was the one! Bastard!

"Mike and Tek told me you were sniffing around for drugs," he said, running his hand over his **unkempt** hair. "I was kinda hoping they'd gotten it wrong. Those two have been known to just make stuff up sometimes, you know?"

My patience was beginning to **dwindle**. The tape that held my recording device in place itched as if it was in sympathy with my feelings. We both wanted him to say something and say it fast.

---

eclipsed: overshadowed or overwhelmed
chicanery: trickery or deception

rendezvous: meeting or date
cunning: slyness or sneakiness

unkempt: messy or scruffy
dwindle: decrease or diminish

"Do you or don't you?" I demanded. "It's not that **convoluted** a question."

"Sure, I know where you can get it. Everyone in this school knows where you can get it," Jon said. "But you shouldn't get involved with that stuff, Kim. It's pointless."

My mouth dropped open. Was he **admonishing** me? Was he, the drug dealer himself, telling me I was a bad girl?

"Right, like *you're* not into that stuff!" I said, pacing around his room.

Jon sat down on his bed and sighed. "No. I'm not."

"You've never done drugs," I said, standing right in front of him. "Give me a break, Jon. You're a musician!" I said, throwing my arm toward the drum set that stood in the corner of his single room. "You wear nothing but black and leather, you snowboard, you drive a jeep. You **exemplify** all the qualities of a user, and you're telling me you've never done drugs."

Of course, he hadn't told me that, but I had gotten to the point that I was acting completely **neurotic**.

"No, I'm not telling you I've never done drugs," Jon said. "I'm telling you I don't do them now."

Something in his tone caused a response in my chest. It sounded too familiar. Like regret, anger, and sadness all mixed into one. Like I felt whenever I thought about Corinne.

And I believed him. In that moment, I knew for sure that Jon had nothing to do with the drug problem at Hereford. Something in his past had caused him to swear off the stuff, and I knew from experience that it was the kind of vow that was impossible to break.

But if it wasn't Jon and it wasn't Marshall and it wasn't David, then who the hell was it? There was no one left on the potential drug-dealer **roster**.

At that moment, I saw a flash of red out the window. The

---

convoluted: complicated or difficult

admonishing: scolding or yelling at

exemplify: embody or epitomize

neurotic: irrational or obsessed

roster: list

luminous floodlights that were always on in the quad at night bathed the area in bright light. I stepped toward the window and saw a familiar form making its way as quickly as possible through the foot of snow that covered the ground.

David Rand.

He crossed the square and disappeared around the side of the girls' dorm, headed toward the outer buildings.

What the hell was David doing out in the middle of the night, running through twelve inches of snow? It was more than a little suspect and couldn't be dismissed as an **inconsequential** development. Something was afoot.

"I have to go," I said, heading for the door.

"Where?" Jon was up like a shot and stood in front of the door, **frustrating** my exit. "You're not going to track down your E, are you?"

"No. Not exactly," I said. "But Jon, you have to let me go."

My heart was starting to panic. If I lost David, I'd never know what he was doing out there. And something inside me told me I had to know.

"Not until you tell me where you're going," he said, firming up his stance and crossing his arms over his chest.

Okay, he couldn't keep me **hostage** here. He was just a scrawny—if sexy—**hermit**, and I was a state-champion fighter. I could totally take him, but what was the point? All it would do was waste precious time.

"Look, I can't explain everything, but I have to get to the outer buildings, and I have to do it now," I said, hoping he'd hear and **comprehend** the **urgency** in my voice just as I'd heard his assertions about his drug use. He looked into my eyes and seemed to realize that I wasn't messing around.

"Well, you're not going alone," he said, reaching by me to grab a couple of jackets off a hook by the wall. He took the leather coat

---

luminous: bright or brilliant	frustrating: blocking or	hermit: loner
inconsequential:	preventing	comprehend: understand
unimportant or insignificant	hostage: prisoner	urgency: insistence or need

and handed me the ski jacket.

"Fine," I said impatiently, shoving my arms into the coat and noticing, even in my anxiety, how it smelled like him—like Ivory soap and sunscreen and sweat. I knew my mother definitely wouldn't approve of bringing along a guy who was a **civilian** *and* a suspect, but I was touched by his **chivalry** and didn't mind having a little company on this particular mission. After everything that had gone wrong that night, I felt out of control and totally clueless. It couldn't hurt to have someone at my side, and I was not ready to call in my mother and her squad just yet.

Not until I **rectified** the situation and figured out where on earth I had gone wrong. I wouldn't have minded having a **culpable** suspect in custody either.

---

civilian: ordinary citizen (as opposed to a soldier or policeman)

chivalry: gentlemanly behavior

rectified: fixed or set right

culpable: guilty

Chapter Thirteen

"Why are we following David Rand?" Jon whispered in the darkness as we trudged across the **barren** soccer field in David's footsteps.

"I can't tell you that right now," I replied.

"But you'll tell me eventually," Jon said.

"Uh . . . yeah."

"That's all I wanted to know."

All *I* wanted to know was where the heck David was headed. I felt like we'd been chasing after him for miles. If we walked much farther, I was sure we were going to hit the fence that **circumscribed** the campus. My breath came in short bursts, and I appreciated Jon's reassuring presence. Not to mention his **scanty** use of words. He was the perfect stakeout partner. Except that he didn't know this was a stakeout.

Suddenly, the **indistinct** outline of a building loomed in the distance. The appearance was so unexpected that I slowed my steps. What had the Hereford people built way out here?

"He's going into the old stables," Jon said, his mouth deliciously close to my ear.

"The old stables? Does anyone ever come out here?" I asked, picking up the pace again.

"Not that I know of," Jon replied. "I used to when I first got here. To be alone."

When David opened the large door at the front of the building, a shaft of dim light appeared, then died as the door closed. I made to follow, but Jon stopped me with a hand on my arm.

"You don't want him to see you?" he whispered.

I shook my head.

---

barren: bare or empty

circumscribed: surrounded or enclosed

scanty: sparse or limited

indistinct: faint or vague

"Follow me," Jon said.

He led me around the back of the **dilapidated** building to an old, rickety ladder that leaned against the **edifice**. In the darkness, it seemed to climb into nothing.

"I am *not* going up there," I hissed. The rungs were covered in snow, and the thing didn't look all that sturdy.

"Trust me?" Jon asked.

For some reason the question made my heart warm. "Yeah," I said honestly.

"Then let's go. I'll be right behind you."

I took a deep breath, held it, and started to climb. My mother would have killed me if she saw how **reckless** I was being. But I was way too caught up in the cloak-and-dagger of it all to back out now. Had David merely constructed the gambling story to **dissuade** me from pursuing him as a suspect? If so, I had fallen for it—hard. I had to know.

The ladder was surprisingly strong and steady and ended at a large, square **aperture** in the wall that provided access to an upper loft. It looked as if a door had been ripped free from its hinges, and the edges of it were **rife** with splinters. I hesitated for a split second and then heard the sound of voices coming from inside. David wasn't alone.

"I'm going in," I said, and crawled through the opening.

The building was so old and out of use that I was afraid the floor might have **eroded** by now, but the boards beneath my feet were solid. A few feet ahead, the loft opened up onto the rest of the stable, which would give me an **aerial** view of whatever was happening below. I could practically taste my own curiosity on my tongue. Hay was scattered here and there, and I could tell that if I walked too heavily my steps would be heard for miles. It was essential that I not call attention to myself. I dropped to the ground and shimmied toward the light that was **emanating** from below.

---

dilapidated: run-down
edifice: building or structure
reckless: careless or irresponsible

dissuade: deter or divert
aperture: hole or opening
rife: abounding or plentiful
eroded: worn away

aerial: from above
emanating: radiating or issuing

In a few agonizingly long seconds, I was able to peek over the edge of the loft. There was David, standing in the middle of the stable, which was illuminated by the light from a single bulb overhead. He was talking to someone, but whoever it was must've been standing just under me, out of view. From my angle, I couldn't **ascertain** who it was.

". . . I'm telling you, you have to get out of here," David was saying, clearly distressed. "She's an undercover cop. Her name isn't even Kim Sharpe."

Jon looked at me with this **confounded** expression. Like, you're a *what?*

I just looked at him and shrugged in a helpless, apologetic way. What was I going to do, explain right then and there? Meanwhile I was **berating** myself for being so careless. I should've had David taken right out of school the second he figured out who I was. But how was I supposed to know that he was all buddy-buddy with the drug dealer? I'd thought running a gambling ring was his only crime.

"And if what I heard on the scanner is right, they've got a whole army of cops coming to take you away," David continued.

But who was he talking to?

Speak up, already!

"That can't be right. Kim? But she's so . . . **cloying**."

At the sound of that voice, I felt as if I had been punched directly in the stomach. All the wind was knocked right out of me as a million thoughts crowded my brain.

Danielle? How could it be *Danielle?* She was so **benign**, so **artless**. I had thought she was all innocent and sweet and so like Corinne—I had even been spurred into action by the thought of protecting her. How could I be so *gullible?*

But the answer was obvious. No one would have ever **ascribed** the crime to a **nonentity** like Danielle. She was **anathema** at this

---

ascertain: determine or figure out
confounded: confused
berating: criticizing

cloying: overly sweet or sentimental
benign: kind or harmless
artless: simple or naïve

ascribed: pinned on or blamed
nonentity: nobody
anathema: something that is hated

school. How could she be the **notorious** drug dealer when no one even wanted to talk to her? I realized at that moment that her entire personality was **contrived**. I didn't even really know who she was.

And did she really think I was *cloying*? That seemed totally unfair.

"Look, I should've told you earlier in the week," David said. "She came to me about the gambling thing, but she told me she wouldn't report me if I didn't blow her cover, so I guess I was scared. And, you know, I wasn't totally sure it was you until . . . until now."

I slipped back out of sight and lifted my wrist to my mouth. It was risky, but we were in the middle of nowhere. If I didn't alert my mother as to our location ASAP, there was a chance that Danielle would **evade** capture.

God! I still couldn't believe she was the bad guy!

"What's going on?" Jon mouthed to me as we moved soundlessly back to the center of the loft.

I lifted one finger to tell him to wait. David was babbling, so all I could do was hope that his voice would mask the sound of my own.

"Attention, Chief Stratford, we're in the old stable past the soccer field to the west of the school. Suspect is here now. All units **converge**."

Jon's face was a mixture of suspicion and **approbation**. It was kinda cool.

"I'll give the orders, Kim. Thanks," my mother's voice said in my ear. Followed by, "All units converge."

I smiled. She hadn't **retracted** my order. Ha!

Then I noticed David had fallen silent. Big fat oops.

"Did you hear something?" Danielle's voice asked.

"We'll be there in five," my mother's voice said in my ear.

And then, all hell broke loose.

I heard a floorboard creak, and half a second later, I noticed something move out of the corner of my eye. I was about to shout a

---

notorious: infamous	**evade:** escape or avoid	**retracted:** taken back
contrived: artificial or made up	**converge:** come together	
	approbation: admiration	

warning when Jon and I both were grabbed from behind and pulled away from each other. Jon's legs flailed out, kicking at the floor, but there was nothing I could do to help him. My own arms were pinned to my sides.

After a **fleeting** moment of panic, I realized that my **assailant** had no idea what he was doing. His arms were locked around my upper body, but he'd left my hands free.

Yet another advantage of being a chick fighter. Those who don't know you don't think you're a threat.

Jon and I were being dragged toward a set of stairs near the far wall. I had no idea what they planned to do with us, but I wasn't going to let them do it. I planted my feet on the ground, leaned forward with all my might, and knocked my attacker off balance. The second he faltered, I bent at the waist and flipped him over my back to the hard floor. Dust rained down from the ceiling, and the **scoundrel** groaned in pain.

He had shaggy hair and a bulky frame and looked vaguely familiar, like I'd seen him in a movie or something, but I couldn't place him.

"What's going on up there?" Danielle's voice called out.

"We'll be right down," the other guy answered from across the loft.

Then I heard a punch crack across a jaw. I turned around to find that Jon had broken free and was wailing on his man. He actually was a pretty **adept** fighter. For a moment, I forgot where I was and simply watched Jon go, impressed. Then my guy got up, grabbed my arm, and twisted it behind my back.

Hello? You're in the middle of a fight!

"Nice try, babe," the guy growled in my ear. "Now why don't you play nice and—"

"Give me a break," I said. I used my free hand and whacked him hard in the nose, then when he was doubled over in pain, I whirled

---

fleeting: brief or passing   **scoundrel:** villain or lowlife   **adept:** skilled
assailant: attacker

easily away from him. This guy had no idea who he was dealing with. He thought a little arm twist could **constrain** me? Ha!

But now I'd pissed him off. He rushed me in an attempt to tackle me to the ground, but I lifted my knee at just the right moment and brought it up into his solar plexus. The guy went sprawling to the floor. He wasn't turning out to be a very **formidable adversary**. I walked over and picked him up by the scruff of the neck.

"Had enough?" I asked, allowing myself a moment of triumph.

"Hardly."

He jabbed backward with his elbow and hit me directly in the gut. I doubled over for a second, surprised, and then he was on his feet again. This time he fought me like a man, but his punches were **imprecise**, and he was no match for my speed. I ducked, weaved, and dodged, and only a couple of his jabs hit home. As we **sparred** our way across the loft, he started to grow winded. He was ungainly, and his fighting was sort of **pedestrian**. In a way, I actually was kind of bored.

As I wore the guy down, I kept wondering what was going on with Jon, whether he was okay, but I couldn't take my eyes off my own opponent. Letting my guard down, even with an **untutored** fighter, could be deadly.

The guy backed me up to the wall and came at me with a powerful punch. I ducked, and his hand went *through* the stable wall. He yelled out in pain, and I could tell it was **excruciating**. All the better for me. I planted my feet firmly on the floor and yanked him free, using my momentum to whirl him halfway across the loft. The guy grasped his bleeding hand, **gaping** at it in wonder. I rushed at him and hit him with an uppercut, ready to finish him off. He stumbled toward the edge of the loft.

Suddenly my heart seized up. He was going to go over! And as much as I wanted to kick his butt, I didn't *really* want to finish him off. I wasn't ready to *kill* somebody.

---

constrain: restrain or hold back	**imprecise:** sloppy	**excruciating:** extremely painful
formidable: fearsome or imposing	**sparred:** fought or dueled	**gaping:** staring open-mouthed
adversary: opponent or enemy	**pedestrian:** ordinary or dull	
	untutored: untrained or inexperienced	

His eyes widened in fear, and I made to grab for him but somehow forgot that a little person like me couldn't stop a big guy like that who was already falling. No matter how strong I was.

We went over the edge, into the **void**—together.

It was over so quickly, I barely had time to register the fact that I was falling. We slammed into the ground, me falling on a few inches of hay, him landing with a thud on the hardwood floor. My landing hurt, but I rolled over as quickly as possible to protect myself from another onslaught.

That little bit of hay turned out to be my **salvation**. The thug, who hadn't been so lucky, was out cold.

"Tag!" Danielle shouted, running over to us. She dropped to her knees next to the **prostrate** body, and suddenly it hit me. I knew where I'd seen this guy before. He was Danielle's boyfriend—the one in the picture on her dresser. They were wrapped up in this drug business together.

I struggled to my feet as Danielle fussed over her boyfriend, who, I was relieved to see, was still breathing. David apparently had fled, because we were the only ones in the room—that is, until the other thug finally succeeded in dragging Jon down the stairs. I looked up to make sure he was okay and instantly my blood ran cold. Jon's hands were **fettered** behind his back with a strip of cloth, and his slimy-looking attacker held a gun to his head.

A trickle of blood ran from Jon's nose, and he stared at me with an unreadable expression in his eyes. Was he angry, scared, begging for help? It was impossible to tell.

"We spotted these two sneaking in upstairs when we were on our way in with the goods," the man said to Danielle, who finally rose to her feet. She turned to look at me, her face pinched, her eyes shiny with tears.

"How could you do this to me?" she demanded. "I thought we were friends!"

---

void: empty space or nothingness

salvation: something that protects or saves

prostrate: horizontal

fettered: tied or bound

My mouth dropped open. She was totally delusional. "How could *I* do this to *you*? Danielle! You're a drug dealer!"

She snorted a laugh. "**Alleged**."

God! Couldn't she even show a **modicum** of regret?

"Kim! We have the place surrounded!" my mother's voice shouted through a bullhorn. They were the most **exquisite** words I'd ever heard. I couldn't help smiling when I saw Danielle's face fall.

"What're you going to do now?" I asked.

Danielle glanced at Tag, who was still **recumbent** on the floor, then looked at the other man. They exchanged some kind of message with their eyes. Then the man threw Jon at me with such force that we tumbled to the ground in a tangled mess of arms and legs. Jon couldn't stop himself, what with his arms tied **inextricably**, and he fell right on top of me. I shoved him away rather **callously** so I could see what was happening. The thug was gone, and Danielle was just disappearing through a back door.

"Stay here," I said to Jon.

And then, without so much as a backward glance, I took off after Danielle.

The first thing I noticed was that my mother did not, in fact, have the place surrounded quite yet. There was no one out back, and Danielle was running along a plowed pathway that seemed to lead back toward the school.

I could feel the adrenaline pumping through my veins as I turned on the speed. I heard shouts back at the barn, and then a gun went off, but I couldn't go back. I had to catch Danielle, the dealer, the person who was peddling drugs to a school full of kids. I just prayed that no one at the barn had been hurt.

My arms and legs pumped as I **accelerated** and started to gain on her. The 400 meters had been my event in high school, and almost no one could catch me on the track. I closed the distance between us and heard her labored breathing. Three feet, two feet, one . . .

---

alleged: supposed but unproven	**exquisite:** beautiful or wonderful	**inextricably:** impossible to untie
modicum: small amount	**recumbent:** lying down	**callously:** heartlessly
		accelerated: sped up

I launched myself into the air and tackled her into a snowbank. "Kim!"

My mother's voice was far off, but not too far. Danielle rolled over, and I pinned her forearms down with my knees. She looked up at me, her eyes defiant as my mother caught up to us. I expected her to confess or beg for forgiveness or cry or something, but she didn't. She just glared at me for a moment, then turned her head away. Somewhere deep, deep inside I was impressed by her **fortitude**. She was caught and she knew it, but she wasn't going to **cower** or cave. She was an entirely different person from the one I had thought I knew.

"I guess you win," she said.

"Damn straight I do."

"Kim! Are you all right?" my mother asked, falling to her knees beside us.

"I'm fine," I replied, standing up so my mother could drag Danielle to her feet and cuff her. "Did you get the other guy?"

"I took him down no problem," my mother said.

Danielle didn't struggle as my mother pulled her arms back and held them with one hand while she fished a pair of handcuffs from her pocket with the other. It all seemed so surreal, standing in the middle of the snow-covered **rural** setting, watching a girl I'd thought was perfectly **amiable** and cool being cuffed.

"What about the gunshot?" I asked, suddenly recalling.

"Eh. He hit the barn," my mother said with a laugh as she secured the cuffs on Danielle's wrists. "A seriously bad shot."

Then she looked at me, and even in the dark I could tell her eyes were beaming with pride. "Good job, Kim," she said. "Really good job."

I grinned and then my mother hauled Danielle off, reading her her rights as they stumbled back toward the stable.

All at once, I felt completely exhausted. Like I could lie down right there and **hibernate** in the snow for the rest of the winter.

---

fortitude: strength or guts   **rural:** countryside   **hibernate:** sleep through
cower: tremble   **amiable:** likable or friendly   the winter

Everything that had happened in the past half-hour pressed down upon me. Danielle's **inimical** posturing, the fight, the fall, the run, the gunplay, the fear and guilt and confusion. As I trudged back to the stable, I felt like I'd pass out with each step. I couldn't wait to get home and back to my own bed.

The double door to the front of the building now yawned open and was already strung with yellow police tape. Dozens of cops bustled around, marking evidence and making notes. I saw Tad duck under the tape to take a look inside. A few shadowy figures were making their way back toward the school—Danielle, Tag, and the slimy guy, each flanked by two officers. I leaned into the stable wall and sighed. How was I ever going to make it all the way back?

And then Jon appeared. He crouched under the crime-scene tape and exited the front door of the stable, looking around. The blood had been cleaned from his face, and he actually looked relaxed. Freed. Happy that it was all over.

But how would he feel about me? The girl who had dragged him into this whole mess and **imperiled** his life?

His eyes finally fell on me, and there was a long tense moment. And then he smiled.

Sweet *relief*!

As he walked over to me, my heart was slamming around in my chest. What would he say? What would *I* say? He didn't even know my real name. Technically, I was as much of a mystery to him as Danielle was to me.

"So," Jon said, his hands stuffed into the pockets of his leather jacket.

"So," I replied.

"Who *are* you?" he asked, leaning against the wall, just inches from me.

I let out an awkward laugh. "I'm Kim Stratford . . . sprinter, karate champ, snowboarder . . . freshman at Stanford University—"

---

inimical: hostile   imperiled: put in danger

Here he made an impressed little frown.

"—and police deputy," I finished.

Jon nodded slowly as if taking this all in. "You thought I was a drug dealer, didn't you?" he asked.

I felt as if someone had doused me in cold water. Oh, God. He was never going to speak to me again.

"You were a suspect . . . yeah," I said. "But I swear I never really thought it was you."

Jon narrowed his eyes. "Even though—what did you say to me before in my room—I fit the **archetypal** profile of a user?"

"That was just the frustration talking," I said desperately. "Don't be mad. I didn't **formulate** the list of suspects, I just investigated them."

"Well, you weren't wrong. I *was* a user," Jon said. "I've been clean for two years and five months."

I swallowed hard. "What made you quit?"

Jon cleared his throat and looked away, off toward the dim lights of the school. "Car accident," he said. "One of my friends was paralyzed from the waist down. I wasn't driving, but the guy who was was high."

"My best friend died last year," I told him, the words tumbling unbidden from my mouth. "We had our prom on a yacht, and she did cocaine with this popular kid she had a crush on. She got all strung out and jumped off the boat and drowned."

Jon looked me in the eye, sending a shiver through me. "I'm sorry."

"I wasn't there to help her. I told her I didn't want to hang out with those people, so she went off alone . . ."

"You couldn't have done anything. People make their own choices," Jon said.

"I know," I said. And I did. Somewhere. My mother, my grief counselors, my teachers, and my friends all had told me this. But I

---

archetypal: typical or classic   **formulate:** put together still felt guilty. I couldn't help it. I probably always would.

But at that moment, I felt kind of light. Lighter than I had since the day it happened. I hadn't told a single soul about Corinne since the day I left Connecticut for California.

"I'm sorry too," I said. "About your friend."

Jon nodded, and we stood there in silence for a moment. I had a hundred emotions whirling through my chest: sorrow over Corinne, the relief of being able to talk about her out loud, the confusion and betrayal over Danielle, and the hope that Jon wouldn't hate me for all **eternity**.

I hazarded a glance at him, and he was watching me closely.

"What?" I said.

"I *knew* you were following me!" he exclaimed, standing up straight and pulling his hands out of his pockets.

I laughed, the **atmosphere** lightened. "I had to! It was my job!"

Then, out of nowhere, he reached out, grabbed the belt loops on my jeans with two fingers, and pulled me to him. My hands pressed into his chest, and my heart stopped beating. Jon smiled down at me.

"I didn't really mind," he said.

And then, he kissed me like I've never been kissed before. His lips were so soft, but his kiss was firm and confident. It was sweet. It was **sensual**. Everyone who had bothered to touch their lips to mine before that moment was instantly forgotten.

This was the real deal.

---

eternity: endless time   **atmosphere:** mood   **sensual:** pleasurable or luxurious

The following afternoon, I went to visit Danielle in her cell at my mother's police station. I had this **prepossessing** need to get her to explain to me what had happened—what had made her do what she'd done. I was nervous to speak to her, not knowing which Danielle was going to greet me—the sweet, funny one I'd first met, the **vindictive** one who had frozen me out for making new friends, or the somewhat scary, intense one who had been arrested the night before.

There were two cells on either side of the small building so that they could separate suspects if they needed to. Tag and the slimy guy, whose name turned out to be Monroe, were in one set of cells; Danielle was alone in the other. My mother opened the outer door for me, and Danielle sat up from her cot. I half expected her to be **stoic** and turn her back on us, but instead she got up and walked over to the bars as if she were psyched to see me.

"I'll be back in ten minutes," my mother said before closing the door.

"Hey," Danielle said tentatively.

"Hey," I replied. Suddenly, even though I had wanted to come here, I had no idea what to say.

"You're not here to **upbraid** me, are you? Because I don't think I can deal with that right now," Danielle said. Her fingers curled around the bars, and it seemed to hit me for the first time. Danielle was in *jail*. And I had put her there. It was so bizarre.

"No," I replied. I pulled a chair out from the wall and sat down across from her. Danielle turned and sat down on the edge of her cot, facing me. "I guess I'm just wondering why."

---

prepossessing: preoccupying or absorbing

vindictive: hurtful or vengeful

stoic: emotionless

upbraid: scold

Danielle sighed and looked at the concrete floor. "I didn't want to do it. Not at first anyway."

"So . . . what, the devil made you do it?" I asked.

"If you're gonna be all sarcastic . . . ," Danielle said.

"You're right. Sorry." I raised my hands in surrender.

"Look, I didn't get sent to Hereford so that I could get into an Ivy," Danielle said, getting up and starting to pace. "I was sent there because Tag and I were caught dealing drugs."

I raised my eyebrows and leaned forward in my seat. "Wait a minute. If you got caught dealing, then why aren't you already in jail?" We both looked at the bars as if seeing them for the first time. "I mean, why *weren't* you in jail, I guess."

"Good lawyers," Danielle said. "They **refuted** every bit of evidence, and we got off. It was totally **expunged** from our records. My parents told me I could never see Tag again, and I was **relegated** to Hereford."

"So then you just set up a new HQ."

"Like I said, not at first," Danielle told me. "I told Tag I wanted out, and he said he did too. For a while everything was fine. We were writing emails, he was talking about this new job his dad got him working at a computer company. I was getting on with my life." She paused, took a deep breath, and let it out slowly. "And then he started asking about the situation at Hereford—was anyone using, did I know of any dealers? At first, it honestly seemed like he was looking out for me."

"But he wasn't," I supplied.

A pained look crossed Danielle's face. "I don't know if I really want to talk about this any more," she said.

But I had a feeling she did. She wanted to confess it all and get it out of her system, or she wouldn't have started babbling in the first place. She needed to spill.

"Why did you get back into it?" I asked.

---

refuted: disproved   **expunged:** wiped out   **relegated:** transferred or handed over

"Cheryl and her idiot friends," Danielle snapped. "God, some-times I think that if they hadn't been such bitches, this would never have happened."

Interesting argument. I didn't think it was going to **exculpate** her in a court of law, but it was intriguing.

"I was totally ostracized. I had no one to talk to. And because they were constantly **browbeating** me, I *needed* someone to talk to," Danielle said, growing fervent. "Tag was the only person who ever stood by me."

"Right, and got you to be the front man for his drug **venture**," I said. "Danielle, he totally **manipulated** you."

Danielle's eyes flashed. "You don't know what it's like," she said. "Cheryl and those girls are so evil to me, and Tag and I . . . we have something that goes beyond stupid high school relationships. We need each other."

Oh, God. I was going to hurl. Did she have any idea how pathetic and programmed she sounded?

"Besides, Tag is **incorrigible**," Danielle said. "The first time he came to visit me at Hereford, I swear there were dollar signs in his eyes."

"Sounds like a real catch," I said under my breath.

Danielle chose to ignore this comment.

"So anyway, the short version is, I wrote a **cryptic** email and sent it out to the entire student body. The people who are looking for drugs know how to decipher these things, and the orders started pouring in."

"To where?" I asked.

"Oh. I said to contact Dee Dee Darko at box 313."

"Huh?"

"Oh yeah. You know Mr. Smoot at the post office? He's in on it," Danielle said **offhandedly**. "I think they're bringing him in right now."

---

exculpate: free from blame
browbeating: bullying
venture: business or operation

manipulated: used or controlled
incorrigible: incurable or a lost cause

cryptic: vague or unclear
offhandedly: casually

"Mr. *Smoot?*" Suddenly, I recalled how happy he had been to see Danielle that day she dropped off the gift for her sister. He'd asked her if she had anything else for him, and she'd said, "Not today." I hadn't thought anything of it. Why would I?

"Yeah, that guy hadn't gotten a raise from Hereford in about fifteen years," Danielle told me. "We gave him two hundred dollars a week, and he **procured** an extra post office box for me. I'd get the orders there, then Tag would bring a shipment to the old stable once every two weeks. I'd give the boxes to Smoot, and he'd distribute them. They were always small enough to fit in the mailboxes so that Jon never touched them."

By this point, my mouth was hanging open with shock and shame. I had *seen* Danielle take a bunch of envelopes out of her mailbox and slip them into her bag. It had seemed like a lot of letters, but I hadn't thought anything of it. She'd done it right in front of me!

Okay, Kim, chill. She wasn't a suspect then. She was never *a suspect until you snagged her.*

Still, it was hard not to feel totally **inadequate**. She hadn't even been **covert** about it!

"It was a pretty good scam, all in all," Danielle said finally, sounding proud.

I had to agree. It was simple, but perfect. As long as Smoot stayed in their pocket, she and Tag were home free. Until I came along, of course.

"Okay, but Dee Dee Darko?" I asked.

"Tag's a big *Donnie Darko* fan," Danielle said, almost **wistfully**. Ugh! She really *did* love that guy. One day, she was going to wake up and realize she'd let him ruin her life, and I felt sorry for her in advance.

"So anyway, that's the story," Danielle said, sitting down again. "David didn't know I was dealing at Hereford until last night. He

---

procured: got hold of   **inadequate:** ineffective or incompetent   **covert:** secret   **wistfully:** sadly or regretfully

heard on the scanner that your mom was coming up to school on a drug bust, and he figured it might be me. I'd told him about me and Tag in a moment of weakness a few weeks after I first got here, so he knew about my past, but not about my present."

"He knew you'd been a dealer and he chose to be friends with you anyway?" I blurted.

"What can I say? The kid believes in **rehabilitation**," she said with a shrug. "Or he did until now, anyway. Besides, he wasn't exactly surrounded by friends either. We fit."

My heart went out to David. He'd spent half the night being interrogated by Quincy, which was at least the lesser of two evils. (It could've been Tad.) According to my mom, he'd been **unburdened** of all blame in the drug scam, but he still must have felt so **wretched** and disappointed. His one friend was sitting in a jail cell right now after he had believed in her.

But then, of course, he always had his gambling ring. It was tough to feel sorry for a guy who was freeing a bunch of people of their **extraneous** cash.

"So . . . are your parents coming to bail you out?" I asked.

Danielle let out a wry laugh. "Yeah. That'll be some **zany** fun." She glanced at the clock behind me, then sighed and rubbed her forehead. "They should be here soon. This day has been **interminable**."

"I can imagine," I said. In my heart, I wanted to feel bad for her too, but why should I? She may have thought Tag was the only person who cared about her, but she had still had a choice. She could have chosen not to deal. She could have chosen to be **strong** and **resilient** and stand up to Cheryl. I know it wouldn't have been easy, but it would have been infinitely wiser than what she'd done. And she would have had a future, whereas she now had a nice, long **incarceration** to look forward to.

She'd had a choice. Just like Corinne could've chosen not to take

rehabilitation: recovery or change for the better	**extraneous:** extra or unnecessary	**interminable:** endless
unburdened: relieved	**zany:** crazy or wacky	**resilient:** strong or tough
wretched: miserable		**incarceration:** imprisonment

that cocaine that had totally strung her out and made her climb up on the boat railing at our prom. Everyone had a choice.

"I probably should go," I said, feeling exhausted and sick to my stomach. There was too much to think about, and none of it was good.

"Thanks for coming by," Danielle said as I stood to go. She sounded so vulnerable and grateful. I turned and did my best to smile for her.

"Good luck," I said.

And then I walked out, salivating for the comfort of my own bed and a nice, long, **insentient** sleep.

*　*　*　*　*

A few days later, the whole Hereford experience seemed like a bad dream. Danielle, Tag, Monroe, and Smoot all had been bailed out and were awaiting trial. I was flying back to Stanford in less than a week and would be able to put the whole thing behind me. Until that summer when I was going to have to sit through hours of depositions with lawyers for all four of the defendants.

Yee-hah.

That Wednesday night, however, I chose not to think about the future but instead to **revel** in the moment. My mother had put together a little party for me as a kind of congratulations and a thank-you for catching the **wily** Hereford drug lord. The entire Morrison force, along with the mayor of Morrison and a few other people I didn't recognize, were **convoked** to the station in semi-formal **attire** to down sparkling cider and eat hors d'oeuvres in my honor. I was beaming the whole night, feeling as if all my hard work was **validated**.

Even if I *had* chased the wrong people for two weeks and then basically stumbled upon the arrest after fortuitously spotting David

---

insentient: out cold
revel: enjoy
wily: clever or sly

convoked: summoned or called together
attire: clothing or dress

validated: confirmed or approved of

out in the quad. I was sure that was how it happened all the time!

I was standing near the back wall, gabbing with Quincy and some of my mother's **colleagues**, when Mom stood up near the front desk and called everyone to attention. I felt my face flush hot. This was going to be embarrassing.

"Thank you, everyone, for coming tonight to recognize the success of my daughter, Kim Stratford, on her first investigation!"

At this, everyone applauded and turned around to smile at me. I raised my hand and grinned at the acclaim, feeling like an **imbecile**. But a happy one.

"You know I'm not the **verbose** type, but I'm very proud of my daughter, and I just wanted to tell all of you that," my mother continued. I felt tears spring to my eyes. It was one of the more perfect moments of my life.

"Kim, I have a little something for you if you want to come up here," she said, waving me over.

There was more applause as I pushed myself away from the wall, surprised, and wove my way through the maze of people. I had no idea what was going on. Had she gotten me some kind of cheesy plastic medal or something?

I stepped up next to her, and the cheering waned. All eyes were on me as I stood there awkwardly, waiting and wondering what was going to happen next.

"Kim, in honor of the great success of your first ever case as a deputy detective—an investigation that led to four arrests," she said, pausing for everyone to take this in, "I'd like to present you with this **commendation**, signed not only by myself and the mayor, but also by the governor himself."

Tad reached forward and handed my mother a framed certificate. My hands were shaking as she handed it to me, but somehow I maintained my **equanimity**. I read the commendation to myself as I grasped the frame with sweaty palms.

---

colleagues: coworkers or partners

imbecile: fool or idiot
verbose: long-winded

commendation: praise or honor
equanimity: calm or composure

This commendation is presented to Ms. Kimberly Ann Stratford in recognition of excellence in the line of duty.

My heart **distended** in my chest over the **accolade**. Wow. I was, like, a real police officer!

A reporter from the local newspaper snapped a few pictures of me and my mom, and of me shaking hands with the mayor. As the flash popped, blinding me, I could have sworn I saw a familiar figure hovering near the door. I blinked rapidly after the photographer was done, and, finally, the person came into focus. It was Jon.

I was about to run over to him and show him the certificate, but my mother grabbed my arm.

"Kim, they want you to say a few words," she told me.

I glanced from the spectators to Jon, longing just to run over to him, grab him, and get the heck out of there, but I couldn't turn down my moment in the spotlight. I stood up there in front of everyone, smiled, and said, "Thanks, everyone! Good night!"

Then I ran.

The crowd behind me laughed, and Jon was shaking his head in amusement when I reached him. He was wearing a shirt and tie under his leather jacket.

"Hey! See what I got?!" I said, holding up the frame.

"I'm impressed," he said. "Not by your award, but by your **eloquence** up there."

"I thought you of all people would appreciate a short **oration**," I said with a smile.

"If it means we can get out of here, then I definitely do."

I grabbed his hand and checked over my shoulder to make sure my mother wasn't watching. She was otherwise occupied, chatting with the mayor and his wife—two people who had originally refused to **endorse** her for chief, but who now seemed completely **enchanted** by her.

---

distended: swelled or stretched
accolade: award or tribute

eloquence: expressiveness or skill at speaking
oration: speech

endorse: give support or backing to
enchanted: charmed or delighted

Funny how quickly things changed.

"Now's our chance," I said to Jon. "Let's go."

*   *   *   *   *

The following week, Jon drove me in his Jeep to the airport. My mother had been called to Hartford to meet with the D.A. about the Hereford case, so we'd said our farewells that morning. I have to say, I was actually kind of glad she wasn't going to be there to see me off. It gave me more time to be alone with Jon.

Over the past few days, we'd been seeing a lot of each other. After classes at Hereford, he would drive to my house, and I would show him around our **prosaic** little town. He'd been going to Hereford since the seventh grade, and he'd never even been to Häagen-Dazs. I guess all of us townies had always given off a serious anti-Hereford vibe.

Jon carried my backpack all the way to the gate, where I was, as always, already late for boarding. As we approached the desk, Jon reached out and squeezed my hand, which only compounded my misery. I handed the check-in attendant my boarding pass and turned to Jon. He was wearing a green shirt that **enhanced** the color of his eyes and made him even more gorgeous. Just looking at him, I couldn't believe how hollow my heart felt. We'd only known each other for a few weeks, but I didn't want to say goodbye.

"Well, this is it," I said. "I guess I'll see you after finals."

May felt like it was **eons** away.

Jon smiled slowly. "Maybe a little sooner," he said. He reached into his pocket and pulled out a folded piece of heavy-stock paper. I took it from his outstretched hand and opened it. It was expensive letterhead with the Stanford seal.

" 'Dear Mr. Wisnewski: We are pleased to inform you that you have been accepted into the Stanford University class of'—Jon!

---

prosaic: dull or ordinary   **enhanced:** intensified or highlighted   **eons:** ages

You're going to Stanford?" I practically screeched, causing the check-in attendant to jump.

Jon tilted his head and shrugged. "Maybe. I haven't actually *seen* the campus yet, and I don't want to make a **rash** decision . . ."

"Omigod! But you'll love it! It's *so* beautiful." I gushed. I was already entertaining **fanciful** daydreams of the two of us next year, walking to class together, eating dinner in the dining hall. My little freshman boyfriend!

"Well, **hypothetically**, if I were going to . . . say . . . fly out there in February, would you know of any place I could crash?" he said, his eyes dancing.

Finally his point sunk in. I took a step closer to him, folded his letter, and stuck it back in his pocket. "I'll give you a world-class tour, by the **culmination** of which you'll never feel the need to look at another school," I said.

"Sounds kinky," Jon said, wrapping his arms around me.

I laughed, stood on my tiptoes, and planted a nice, long kiss on his lips. I'd been dreading this all day, certain that it would be our last. But now, it was perfectly **sublime**.

I knew it was going to be the first of many.

---

rash: hasty or thoughtless
fanciful: fantastic or imaginary

hypothetically: in theory or for the sake of thought

culmination: end or conclusion
sublime: magnificent

A

abased: *v* humiliated (92).

abdicated: *v* abandoned (5).

aberration: *n* irregularity or freak (45).

abhor: *v* hate (2).

abject: *adj* miserable (33).

abjuring: *v* rejecting (118).

abode: *n* dwelling or home (49).

abolish: *v* put a stop to (82).

abominable: *adj* terrible (126).

abort: *v* stop or terminate (105).

abound: *v* are plentiful (44).

abrasive: *adj* grouchy or irritating (16).

abscond: *v* run away (15).

absolution: *n* forgiveness (68).

absolve: *v* pardon (83).

abstain: *v* refrain or avoid (53).

abstemious: *adj* self-denying (82).

abstruse: *adj* puzzling (111).

absurd: *adj* strange or ridiculous (55).

abysmal: *adj* very bad (106).

accelerated: *v* sped up (156).

accentuated: *v* drew attention to (44).

accessible: *adj* reachable (106).

acclaim: *n* praise (16).

acclimated: *adj* adjusted (67).

accolade(s): *n* praise or compliments (44), award or tribute (168).

accomplice: *n* partner in crime (119).

accomplished: *adj* talented or skillful (105).

accosted: *v* confronted or attacked (92).

acerbically: *adv* bitterly or sarcastically (8).

acknowledged: *v* recognized or accepted (61).

acquiescent: *adj* passive or unresisting (12).

acrimonious: *adj* unfriendly or bitter (6).

acumen: *n* insight or shrewdness (119).

acutely: *adv* sharply or intensely (69).

adamant: *adj* stubborn (11).

adept: *adj* skilled (153).

adjacent: *adj* next to (2).

administration: *n* officials (51).

admonishing: *v* scolding or yelling at (145).

adroit: *adj* skillful (92).

adulation: *n* admiration (92).

adversary: *n* opponent or enemy (154).

adverse: *adj* negative or bad (114).

aerial: *adj* from above (150).

affable: *adj* friendly or pleasant (109).

affinity: *n* liking (22).

aggression: *n* anger or violence (92).

aggrieved: *adj* distressed (142).

aghast: *adj* shocked or stunned (114).

agility: *n* swiftness or dexterity (44).

agitated: *adj* restless or disturbed (107).

akin: *adj* similar (38).

alias: *n* false name (19).

alien: *adj* foreign or unknown (123).

allayed: *v* put to rest (20).

alleged: *adj* supposed but unproven (156).

alleviate: *v* lessen (71).

aloof: *adj* distant or cold (21).

altercation: *n* argument (8).

amassed: *v* collected or accumulated (53).

amenable: *adj* agreeable (21).

amended: *v* revised or corrected (108).

amends: *n* peace or compensation (105).

amiable: *adj* likable or friendly (157).

anathema: *n* something that is hated (151).

anguished: *adj* pained or agonized (68).

angular: *adj* lean or bony (50).

animated: *adj* excited or lively (117).

animosity: *n* hostility or ill will (34).

anticipation: *n* expectation (74).

antiquated: *adj* old-fashioned or out-of-date (79).

antiseptic: *adj* sterile or bland (22).

aperture: *n* hole or opening (150).

aplomb: *n* self-confidence or ease (15).

appalled: *adj* shocked or horrified (140).

appalling: *adj* awful or dreadful (1).

appraising: *v* judging or evaluating (141).

appreciate: *v* value (12).

apprehensive: *adj* worried or nervous (101).

approbation: *n* admiration (152).

approve: *v* agree with or support (40).

archetypal: *adj* typical or classic (159).

ardent: *adj* eager or intense (120).

arduous: *adj* difficult or tiring (55).

aroma: *n* smell (33).

arrogant: *adj* proud or conceited (31, 124).

artless: *adj* simple or naïve (151).

ascent: *n* rise (6).

ascertain: *v* determine or figure out (151).

ascribed: *v* pinned on or blamed (151).

aspect: *n* part or phase (81).

assailant: *n* attacker (153).

assailed: *v* beat or attacked (93).

assault: *n* attack (122).

asserted: *v* stated or declared (129).

assertions: *n* statements or claims (70).

assessments: *n* judgments or opinions (34).

assumed: *v* took on (87); supposed or took for granted (106).

assured: *v* promised (70).

astonishing: *adj* incredible or unbelievable (35).

astute: *adj* smart or clever (81).

atmosphere: *n* mood (160).

attentive: *adj* caring or kind (120).

attire: *n* clothing or dress (166).

attributes: *n* traits (60).

audacious: *adj* bold or daring (11).

audible: *adj* capable of being heard (45).

auspicious: *adj* positive or favorable (111).

authentic: *adj* genuine (72).

avalanche: *n* landslide (80).

awed: *adj* impressed (47).

B

baffled: *adj* puzzled (93).

balked: *v* blocked (93).

balmy: *adj* mild or pleasant (111).

banal: *adj* ordinary or predictable (61).

bane: *n* curse or great annoyance (116).

banned: *v* barred (135).

barren: *adj* bare or empty (149).

basking: *v* reveling or indulging (52).

bastion: *n* stronghold (72).

befuddled: *adj* confused (91).

belittle: *v* put down (46).

bemoaning: *v* complaining about (92).

bemused: *adj* puzzled (113).

benevolent: *adj* kind or generous (101).

benign: *adj* kind or harmless (151).

berating: *v* criticizing (151).

beseeched: *v* begged or pleaded (69).

betray: *v* give away (81).

betraying: *v* being disloyal or treacherous to (92).

bevy: *n* crowd (34).

bewildered: *adj* dazed or confused (114).

biased: *adj* unfair or prejudiced (33).

bilk: *v* trick (34).

billowed: *v* fluttered or waved (37).

bizarre: *adj* strange (7).

blanched: *v* grew pale (29).

blasphemy: *n* serious disrespect to beliefs (34).

blatantly: *adv* obviously (106).

bliss: *n* pleasure or enjoyment (5).

blithely: *adv* casually (74).

blunt: *adj* dull (122).

blustery: *adj* windy (133).

boisterous: *adj* lively or noisy (60).

bolstering: *v* giving a boost to (79).

boorish: *adj* rude (80).

braggart: *n* someone who brags or boasts (51).

brawn: *n* strength or brute force (55).

brazen: *adj* bold or shameless (116).

bridle: *v* get angry or annoyed (101).

brilliant: *adj* clever or inspired (81).

brink: *n* edge (133).

brittle: *adj* fragile or dry (91).

browbeating: *v* bullying (163).

brunt: *n* weight or burden (2).

buffeted: *v* beat or battered (46).

bulky: *adj* large or massive (70).

burgeoning: *adj* budding or growing (129).

bustled: *v* hurried (22).

C

cacophony: *n* harsh noise (49).

cadence: *n* beat or rhythm (116).

cajole: *v* coax or sweet-talk (118).

calamity: *n* disaster (94).

calculated: *adj* deliberate or plotted (32).

callously: *adv* heartlessly (156).

callow: *adj* immature (37).

camaraderie: *n* friendship or brotherhood (112).

candid: *adj* open or honest (134).

candor: *n* openness or honesty (71).

canvas: *n* background or setting (117).

capacious: *adj* large or roomy (116).

capitulate: *v* submit or give in (123).

carousing: *adj* partying (117).

catalyzed: *v* inspired or incited (70).

caustic: *adj* sharp or bitter (32).

cavalierly: *adv* casually or offhandedly (73).

cavernous: *adj* huge or vast (43).

cavorting: *v* horsing around (67).

ceremoniously: *adv* formally or properly (82).

certitude: *n* confidence or certainty (116).

chaos: *n* commotion or madness (60).

charitable: *adj* generous (91).

charlatan: *n* fraud or faker (140).

chasten: *v* scold or punish (124).

chastise: *v* yell at (115).

chicanery: *n* trickery or deception (144).

chivalry: *n* gentlemanly behavior (147).

circumscribed: *v* surrounded or enclosed (149).

circumspect: *adj* cautious or guarded (94).

circumvented: *v* dodged or sidestepped (137).

civilian: *n* ordinary citizen (as opposed to a soldier or policeman) (147).

clairvoyant: *adj* psychic or mind-reading (37).

clamoring: *v* shouting or crying out (94).

clandestine: *adj* secret (95).

clarified: *v* explained or made clear (17).

clasped: *v* held or grasped (32).

clemency: *n* forgiveness (84).

cloying: *adj* overly sweet or sentimental (151).

coddle: *v* overprotect or fuss over (92).

coerced: *v* tempted or pressured (113).

colleagues: *n* coworkers or partners (167).

colluding: *v* plotting or scheming (112).

commencement: *n* start or beginning (21).

commendation: *n* praise or honor (167).

commingled: *adj* mixed or blended (61).

commit: *v* perform or do (83).

compelling: *adj* convincing or forceful (132).

compiling: *v* putting together (50).

complacently: *adv* smugly or self-assuredly (123).

complicit: *adj* associated with or involved in (112).

compliment: *n* praise or flattery (19).

compounded: *v* made worse (47).

comprehend: *v* understand (147).

compromise: *v* middle ground (135).

compunction: *n* guilt (54).

conceding: *v* admitting (48).

conceited: *adj* vain or stuck-up (102).

conciliated: *v* made peace with (135).

concoct: *v* make up (140).

concrete: *adj* rock-solid or tangible (132).

concur: *v* agree (132).

condescending: *adj* snobby or superior (102).

confidant: *n* someone to talk to (91).

confounded: *v* confused (151).

confront: *v* challenge or face (64).

congenial: *adj* friendly (35).

conspicuous: *adj* noticeable (94).

conspiratorially: *adv* sneakily or secretively (36).

constituted: *v* amounted to (134).

constrain: *v* restrain or hold back (154).

construed: *v* interpreted (94).

consumed: *v* overwhelmed (70); eaten (82).

contagion: *n* virus (90).

contemplating: *v* considering or thinking over (65).

contempt: *n* dislike (80).

contender: *n* candidate or rival (80).

contradictory: *adj* conflicting (136).

contravene: *v* disobey (8).

contrite: *adj* sorry or ashamed (115).

contrived: *adj* artificial or made up (152).

conundrum: *n* puzzle or mystery (118).

convened: *v* met or gathered (39).

converge: *v* come together (152).

convey: *v* express or get across (58).

convict: *v* find guilty (82).

convivial: *adj* warm or friendly (23).

convoked: *v* summoned or called together (166).

convoluted: *adj* complicated or difficult (145).

copious: *adj* numerous or plentiful (118).

cordial: *adj* warm or friendly (117).

correspondence: *n* mail or communication (73).

corroborated: *v* confirmed (57).

corroding: *adj* crumbling or decaying (88).

corrupt: *adj* shady or dishonest (111).

counsel: *v* advise (116).

courtesy: *n* good manners (55).

covert: *adj* secret (164).

covetous: *adj* jealous (86).

cowed: *v* scared or intimidated (60).

cower: *v* tremble (157).

coy: *adj* shy or timid (114).

crass: *adj* rude or insensitive (90).

craving: *n* hunger or desire (58).

credited: *v* given recognition (63).

cringing: *v* wincing or flinching (57).

crisis: *n* disaster or emergency (121).

crucial: *adj* essential or important (86).

crude: *adj* vulgar or offensive (13).

cryptic: *adj* vague or unclear (163).

cuisine: *n* cooking (33).

culmination: *n* end or conclusion (170).

culpable: *adj* guilty (147).

culprits: *n* criminals (91).

cunning: *adj* slyness or sneakiness (14, 144).

curb: *v* hold back (104).

currency: *n* money (74).

cursory: *adj* quick or hurried (112).

curt: *adj* abrupt or rude (27).

curtailing: *v* holding back (14).

D

dabble: *v* mess around (50).

daunted: *v* frightened or intimidated (40).

dawdle: *v* hang around or waste time (112).

daze: *n* fog or haze (87).

dearth: *n* shortage or lack (23).

debacle: *n* incident (142).

debunked: *v* exposed as untrue (31).

decade: *n* ten years (57).

deception: *n* trickery (116).

decided: *adj* definite or certain (131).

decipher: *v* figure out (88).

decorously: *adv* properly or decently (21).

dedicated: *adj* enthusiastic or devoted (100).

deduced: *v* figured out (58).

deemed: *v* judged or considered (57).

defaced: *adj* vandalized (117).

defer: *v* postpone (91).

deficient: *adj* poor or lacking (74).

deflated: *v* lessened in size (86).

deft: *adj* nimble or quick (93).

defunct: *adj* no longer functioning (132).

defy: *v* disobey or challenge (40).

deity: *n* god (94).

dejected: *adj* unhappy or depressed (119).

deleted: *v* erased (126).

deliberate: *v* think or ponder (85).

delinquent: *adj* careless or irresponsible (29).

delusional: *adj* crazy or hallucinating (102).

denigrate: *v* talk down to (45).

depicted: *v* showed (16).

deprivation: *n* lack (72).

deranged: *adj* crazy or insane (79).

derisive: *adj* scornful or mocking (6).

descent: *n* move downward (27).

deserted: *adj* empty or isolated (64).

desolate: *adj* unhappy or depressed (90).

despise: *v* hate (90).

despondent: *adj* miserable or pessimistic (106).

detain: *v* delay or hold back (31).

deteriorating: *v* decaying or falling apart (142).

deterred: *adj* discouraged (12).

detests: *v* hates (33).

devastating: *adj* damaging (91).

devious: *adj* tricky or dishonest (117).

devoid: *adj* empty (67).

devotee: *n* fan or enthusiast (17).

devoured: *v* ate quickly (64).

dialogue: *n* conversation (94).

diffident: *adj* hesitant or timid (70).

dilapidated: *adj* run-down (150).

dilatory: *adj* slow (120).

diligently: *adv* thoroughly or industriously (5).

diminutive: *adj* tiny (5).

disaffected: *adj* discontented or rebellious (120).

discarded: *adj* thrown away (3).

discern: *v* make out (117).

discomfited: *adj* uncomfortable (45).

disconcerting: *adj* upsetting or disturbing (135).

disconsolate: *adj* depressed or sad (77).

discordant: *adj* conflicting or incompatible (120).

discrepancy: *n* difference (81).

disdain: *n* disrespect or ill will (27).

disgruntled: *adj* irritated or discontented (78).

disheartened: *adj* discouraged or dispirited (46).

disinclined: *adj* reluctant or hesitant (126).

dismal: *adj* dreary or miserable (109).

disparate: *adj* different or dissimilar (120).

dispassionately: *adv* without emotion (78).

dispatch: *v* send out (20).

dispensing: *v* giving out (137).

disperse: *v* scatter (94).

dispose: *v* destroy or get rid of (126).

disquieting: *adj* disturbing or unsettling (68).

disreputable: *adj* dishonest (62).

disrupted: *adj* interrupted or disturbed (17).

dissipating: *v* dissolving or fading (101).

dissuade: *v* deter or divert (150).

distended: *v* swelled or stretched (168).

distinct: *adj* clear (27).

distinction: *n* honor or worth (79).

distorted: *adj* misshapen (123).

distracted: *adj* thinking about something else (108).

distraught: *adj* upset (68).

dither: *v* hesitate or waste time (131).

divert: *v* distract (137).

divulge: *v* make known (51).

domestic: *adj* made in this country (137).

domicile: *n* dwelling or home (49).

dominated: *v* been in control (47).

domineering: *adj* dominant (14).

dour: *adj* stern or unfriendly (43).

drab: *adj* dull or dingy (49).

dramatic: *adj* staged or theatrical (46).

droll: *adj* funny or entertaining (137).

dubious: *adj* doubtful (11).

dumbfounded: *adj* astonished or speechless (16).

dunce: *n* fool or idiot (15).

duplicitous: *adj* two-faced or dishonest (36).

dwindle: *v* decrease or diminish (144).

E

ebullient: *adj* bright and cheerful (3).

eclectic: *adj* varied or quirky (2).

eclipsed: *v* overshadowed or overwhelmed (144).

ecstatic: *adj* delighted or overjoyed (28).

eddy: *n* gust or current (77).

edifice: *n* building or structure (150).

efface: *v* erase or wipe out (105).

effervescence: *n* sparkle (1).

efficacious: *adj* effective or successful (13).

effulgent: *adj* bright or beaming (3).

ejection: *n* kicking out (74).

elaborate: *adj* complex or complicated (138).

elated: *adj* excited or overjoyed (71).

elicit: *v* extract or draw out (128).

eloquence: *n* expressiveness or skill at speaking (168).

elucidated: *v* made clear (139).

eluded: *v* escaped from (40).

emanating: *v* radiating or issuing (150).

embarked: *v* began or started (138).

embellished: *v* decorated (77).

emblazoned: *v* inscribed or decorated (107).

embroiled: *v* involved (68).

emissary: *n* representative or agent (15).

emulate: *v* imitate (137).

enamored: *adj* in love with (59).

enchanted: *adj* charmed or delighted (168).

encounter: *n* meeting (57).

encrypted: *v* protected or hidden with a secret code (83).

encumbered: *v* burdened (12).

endangering: *v* putting in danger (5).

endeavored: *v* tried (39).

endorse: *v* give support or backing to (168).

endured: *v* lasted (109).

engender: *v* produce (15).

enhanced: *v* intensified or highlighted (169).

enigma: *n* mystery or puzzle (128).

enmeshed: *adj* trapped or tangled (135).

enmity: *n* hostility or ill will (22).

ennui: *n* boredom (9).

ensconce: *v* install (79).

enthralled: *adj* fascinated or gripped (79).

entice: *v* tempt (137).

enumerating: *v* listing or naming (16).

enveloped: *v* surrounded or enclosed (117).

eons: *n* ages (169).

epiphany: *n* sudden realization or awakening (3).

epitome: *n* ultimate example (78).

equanimity: *n* calm or composure (167).

era: *n* time period (77).

eradicated: *v* wiped out (137).

eroded: *v* worn away (150).

erudite: *adj* well-educated (129).

eschewing: *v* avoiding (19).

eternity: *n* endless time (160).

ethics: *n* morals or principles (51).

eulogy: *n* speech given at a funeral (1).

euphoria: *n* exhilaration or joy (3).

evade: *v* escape or avoid (152).

evinced: *v* displayed (25).

exacerbated: *v* intensified or made worse (7).

exaggeratedly: *adv* overly or excessively (127).

exalted: *adj* lofty or high-ranking (31).

exasperation: *n* frustration or annoyance (31).

excavate: *v* dig out (3).

excise: *v* cut out (60).

exclusive: *adj* private or restricted (63).

excruciating: *adj* extremely painful (154).

exculpate: *v* free from blame (163).

excursion: *n* outing or detour (114).

execrable: *adj* terrible or disgusting (1).

exemplify: *v* embody or epitomize, serve as an example of (14, 145).

exertion: *n* physical effort (47).

exigent: *adj* difficult or tricky (40).

exonerated: *v* cleared or acquitted (127).

exorbitant: *adj* excessive or outrageous (112).

expeditiously: *adv* quickly (116).

exploits: *n* deeds or activities (122).

expunged: *v* wiped out (2, 162).

exquisite: *adj* beautiful or wonderful (156).

extemporaneous: *adj* sudden or improvised (126).

extended: *v* gave or offered (131).

extension: *n* product or outgrowth (15).

extensive: *adj* large or far-reaching (77).

extinguish: *v* put out or turn off (118).

extolling: *v* praising (2).

extracting: *v* pulling out (85).

extraneous: *adj* extra or unnecessary (165).

extricate: *v* pull out or extract (104).

exultant: *adj* thrilled or overjoyed (87).

F

fabricate: *v* make up (86).

façade: *n* false appearance (35).

facet: *adj* aspect or part (70).

facetiously: *adv* jokingly (44).

facilitate: *v* make easier (51).

fallacious: *adj* incorrect (18).

faltering: *v* weakening or hesitating (69).

fanatic: *n* enthusiast or maniac (50).

fanciful: *adj* fantastic or imaginary (170).

fastidious: *adj* careful or attentive (2).

fatuous: *adj* stupid or childish (59).

feasible: *adj* possible (64).

feeble: *adj* weak (11).

feigning: *v* faking or simulating (50).

felicitous: *adj* fortunate (24).

fervent: *adj* hot-blooded (12).

fettered: *adj* tied or bound (155).

fiasco: *n* disaster or mess (119).

fickle: *adj* unpredictable or unreliable (16).

fictional: *adj* imaginary (53).

fidgeting: *v* playing with nervously (91).

finesse: *n* grace or flair (14).

flabbergasted: *adj* stunned (7).
flagrant: *adj* obvious or glaring (58).
fleeting: *adj* brief or passing (153).
flinch: *v* cringe or start (29).
flourish: *n* showy gesture (21); *v* thrive or prosper (129).
flustered: *adj* tense or uncomfortable (108).
focus: *n* concentration (60).
foiling: *v* blocking or thwarting (40).
folly: *n* foolishness (85).
forbearance: *n* patience (118).
forerunner: *n* predecessor (33).
foresee: *v* predict (90).
forestall: *v* prevent (131).
forgo: *v* give up (121).
forlorn: *adj* sad or unhappy (24).
formidable: *adj* fearsome or imposing (154).
formulate: *v* put together (159).
forsake: *v* abandon (21).
forthright: *adj* direct or upfront (102).
fortitude: *n* strength or guts (157).
fortuitous: *adj* lucky (2).
forum: *n* environment (131).
fractious: *adj* touchy or irritable (109).
fragile: *adj* delicate (78).
frail: *adj* fragile (93).
fraud: *n* fake or phony (35).
frenetically: *adv* wildly or frantically (20).
frenzied: *adj* wild or furious (93).
frenzy: *n* flurry or storm (141).
fret: *v* worry (122).
frigid: *adj* freezing (37).
frustrating: *v* blocking or preventing (146).
fundamental: *adj* important or deep (99).
furrowing: *v* creasing or wrinkling (67).
furtive: *adj* sly or sneaky (18).
futile: *adj* useless or unsuccessful (60).

G

galling: *adj* painful or maddening (124).
gamely: *adv* eagerly or cheerfully (61).
gaping: *v* staring open-mouthed (154).
garbled: *adj* muddled or inaudible (139).
garish: *adj* bright or gaudy (137).
garner: *v* gain or collect (50).
garrulous: *adj* talkative (49).
gaunt: *adj* thin or bony (44).
general: *adj* common or universal (29).
genial: *adj* friendly (16).
genially: *adv* in a friendly manner (78).
genius: *n* brilliant person or mastermind (33).
gibes: *v* taunts or jokes (134).

girth: *n* size or thickness (72).
glowered: *v* looked angrily (45).
gluttons: *n* people who overeat or eat greedily (90).
gratified: *adj* satisfied (88).
gratuitous: *adj* unnecessary or unreasonable (71).
gravity: *n* seriousness (124).
gregarious: *adj* social or talkative (54).
gross: *adj* disgusting (115).
grovel: *v* beg or plead (122).
grudgingly: *adv* unwillingly (80).
guileless: *adj* straightforward or upfront (117).
gulf: *n* gap (89).
gullible: *adj* easy to fool (87).

H

hallowed: *adj* sacred or respected (14).
hampers: *v* gets in the way of (78).
haphazardly: *adv* randomly or messily (78).
hapless: *adj* unlucky (78).
harangue: *n* lecture or criticism (14).
harass: *v* bother or pester (143).
harbored: *v* hid or guarded (89).
haughty: *adj* proud or conceited (17).
hazardous: *adj* dangerous (60).
heckled: *v* harassed or jeered at (62).
hedonist: *n* someone who seeks pleasure (74).
heinous: *adj* terrible or offensive (46).
heir: *n* successor or inheritor (74).
heralding: *v* signaling (84).
heredity: *n* inherited traits (11).
heretofore: *adv* up to this point (60).
hermit: *n* loner (146).
hibernate: *v* sleep through the winter (157).
hidebound: *adj* narrow-minded (134).
hilarious: *adj* very funny (100).
hinder: *v* get in the way of (35).
hoarding: *v* saving or stockpiling (134).
hone: *v* sharpen (18).
horizontal: *adj* parallel to the ground (45).
hors d'oeuvres: *n* appetizers (137).
hostage: *n* prisoner (146).
hostile: *adj* unfriendly or resentful (85).
humble: *adj* modest or lowly (49).
hurdle: *v* jump over (120).
hyperbole: *n* exaggeration (101).
hypocritical: *adj* two-faced or deceitful (99).
hypothetically: *adv* in theory or for the sake of thought (170).

I

idolized: *v* worshipped (107).

ignominious: *adj* humiliating (46).

illicit: *adj* illegal (119).

illuminated: *v* lit up (103).

illusion: *n* fantasy or daydream (136).

illustrating: *v* showing (124).

imbecile: *n* fool or idiot (167).

immeasurable: *adj* huge (121).

immense: *adj* enormous (139).

imminent: *adj* coming up (36).

immune: *adj* untouchable or exempt (53).

impassive: *adj* emotionless (29).

impediment: *n* obstacle or barrier (74).

impeding: *v* getting in the way of (40).

impending: *adj* coming up soon (85).

imperative: *adj* necessary (49).

imperiled: *v* put in danger (158).

imperious: *adj* bossy or commanding (11).

impertinent: *adj* impolite or disrespectful (48).

impervious: *adj* solid or watertight (2).

impetuously: *adv* suddenly or without planning (113).

implant: *v* insert or place (32).

implement: *v* tool or instrument (122).

implicate: *v* point the finger at (74).

implore: *v* plead (86).

implying: *v* suggesting (102).

import: *n* importance (79).

imposing: *v* being a burden or annoyance (107).

impound: *v* seize (142).

imprecise: *adj* sloppy (154).

improbable: *adj* unlikely (80).

improvised: *v* made up or ad-libbed (48).

impulse: *n* sudden urge or whim (72).

inadequate: *adj* ineffective or incompetent (164).

inadvertently: *adv* by accident (86).

inane: *adj* silly or stupid (100).

inarticulate: *adj* speechless or incoherent (80).

inaudibly: *adv* faintly (33).

inaugural: *adj* first (88).

incarceration: *n* imprisonment (165).

incarnate: *adj* in material form (69).

incendiaries: *n* people who stir up trouble (8).

incensed: *adj* angry or furious (88).

incessantly: *adv* continually or relentlessly (31).

incidental: *adj* beside the point (139).

incisive: *adj* sharp or perceptive (58).

inciting: *v* provoking or stirring up (101).

inclined: *adj* ready or feeling like (120).

incoherent: *adj* jumbled or garbled (88).

incompetent: *adj* useless or bungling (142).

incongruous: *adj* strange or out of place (37).

inconsequential: *adj* unimportant or insignificant (146).

inconstant: *adj* unreliable or unpredictable (140).

incorrigible: *adj* incurable or a lost cause (163).

incredulous: *adj* amazed or disbelieving (101).

indecipherable: *adj* unreadable (117).

indecision: *n* uncertainty (139).

index: *n* directory (124).

indifferent: *adj* uncaring or unconcerned (32).

indigenous: *adj* native (5).

indigent: *adj* poor or needy (13).

indignation: *n* anger or annoyance (119).

indistinct: *adj* faint or vague (149).

indomitable: *adj* unconquerable (1).

ineffectual: *adj* useless or weak (104).

inept: *adj* clumsy or unskilled (15).

inevitable: *adj* certain or unavoidable (133).

inextricably: *adv* impossible to untie (156).

infamous: *adj* well-known or legendary (46).

infantility: *n* immaturity or childishness (89).

inferior: *adj* lesser or worse (62).

inferred: *v* assumed (71).

infiltrate: *v* break into (32).

inflated: *adj* puffed up or overblown (35).

infuse: *v* fill or introduce (5).

ingenious: *adj* clever or inspired (1).

ingénue: *n* naïve or inexperienced girl (101).

ingenuous: *adj* innocent or naïve (130).

ingratiate: *v* suck up to (61).

inherent: *adj* natural or inborn (67).

inhibit: *v* stop or discourage (141).

inimical: *adj* hostile (158).

iniquitous: *adj* evil or unfair (133).

initiate: *v* start (79, 101).

initiative: *n* lead or control (127).

inkling: *n* hunch or idea (63).

innocuous: *adj* harmless (33).

inordinately: *adv* overly or excessively (83).

insentient: *adj* out cold (166).

insidious: *adj* sinister (126).

insight: *n* knowledge (101).

insinuate: *v* weasel a way into (64).

insipid: *adj* dull (2).

insomnia: *n* sleeplessness (59).

integral: *adj* essential (82).

intellectual: *n* thinker or scholar (102).

intemperate: *adj* hotheaded (63).

intense: *adj* forceful or extreme (36).

intensifying: *v* increasing or deepening (136).

interminable: *adj* endless (165).

internally: *adv* on the inside (104).
interrogate: *v* interview or cross-examine (58).
intervene: *v* get involved (89).
intricate: *adj* elaborate or fancy (138).
intrigued: *adj* interested or absorbed (7).
introvert: *v* shy person (37).
intuition: *n* instinct (71).
intuitive: *adj* sensitive or perceptive (103).
inundating: *v* overwhelming (43).
inured: *v* accustomed (128).
invective: *n* criticism or attack (68).
invigorating: *adj* energizing or refreshing (99).
irate: *adj* angry (114).
iridescent: *adj* shimmering (117).
irk: *v* annoy (124).
ironic: *adj* opposite to what was expected (30).
irrefutable: *adj* unquestionable (130).
irreproachable: *adj* perfect (80).
irreverence: *n* sassiness or cheekiness (55).
isolate: *v* separate (50).
issue: *v* emerge (72).

J

jeopardy: *n* danger (122).
jolly: *adj* cheerful (128).
jovially: *adv* merrily or gleefully (47).
jubilant: *adj* joyful (24).
justifiably: *adv* rightly or understandably (70).
jutted: *v* stuck out (72).
juxtaposition: *n* side-by-side comparison (111).

K

knell: *n* ring or chime (120).

L

labyrinth: *n* maze (43).
laceration: *n* cut or gash (92).
lackluster: *adj* lifeless or mediocre (93).
laconic: *adj* quiet or curt (107).
lamenting: *v* crying about (62).
languishing: *v* wasting away (110).
lapse: *n* error (81).
largesse: *n* generosity (87).
latent: *adj* hidden or buried (102).
lauding: *v* praising (81).
lavish: *adj* fancy or extravagant (74).
lax: *adj* careless (106).
legible: *adj* readable (77).
legitimate: *adj* valid or genuine (52).
levity: *n* humor (77).
liable: *adj* legally responsible (124).
linchpin: *n* key player (95).

listless: *adj* limp or lacking energy (77).
lithe: *adj* flexible or graceful (99).
livid: *adj* furious (60).
loathed: *v* hated (85).
logical: *adj* rational or reasonable (126).
loiter: *v* hang around (71).
loomed: *v* appeared or rose up (43).
lumbered: *v* walked heavily (106).
luminous: *adj* bright or brilliant (146).
lurid: *adj* racy or explicit (142).
lush: *adj* luxuriant (106).
luxurious: *adj* fancy or deluxe (101).

M

magnanimous: *adj* generous or noble (102).
maintain: *v* keep up (29).
malevolent: *adj* wicked (113).
malleable: *adj* flexible or manipulable (7).
manipulated: *v* used or controlled (163).
massive: *adj* huge (125).
materialism: *n* love of luxury items (72).
maverick: *n* rebel (20).
maximize: *adj* increase as much as
  possible (132).
mayhem: *n* confusion or chaos (142).
meandered: *v* wandered or zigzagged (77).
medieval: *adj* from the Middle Ages (5th–15th
  centuries A.D. (122).
mediocre: *adj* average or second-rate (58).
medley: *n* jumble or mix (21).
meekly: *adv* timidly or tamely (141).
melancholy: *n* gloom or sadness (100).
mellow: *adj* calm or laid-back (134).
melodramatic: *adj* sensational or dramatic (140).
menacing: *adj* threatening (67).
mendacious: *adj* dishonest or misleading (95).
mercurial: *adj* changing or unpredictable (114).
mesmerized: *v* captivated or entranced (99).
metamorphosis: *n* transformation or
  change (128).
meticulously: *adv* carefully or thoroughly (3).
mettle: *n* nerve or guts (141).
mimicking: *v* imitating (55).
mischievous: *adj* naughty or playful (52).
modicum: *n* small amount (156).
mollify: *v* calm or pacify (134).
momentum: *n* force of motion (4).
mordantly: *adv* bitingly or sarcastically (79).
morose: *adj* gloomy or glum (83).
mortifying: *adj* shameful (3).
motivation: *n* reason or incentive (31).
multifarious: *adj* various (44).

munificence: *n* kindness or generosity (117).
mural: *n* wall painting (117).
mused: *v* thought (86).
mustering: *v* gathering (3).
muted: *v* muffled or quieted (21).
mutinous: *adj* defiant (79).
mutual: *adj* common or shared (135).
myriad: *n* countless (43).

N

nadir: *n* lowest point (94).
naïve: *adj* gullible or simple (72).
nefarious: *adj* evil or wicked (27).
negligent: *adj* careless or inattentive (123).
negotiating: *v* discussing or bargaining (139).
neophyte: *n* beginner (86).
neurotic: *adj* irrational or obsessed (145).
newfangled: *adj* new or original (77).
nimble: *adj* quick or agile (93).
nocturnal: *adj* active at night (3).
noisome: *adj* harmful or nasty (27).
nonchalantly: *adv* casually or coolly (30).
nonentity: *n* nobody (151).
nook: *n* corner (82).
nostalgia: *n* longing for the past (70).
notable: *adj* prominent or noticeable (71).
notorious: *adj* infamous (152).
novice: *n* beginner (4).
noxious: *adj* poisonous or harmful (61).
nurture: *v* encourage or foster (129).

O

obese: *adj* fat or overweight (29).
objective: *adj* neutral (82).
obligatory: *adj* unavoidable or necessary (4).
oblique: *adj* indirect or meandering (2).
obliterated: *v* wiped out (77).
oblivious: *adj* unaware (63).
obnoxious: *adj* annoying or intolerable (34).
obscure: *adj* little-known (73).
obsequiously: *adv* in an overly flattering or polite manner (61).
obsessing: *n* worrying or fixating (29).
obsolete: *adj* out-of-date (59).
obstinate: *adj* stubborn (8).
obstreperous: *adj* loudmouthed or unruly (60).
obstructed: *v* blocked (139).
obtuse: *adj* stupid or simple-minded (115).
odious: *adj* horrible (27).
offhandedly: *adv* casually (163).
ominous: *adj* threatening (89).
omnipotence: *n* power (52).

opiate: *n* drug or narcotic (115).
opportunist: *n* someone who takes advantage of people or circumstances (115).
optimism: *n* confidence or hopefulness (73).
opulent: *adj* fancy or extravagant (73).
oration: *n* speech (164).
oscillating: *v* moving back and forth (95).
ostensibly: *adv* supposedly (51).
ostentatious: *adj* showy or flamboyant (49).
ostracized: *v* disliked or did not accept (36).
outcast: *n* outsider (37).
overbearing: *adj* bossy or domineering (36).
overestimated: *v* overrated or hyped (34).
overstating: *v* exaggerating (101).
overwrought: *adj* emotional or overexcited (83).

P

pacify: *v* calm (142).
painstakingly: *adv* carefully or meticulously (70).
palatable: *adj* tasty or delicious (128).
pall: *n* gloom (93).
palliate: *v* excuse or cover for by apologizing (142).
pallid: *adj* pale (18).
palpable: *adj* physical or solid (61).
paradigm: *n* example or model (20).
parallels: *n* similarities (70).
paramount: *adj* of greatest importance (69).
paranoid: *adj* unreasonably suspicious (51).
parched: *adj* very thirsty (137).
pariah: *n* outsider or reject (69).
passionate: *adj* hot-blooded or fervent (22).
patronizing: *adj* condescending or belittling (72).
pauper: *n* poor person (107).
pealed: *v* rang (4).
peccadillo: *n* small crime or wrongdoing (83).
pecuniary: *adj* financial (83).
pedestal: *n* high position (72).
pedestrian: *adj* ordinary or dull (154).
peer: *v* colleague or equal (19).
peevish: *adj* cranky or irritable (75).
pejorative: *adj* negative or uncomplimentary (93).
penitent: *adj* apologetic (12).
penultimate: *adj* second-to-last (92).
permeate: *v* penetrate (1).
perpetrating: *v* committing (89).
perpetuate: *v* keep up (87).
perplexed: *adj* confused (106).
persecute: *v* bully or harass (89).
persistent: *adj* constant (19).
pertained: *v* related (106).

pertinacious: *adj* constant (14).

pertinent: *adj* important or relevant (52).

perturbed: *adj* bothered or disturbed (55).

peruse: *v* read carefully (118).

pervaded: *v* spread through (118).

petty: *adj* low or small-minded (108).

pilgrimage: *n* journey (100).

pinnacle: *n* height or peak (93).

piqued: *v* awakened or aroused (75).

pivotal: *adj* important or crucial (39).

placid: *adj* calm (128).

plaintively: *adv* sadly (115).

plausible: *adj* possible or believable (67).

plethora: *n* excess or large number (1).

poignant: *adj* moving or touching (82).

poise: *n* self-assurance or composure (67).

ponder: *v* think or meditate about (55).

pontificate: *v* preach (143).

potential: *adj* possible (80).

prattle: *v* babble or chatter (123).

precariously: *adv* unsteadily (106).

precipitate: *adj* reckless or hasty (19).

precisely: *adv* exactly (111).

preconceived: *adj* existing beforehand (137).

predecessor: *n* person who held the job previously (143).

predicament: *n* problem or dilemma (7).

preen: *v* swell with pride (13).

prematurely: *adv* quickly or too early (107).

premeditated: *adj* thought out beforehand (82).

preoccupied: *adj* worried or fixated (118).

preponderance: *n* excess or surplus (73).

prepossessing: *adj* preoccupying or absorbing (161).

preposterous: *adj* ridiculous or unbelievable (87).

prerogative: *n* choice or right (143).

prescient: *adj* prophetic (21).

pressed: *v* questioned persistently (23).

presumptuous: *adj* conceited or presuming (23).

pretense: *n* deceit or falseness (129).

prevail: *v* win or succeed (59).

primary: *v* main or most important (131).

prime: *adj* major or foremost (24).

priorities: *n* goals or concerns (131).

probe: *n* search or investigation (81).

procured: *v* got hold of (164).

profound: *adj* intense or overwhelming (87).

propensity: *n* tendency (13).

prosaic: *adj* dull or ordinary (169).

prostrate: *v* horizontal (155).

proverbial: *adj* well-known or commonly spoken of (53).

provoked: *v* irritated or aggravated (19).

puerile: *adj* childish (32).

punctuality: *n* being on time (107).

pungent: *adj* sharp or strong (106).

Q

quagmire: *n* swamp (126).

quaint: *adj* old-fashioned or charming (4).

qualms: *n* doubts or worries (117).

quandary: *n* dilemma (113).

queasy: *adj* sick or uneasy (59).

quench: *v* satisfy (137).

queries: *n* questions (31).

querulous: *adj* grouchy or difficult (107).

quotidian: *adj* daily (57).

R

radical: *adj* extreme or revolutionary (143).

rampant: *adj* widespread (125).

rancid: *adj* rotten (32).

rancor: *n* bitterness or resentment (113).

randomly: *adv* by chance (112).

ranted: *v* shouted or raged (141).

rapacious: *adj* aggressive or predatory (30).

rash; *adj* hasty or thoughtless (170).

rashly: *adv* hastily or without thinking (113).

rational: *adj* sensible or reasonable (136).

raucous: *adj* wild or rowdy (34).

reassure: *v* encourage or give confidence (135).

rebuffed: *v* rejected or snubbed (32).

receptacle: *n* container (38).

reciprocating: *v* returning (90).

reckless: *adj* careless or irresponsible (150).

reclined: *v* sat back or lay back (52).

recoiled: *v* shrank away (93).

rectified: *v* fixed or set right (147).

recumbent: *adj* lying down (156).

refrain: *v* avoid (35).

refurbishment: *n* restoration or renovation (57).

refuted: *v* disproved (162).

regale: *v* entertain or please (82).

regime: *n* rulers or commanders (63).

regurgitate: *v* repeat (23).

rehabilitation: *n* recovery or change for the better (165).

reigned: *v* ruled (39).

relegated: *v* transferred or handed over (162).

relented: *v* gave in (90).

relished: *v* enjoyed (58).

reluctantly: *adv* unwillingly (14).

remedial: *adj* meant for slower learners (62).

remotely: *adv* the least bit (80).
rendezvous: *n* meeting or date (144).
replete: *adj* filled or full (11).
reprehensible: *adj* wrong or blameworthy (46).
repress: *v* hold back or keep inside (38).
reprimand: *n* scolding or lecture (59).
reproach: *n* criticism (27).
reproving: *adj* disapproving (12).
repudiating: *v* rejecting (126).
repugnant: *adj* disgusting (86).
reputable: *adj* highly regarded (62).
requisite: *adj* required or necessary (18).
rescinded: *v* taken back (88).
resigning: *v* giving up or yielding (28).
resilient: *adj* strong or tough (165).
resolute: *adj* firm or steadfast (14).
resolution: *n* determination or firmness (11).
resolved: *v* determined (100).
resonating: *v* echoing or booming (136).
resounding: *adj* echoing or booming (93).
respite: *n* break (127).
restraint: *n* self-control (122).
retain: *v* preserve or maintain (73).
retaliated: *v* struck back (93).
reticent: *adj* quiet or reserved (120).
retracted: *v* taken back (152).
reveal: *v* tell (122).
revel: *v* enjoy (166).
revelation: *n* confession or admission (123).
reverberated: *v* echoed or boomed (57).
revered: *adj* respected (129).
reverently: *adv* respectfully (117).
revived: *v* reenergized (117).
ribald: *adj* vulgar or bawdy (7).
rife: *adj* abounding or plentiful (150).
rigid: *adj* firm or stiff (15).
riled: *adj* angered or annoyed (73).
rival: *n* competitor or challenger (141).
roster: *n* list (145).
rotund: *adj* fat or round (9).
ruffled: *v* bothered or intimidated (30).
ruminate: *v* think over (4).
rural: *adj* countryside (157).
ruse: *n* trick or hoax (36).
rustic: *adj* old-fashioned or rural (5).

S

saccharine: *adj* overly and falsely sweet (78).
salvation: *n* something that protects or saves (155).
sanguine: *adj* confident or optimistic (129).
sardonic: *adj* mocking or scornful (17).

savoring: *v* enjoying (140).
scant: *adj* tiny or minimal (72).
scanty: *adj* sparse or limited (149).
scathing: *adj* mocking or wounding (34).
scenario: *n* situation (96).
scent: *n* smell (39).
scholarly: *adj* intellectual (62).
scoffed: *v* jeered or laughed at (12).
scorn: *n* ridicule or annoyance (50).
scoundrel: *n* villain or lowlife (153).
scrutiny: *n* study or inspection (73).
sedate: *adj* dull (1).
sedentary: *adj* inactive (9).
self-deprecating: *adj* self-critical (70).
sensual: *adj* pleasurable or luxurious (160).
sequestered: *adj* isolated or apart (1).
serendipity: *n* luck (9).
serene: *adj* peaceful or calm (7).
shiftlessness: *n* laziness (19).
shilling: *v* selling or promoting (115).
shrewd: *adj* sharp or clever (111).
shunning: *v* rejecting (91).
sinister: *adj* menacing or creepy (80).
sinuous: *adj* graceful (9).
slovenly: *adj* sloppy or messy (70).
sly: *adj* sneaky or secretive (117).
smug: *adj* self-satisfied (114).
snubs: *v* ignores or rejects (80).
sober: *adj* serious or dreary (93).
soiree: *n* evening party (143).
solicitous: *adj* attentive or concerned (128).
solo: *adj* alone (38).
sophomoric: *adj* immature (6).
sparred: *v* fought or dueled (154).
spontaneously: *adv* suddenly or without thought (82).
sporadic: *adj* occasional or intermittent (64).
squelched: *v* suppressed or held back (74).
staid: *adj* serious or dull (1).
stance: *n* position or viewpoint (14).
stealthy: *adj* quiet or sneaky (64).
stereotype: *n* commonly held belief that may be wrong (119).
stern: *adj* harsh or serious (78).
stoic: *adj* emotionless (161).
stupendous: *adj* amazing or wonderful (129).
subjugate: *v* overcome or suppress (129).
sublime: *adj* magnificent (170).
subtle: *adj* delicate or restrained (110).
sullen: *adj* gloomy or morose (19).
superb: *adj* wonderful (90).
superficial: *adj* shallow or insincere (134).

superfluous: *adj* extra or unnecessary (6).

surly: *adj* rude or abrupt (50).

surmise: *v* guess (55).

surpassed: *v* beat or outdid (33).

surreptitiously: *adv* sneakily or secretly (38).

systematically: *adv* thoroughly or methodically (122).

T

tacit: *adj* unspoken or implied (105).

taciturn: *adj* quiet or distant (79).

tactic: *n* strategy or plan (122).

tamper: *v* tinker or meddle (123).

tantamount: *adj* roughly the same as (80).

tedious: *adj* boring or tiresome (2).

temper: *v* control or regulate (124).

tentatively: *adv* cautiously or hesitantly (45).

thaw: *v* melt or defrost (109).

theorized: *v* guessed or speculated (54).

therapeutic: *adj* good for the health (43).

thrive: *v* prosper or blossom (34).

thwart: *v* block (51).

tinged: *v* tinted or shaded (107).

tirade: *n* outburst (16).

tolerant: *adj* open-minded (61).

tolerate: *v* put up with (107).

tomes: *n* books (2).

trajectory: *n* route or flight path (79).

trammel: *v* get in the way of (41).

tranquil: *adj* peaceful or calm (99).

transgression: *n* wrongdoing or intrusion (105).

transient: *adj* temporary (102).

transmute: *v* change (105).

transparent: *adj* obvious or see-through (105).

trek: *n* hike (101).

tremor: *n* vibration or tremble (84).

tremulous: *adj* unsteady or trembling (7).

trepidation: *n* fear or nervousness (16).

trilled: *v* spoke musically or warbled (6).

truncating: *v* cutting short (59).

turbulent: *adj* chaotic or restless (79).

turgid: *adj* stiff or stilted (2).

turmoil: *n* confusion or chaos (109).

U

umbrage: *n* offense (34).

unabashed: *adj* unembarrassed or unashamed (30).

unabridged: *adj* full-length (2).

unalloyed: *adj* pure or absolute (119).

unaltered: *adj* unchanged (100).

unbiased: *adj* neutral or open-minded (100).

unburdened: *v* relieved (165).

uncanny: *adj* unnatural or extraordinary (1).

uncouth: *adj* crude or offensive (63).

undermined: *v* damaged (20).

underscored: *v* emphasized (113).

undertaking: *n* job or task (107).

unfathomable: *adj* unbelievable (92).

unflinchingly: *adv* fearlessly or determinedly (101).

universal: *adj* common or widespread (83).

unkempt: *adj* messy or scruffy (144).

unprecedented: *adj* first-time or extraordinary (87).

unremittingly: *adv* endlessly or relentlessly (137).

unscrupulous: *adj* immoral or wicked (88).

untutored: *adj* untrained or inexperienced (154).

unwary: *adj* innocent or unsuspecting (82).

unwholesome: *adj* dishonest or indecent (63).

unwittingly: *adv* unknowingly (83).

upbraid: *v* scold (161).

urgency: *n* insistence or need (147).

V

vain: *adj* proud or conceited (59).

valid: *adj* real or legitimate (120).

validated: *v* confirmed or approved of (166).

vanquishing: *v* defeating or crushing (44).

vapid: *adj* dull or bland (64).

variegated: *adj* multicolored or flecked (99).

vehemently: *adv* heatedly or intensely (134).

venture: *n* business or operation (163).

verbose: *adj* long-winded (167).

verify: *v* prove or confirm (84).

vestiges: *n* traces or remnants (5).

vindicated: *adj* blameless or proven right (130).

vindictive: *adj* hurtful or vengeful (161).

vitriolic: *adj* cruel or spiteful (128).

vociferous: *adj* vocal or enthusiastic (41).

void: *n* empty space or nothingness (155).

volatile: *adj* unstable or explosive (141).

voluptuous: *adj* sexy or sensual (72).

vulnerable: *adj* weak or defenseless (69).

W

wallowing: *v* remaining helpless or self-pitying (2).

wavering: *v* shaking or trembling (40).

whetted: *v* awakened or aroused (85).

wily: *adj* clever or sly (166).

winced: *v* flinched or cringed (139).

wistfully: *adv* sadly or regretfully (164).

withering: *adj* sneering or hateful (88).
wizened: *adj* wrinkled or aged (78).
wretched: *adj* miserable (165).

Y
yoke: *n* join or attach (128).

Z
zany: *adj* crazy or wacky (165).